Praise for *Lesley Crewe*

The Spoon Stealer

Globe & Mail bestseller; Canada Reads 2022 longlist

"I loved *The Spoon Stealer* so much, for so many reasons....I laughed, I cried through scenes both charming and horrifying, and I was emotionally attached to every character. Like with every one of Ms. Crewe's books, each scene and character was expertly crafted, and I was left wishing the story would never end. An absolutely wonderful, heartfelt story of family and redemption, forgiveness and love."
–**Genevieve Graham**, bestselling author of *The Forgotten Home Child*

"Lesley Crewe artfully threads history and humour through this touching story of family, friendship, and the preciousness of memories. With its indomitable spirit, down-to-earth wisdom, and a dash of gutsy sass, *The Spoon Stealer* might just steal your heart."
–**Amy Spurway**, award-winning author of *Crow*

Mary, Mary

Leacock Memorial Medal for Humour longlist

"A funny and charming story of a dysfunctional Cape Breton family, and the irony of the "white sheep" who stands out like a sore thumb."
–**Atlantic Books Today**

Amazing Grace

National bestseller

"A fast-paced novel written in Crewe's breezy, chatty style. [She] has a gift for creating delightful characters."
–**Halifax Chronicle Herald**

Vagrant Press is an imprint of
Nimbus Publishing Limited
3660 Strawberry Hill St, Halifax, NS, B3K 5A9
(902) 455-4286 nimbus.ca

Printed and bound in Canada

Editor: Penelope Jackson
Editor for the press: Whitney Moran
Cover design: Heather Bryan
NB1600

*This is a work of fiction. While certain characters are inspired by persons no longer
living, and certain events by events which may have happened, the story is a work
of the imagination not to be taken as a literal or documentary representation of its
subject.*

Library and Archives Canada Cataloguing in Publication

Title: Nosy Parker / Lesley Crewe.
Names: Crewe, Lesley, 1955- author.
Identifiers: Canadiana (print) 20210380616 | Canadiana (ebook) 20210380624
ISBN 9781774710425 (softcover) | ISBN 9781774710784 (EPUB)
Classification: LCC PS8605.R48 N67 2022 | DDC C813/.6—dc23

Nimbus Publishing acknowledges the financial support for its publishing
activities from the Government of Canada, the Canada Council for the Arts,
and from the Province of Nova Scotia. We are pleased to work in partnership
with the Province of Nova Scotia to develop and promote our creative indus-
tries for the benefit of all Nova Scotians.

Nosy Parker

LESLEY CREWE

Vagrant
PRESS

A love letter to my dad, John Brown
The real writer in the family·

Chapter One

I know that old fella across the street with one leg is a murderer. He's come home in the middle of the night, and it's pouring rain so hard that it's bouncing off the pavement. A taxi pulled up, dropped him off, and whished away. He limped up the front stoop with his crutch and is leaning on the railing, wearing a trench coat and a fedora pulled down over his eyes. The kind hitmen wear when they lurk in dark alleys. Now he's lighting a cigarette. The red glow resembles a miniature dinosaur eye.

He's brooding about the execution. How else could he have done it? He needed that cab. One-legged men can't drive cars.

He disappears into his duplex and I wait, but the indoor lights never come on. His windows are always dark. Who doesn't turn on a light?

Assassins.

I'm so busy ruminating about how he might bump me off one night that I don't hear Dad's typewriter stop clacking.

"Audrey Rosemary Parker. What are you doing behind the living room curtains?"

"I'm not here."

"The curtains are sheer. I can see you."

"You're dreaming."

"Christ almighty. Get to bed."

It's my policy to always wait for my father to curse before I obey him. His list of swear words are in my notebook, but so far, I haven't had to write down the big enchilada. Dad thinks I've never heard this word, and that he's being a proper parent by never saying it out loud.

But the day we moved in, the first thing the kid next door said to me was "Fuckin' Anglais." Welcome to the neighbourhood.

I shuffle across the living room rug and take baby steps down the hall.

"Go to the bathroom."

"Meet me in my room with a glass of Pepsi."

He growls. A low rumbling in his throat. He does that a lot.

My very small bedroom is off the kitchen, and this arrangement suits me just fine. The window faces the back alley and I can peer into the rear windows of the houses one street over. It's just a matter of pulling up a chair to spy on the people who live there, and the kitchen is close enough that I can make a peanut butter sandwich and eat it while holding my mother's opera glasses up to my eyes. Dad doesn't know I found them.

I get into bed and lean against the pillows until Dad comes in and sits beside me, handing me a glass with two inches of Pepsi in it.

"You look tired," I say. His black, square-framed glasses are shoved up on the top of his wavy grey hair, which always happens when I interrupt him at his desk. "Were you writing something important?"

"'The Ultimate Society,' what else."

"You've been writing that book since I was born."

"Audrey, you've got to sleep at night."

"So do you." I drink the Pepsi in one gulp. "Thank you."

"Aunt Maureen would now tell you to brush your teeth."

"Can't. Have to sleep. Goodnight, Daddio." I throw the covers over my head.

"Goodnight, Nosy." Dad gets up and pats the blanket but misses my body.

"Hey. I'm not nosy. I'm inquisitive."

"Do you have my thesaurus, by any chance?"

My hand reaches out from underneath the sheets to give it to him. "Thanks."

———

It's dawning on me that my father is ancient. Prehistoric. In his dotage. I'm twelve and he's fifty-five. Sometimes I tell people he's my grandfather just to keep them from asking questions. Because he tends to act like an old man. He doesn't have the time or the patience for anything he's not interested in. So aside from writing, philosophy and history books, great literature, classical music, playing the piano, MGs, pipes, alcohol, and good food, he couldn't care less.

We moved into this downstairs stone-clad duplex in NDG because Dad got fed up with his sister Maureen constantly nagging him: "An apartment is no place to raise a child."

Hey, I liked our apartment. The superintendent kept a big turtle in the tropical water fountain in the lobby. The palm trees were fake, but the turtle didn't care. He lived for lettuce. And a garbage chute is the most exciting thing in the world. But the best day of my life was when the super sat outside the front doors and wouldn't let kids come into the building on Halloween night. There were only a few kids who lived in the complex, so we zoomed up and down on the elevator, knocking on every apartment door. The folks were very happy to see us, and most of them ended up dumping everything in our bags. At one point I ran back to our apartment to get a pillowcase.

Ideally, Maureen would have liked Dad to buy a house, but you can only push a stubborn old goat so far.

We turned the key to our new home on April 28, the day Expo 67 opened to the world, which wasn't great planning on our part, since the city of Montreal was a zoo. The traffic was hideous, with everyone and their out-of-town relatives trying to be the first ones through the gates.

It's now the first of June, and Dad still hasn't gotten around to taking me to this amazing world's fair. Something else Aunt Maureen mentioned just the other day.

"If it bothers you so much, Maureen, then please feel free to take her yourself."

"Into a crowd of tens of thousands of people? Are you nuts?" She glances at me and flicks her cigarette ash in the kitchen sink. "This child is a jackrabbit. She'll take off and I'll never find her again. I'm not having that on my conscience."

My aunt has never gotten over the time she took me shopping downtown at Ogilvy's and thought she lost me for an entire hour. I had her under surveillance the whole time from my hiding place. She was so distraught, she approached a security guard and babbled incoherently about losing her baby girl.

"Don't worry, madam. We'll find her. What does she look like?"

"A real mess! Unbrushed hair, dirty, freckled face…"

The guard gave her a confused look. "How big is she?"

Maureen held her hand over her head.

"So, not a toddler?"

"No! She's ten, tall and gangly. Looks like a crane fly. I'll kill her when I find her."

When they eventually spotted me, I was crouched down in the middle of a circular rack of women's sweater sets. Maureen grabbed my arm and pulled me out, dragging me through the store, absolutely mortified.

"Why on earth did you embarrass me like that?"

"I was tailing a shoplifter. I would've had the evidence, too, if you hadn't shown up."

"Not one word to your father, do you hear me?"

Aunt Maureen is too bossy. Domineering. Overbearing. And really stubby. Her husband died recently out on his lawn chair in their backyard. They'd had an argument and Aunt Maureen thought he was just stubbornly sitting out there ignoring her. Finally, at dusk, she marched over to him to tell him to knock it off. She shoved the back of his shoulder and he fell right over and hit the ground.

Her two sons came home for the funeral and then left again. They live in Toronto.

The next morning I'm pouring Cap'n Crunch into our bowls for breakfast when the doorbell rings. I hear "Shit!" from the bathroom.

"I told you not to move so close to her."

The front door opens. "Only me."

Dad walks into the hallway in his work trousers and sleeveless undershirt, wiping a few spots of shaving cream off his face with a hand towel. "Maureen, why are you here at the crack of dawn?"

She waves a cigarette and limps past him. "Nothing else to do."

"What happened to you?"

"Tripped over Jerry's damn cat. I should've buried the bloody animal with him."

She sits at our green Formica kitchen table, pulling a glass ashtray closer to her. "Hello, you."

I plunk both bowls of cereal on the table. "Hey, Moo. Want some?"

She shakes her head. "You should be eating thick porridge with lots of brown sugar and cream. You need to fatten up."

I go to the fridge, take out chocolate milk, and pour it over our cereal. Dad sits down with his newspaper and starts eating.

Aunt Maureen stares. "Is that what I think it is?"

Nodding, I take a big spoonful and Cap'n Crunch away. "Mm-hmm."

"You let her eat cereal with chocolate milk?"

"Mm-hmm," Dad replies, still looking at the headlines.

Aunt Maureen takes a long drag off her cigarette and blows the smoke straight up over the table. "Now I've seen everything. I better move in here and take charge."

"NO!" both Dad and I yell with our mouths full.

She gives us a startled look. "Thanks a bunch. It's nice to know my family loves me."

Dad gathers his wits. "Of course we love you, Maureen. When you suggested we move here, I was happy to know we'd see each other more often, but this doesn't mean you can come in here at all hours of the day telling us what to do."

"And I didn't know my selfish husband would drop dead in the meantime. I have no one else now."

"You are hardly alone. You have two grown sons, four grandchildren, and six siblings."

"My two live in another province and our family grunts at each other once a year, so how does that help? You know, Jack, you never would've managed without me when Audrey was little."

"That's very true, and I'll always be grateful, but she's grown up now."

"She's only eleven, you foolish man."

I'm still crunching. "I'm twelve today, as a matter of fact."

They both look at me, horrified. "How did we forget your birthday?!" Dad shouts.

"We've been busy moving. No point in having a party if I have no one to invite. Buy me a box of Creamsicles and I'm good to go."

"Goddammit, Audrey. I'm sorry, I feel like a louse."

"It's okay. I'm autarkic."

"No." Dad points his spoon at me. "Wrong usage. You are self-sufficient. Able to stand on your own two feet."

Aunt Maureen looks under the table. "This sweet birthday girl is standing on her own two feet with a hole in the toe of her sneakers. There's also a huge ink stain on her blouse, not to mention her fingers. Is this how she goes to school?" She takes another puff of her cigarette and crushes it into the ashtray. "I wasn't lucky enough to have a daughter of my own, but if I did, you can be sure she'd look like she came out of a band box. Audrey needs all the help she can get. I know how kids can be. She shouldn't go around looking like a waif. Especially in a new school. Thank God she has to wear a uniform, or it would be worse."

And with that, she gets up and leaves, but then she comes back. "And another thing. You are the only member of this family who's actually made it in the world, Jack. Need I remind you that we come from a tenement building in Point Saint Charles, and most of us still have nothing? But you make a decent living. So why is your daughter walking around in holey shoes?"

"Dad and I don't care about money. We are unfettered and don't need much, do we, Daddio?"

"You heard the girl."

"You two deserve each other. Happy birthday, honey."

This time she does leave, and she slams the door on her way out for good measure.

Dad shrugs, shakes his paper, and continues to read. I finish off my cereal and go into his study to open my favourite book.

Waif. Guttersnipe. Stray.

Back to the kitchen. "Am I really a guttersnipe?"

"No. You are not an orphan."

"But apparently I look like one."

He growls softly, more like a purr. "You could brush your hair now and again."

That hurt. He sees it on my face.

"You are perfect, Aud. Oddly perfect, just as you are. I'm late. Is my coffee ready?"

"Indeed."

He does his usual dance around to get his shirt and tie and suit jacket on, then gathers papers off his desk to put them in his briefcase while I pour his coffee into a mug that reads *World's Greatest Dad*.

"Two cream, two sugar," he says.

"I'm not stupid."

"Find another word."

"I'm not a peabrain."

"Better."

While I hold the mug by the front door, it's time to go through the list. "Do you have your glasses?"

He feels the top of his head and brings them down to rest on his large Roman nose. I know that's what it's called because he looks just like the statue of Julius Caesar. He also has what's called a strong jaw. I think I do too. Chewing meat is very easy for me. "Check."

"Your wallet?"

He pats his pocket. "Check."

"Keys?"

Pats the other pocket. "Check."

"Umbrella?"

"Good thinking." He takes it off the coat rack.

"Hat?"

"Right."

That's on the chair where we put the mail.

"What are we having for supper?" he asks.

"Swanson TV Dinner. Fried chicken."

"My favourite." He takes the mug, and since his hands are full, he leans down and pecks the top of my messy head. "Try not to get into trouble today."

"Check."

"OH! And happy birthday, Nosy Parker."

And out he goes to drive downtown in bumper-to-bumper traffic, so he can sit at his magnificent desk in the iconic Linton Apartment Building on Sherbrooke Street West, where he has his own publishing company on the first floor. He tells me he writes, edits, sells, hustles, has two-martini lunch meetings at the AAA Club, and hobnobs with artsy types in the Montreal literary world. He's met Mordecai Richler. I had to look him up. If he does all that and has to look after me as well, it's no wonder it's taken the poor man twelve years to write his own book.

I've spent many a day hiding under that desk. Once I tied his shoelaces together. I'll never do that again.

Time to gaze at my hair in the bathroom mirror. You can't brush curls. Curly hair is messy. Hence the phrase, *a mess of curls*. Doesn't anyone know anything? And besides, no one notices the tangles. They're too dazzled by the colour. Dad's barber called it strawberry blonde, and that sounds delicious, so I'm satisfied. (Even though Aunt Maureen almost fainted when she found out Dad was taking me to a barber.)

But I do take another wrinkled blouse out of the hamper and throw the ink-stained one back in. I'm brushing my teeth when a sound piques my interest. I put the water glass up to the bathroom wall and hear Mrs. Weiner (the best name ever) yell at her boys about being late for school.

Our duplex is smack-dab in the middle of a street that has an elementary school at the top and a high school at the bottom. This is a plus when trying to figure out when I should head out the door. If there's only a few kids on the sidewalk, I have time. If I look out and a flood of minors are running up the street and awkward, pimply teenagers are meandering down, I need to get going.

And right now, the street is crawling with offspring, so I shove a couple of tissues in the hole of my shoe, pick my book bag up off the coat rack it's been hanging on since I put it there yesterday, and grab my key. Once the door is locked, I put the string around my neck and hide it under my blouse.

We might only live a half a block away from the school, but I drag the gold bike Dad bought for me when we moved here out from behind the front hedge and proceed to pedal down the sidewalk. The bike is too big for me, as Aunt Maureen pointed out, but Dad wisely reasoned that I'll grow into it and the scabs on my knees and elbows will heal.

I'm almost to the end of the block when I glance down one of the paved driveways between the buildings and see a fat-bellied man shaking his finger in the face of a skinny adolescent. He shouts and throws his hand around like there's a bee in his face. This could be a police matter. I hop off my bike and let it fall on the grass of someone's lawn, sneak over to the nearest front porch, then tiptoe to the edge of the brick duplex. Stone. Brick. Stucco. This street has no uniformity at all. By this time, I have my trusty notepad and pencil out of my jacket pocket.

The particulars are as follows:

Fat guy. Old. Mustache. Beady eyes. Yelling in a foreign language. Somewhat threatening manner.

Young guy. Skinny. Trying to grow a mustache but not having much luck. Can't get a word in edgewise.

Time—I look at my Mickey Mouse watch—8:57 A.M. *Date: Thursday, June 1, 1967.*

Just as I look up again, the flabby guy gives the young one two swats. One on his cheek and one on the back of his head. Then he shoves him away with a wave of dismissal and disappears into a garage.

The young man walks down the driveway with his hands in his pockets. When I burst out from behind the brick wall, he jumps with fright. "*Merda!*"

"I saw the whole thing! We can call the police and arrest that man for assault!"

"What the hell are you talking about? Beat it, squirt."

"I saw him hit you. I can be a witness."

"He didn't hit me. He's my pops."

My pencil is poised over my notebook. "And what's his name?"

"What's it to ya? Now buzz off, you little weirdo. And get that bike off our lawn."

He keeps walking towards the high school. I put my notebook and pencil in my pocket and pick up my bike. That's the thanks I get for trying to be a good citizen.

Of course, when I pull into the schoolyard, all the kids are inside and the bike racks are taken. Once again, I have to put my bike down on its side, because it never seems to stay up on its stand. It's going to be totally scratched at this rate.

My new elementary school is a huge, dark brown, rectangular brick building that takes up an entire block if you include the playground. And every couple of feet along the facade of this four-storey prison there are enormous multi-paned windows. A five-year-old could've drawn this on an Etch-a-Sketch, so who was the brilliant architect on this project? It reminds me of Aunt Maureen's dry meatloaf, without the ketchup on top.

I've only been here a month, but I know that my seventh-grade teacher, Mrs. Fuller, will have a scowl on her face when I show up. She always looks like she has indigestion, and she throws chalk at us. Maybe there's a connection.

There are hooks outside the classroom, and I put my jacket over Yana's sweater. She's a chubby girl and the only one who doesn't seem to mind my jacket. But maybe she does. She doesn't usually talk, so I'm not exactly sure.

Everyone is standing singing the national anthem accompanied by music piped in over the intercom. Mrs. Fuller sees me in the doorway and points a bright red claw in my direction, which means *stay where you are.*

If only I sat in the back of the room, but no. Mrs. Fuller decided that I need her special supervision, so I get to be across the room by the windows in the very first seat next to her desk, which means every student watches me slink over to my spot when "O Canada" is over.

"Late again, Audrey. I will have no choice but to contact your mother if this continues."

"Good luck with that," I mumble.

"Excuse me?"

"Yes, Mrs. Fuller. I'm sorry I'm late. I almost had to call the cops."

The whole class bursts into laughter. This is why she hates me.

"Sit down and keep your mouth shut. Everyone, open your math books, please."

But there are advantages to this location. It seems I'm surrounded by nice-looking boys, the ones who cause trouble. Mrs. Fuller obviously likes the rebels to be within grabbing distance.

The only exception is the boy behind me. He's Norwegian. I asked him if he was from Norway and he nodded, although there was really no need. He looks exactly like the triplet boys in the *Snipp, Snapp, Snurr* series. I mentioned it in passing one day, but I don't think he heard me. I'm secretly in love with him and want to go to Norway someday.

But Derek beside me is a pill. The only thing he pays attention to is girls' chests. Only one girl in our class has actual breasts. Pamela. She's pretty popular. I didn't think I had any, until Derek made a curved gesture to his friend when I leaned against the front edge of my desk one day. I looked down and then sat straight up.

"Mind your beeswax," I hissed at him.

"Aud-ball. Get it? Aud-ball. Or did that go right over your head?"

"For you to say anything that would go over my head, you'd have to stand on a chair."

At recess we pour out of the room like a tidal wave, the boys pushing ahead to get to what looks like a baseball diamond at the back of the paved schoolyard. They aren't allowed to play actual baseball with bats and whizzing balls flying through the air, which makes total sense. No one needs to be concussed while eating their Lik-M-Aid. The game seems to be a cross between soccer and kick-ball. Only the Grade Sevens are allowed there, since they run the school.

The playground equipment is also popular, consisting of a ten-foot-high monkey bar, a metal slide that burns your legs when the sun hits it, the maniacal roundabout, and three crotch-destroying see-saws. To avoid these deathtraps, I stand by the chain-link fence and watch the girls play double Dutch with their skipping ropes or jump on one leg through hopscotch mazes drawn in coloured chalk. My real interest is the little boys playing with marbles. Every single one of them has a soft cloth bag with a drawstring, and they crouch down to flick them with the front of their thumbs on the pavement. It's beyond me why they do it, but it keeps their interest. It seems there's a marble called a cat's eye, and this intrigues me. Might have to put it on my Christmas list. Not that Dad ever reads it, since it's usually several pages long.

A rubber ball bounces my way, so I pick it up and see the owner come running over. I bounce it a few times and then toss it to her. "Hi, Gloria."

"Hi, Audrey. Thanks. Wanna come to my house for lunch tomorrow? My mom said to invite you since you're new to the neighbourhood."

"Sure. Where do you live?"

"The first house on your street. The white one."

One of the few detached houses on a street full of duplexes. "Are you rich?"

"No, we're Greek. See ya."

Off she goes, whacking at her ball.

Pamela and her equally chesty friend from the other Grade Seven class saunter by and eye me up and down. "You've got Kleenex coming out of your shoe."

"Thanks! I've been looking all over for that." I reach down and pull the tissue out of the toe hole and blow my nose with it.

Pamela rolls her eyes and they keep walking.

Every day a different teacher is on duty during recess and lunch hour. My favourite day is when the kindergarten teacher, Mrs. Brown, strolls through the yard. She has the nicest smile and all the little kids love her. Her pretty face looks like the portrait of the young Queen Elizabeth that hangs on our classroom wall. She is a new addition to my *Women I Admire* notebook. I've kept one since I was seven, when it intellectually occurred to me that I didn't have a mother. The first woman I put on the list was Aunt Maureen, but that was more out of family obligation. I love the woman, but she can be strange. Wacky. Weird.

I happen to walk close to where Mrs. Brown is standing, pretending this was my destination all along.

"Hello, Audrey. How are you getting along, dear? I hope you're meeting new friends."

"Yes, I've met a few nice girls and some boys who are real finks."

Mrs. Brown holds her hand up to her mouth so I can't see her smirk. She points at a girl rocking back and forth, waiting for the right moment to jump in the middle of a swinging skipping rope. "That's Jane Andrews. You'd like her. I know her mother well. Jane is a Girl Guide. That might be something you'd be interested in. They meet in the basement of St. John's United Church every Monday evening at six."

"I've always wondered about Girl Guides. Are you sure they aren't a cult?"

Mrs. Brown laughs out loud. "Oh, Audrey. I have a feeling your parents have their hands full."

"Well, one does, anyway."

The deafening buzzer goes off, letting the entire district know that recess is over. We all scatter, the boys running to the boys' entrance on the left and the girls gathering in two lines to the right. Which makes absolutely no sense to me, because the minute we troop up the stairs and pass through the heavy panelled glass doors, we mingle back together again.

I have my doubts about adults and their rules.

The only noteworthy moment after recess is when Mrs. Fuller throws a piece of chalk from the blackboard and it lands down the front of Pamela's blouse at the back of the room. The boys go out of their minds. It's at least fifteen minutes before things calm down. I'm annoyed on Pamela's behalf. She looks humiliated. I write down the details of this travesty to present to the principal at a later date. It's possible I'll need a few more incidents to make a tighter case against Mrs. Fuller.

After an excruciating French lesson (*ouvrez la fenêtre; fermer la porte; j'ai été kidnappée*), the equally rattling lunch buzzer goes off and once more the spawn of countless nearby couples migrate home for their noonday meal.

It takes me about forty-five seconds to bike to our abode. Who's standing on the porch but Moo. It's quite warm out, but she's wearing an all-weather coat that goes to her ankles. All her clothes do, since she's so elfin. Mrs. Weiner leans on her side of the railing in her zippered housedress, laughing to kill herself while they puff away.

"There she is," Aunt Maureen says cheerfully. A little too jovial, if you ask me. She might be annoyed.

Mrs. Weiner has short, jet-black hair but the top of her head is teased to a great height, with a curl hairsprayed flat in front of each ear.

She nods her head like one of those little suede dogs on a car dashboard. "Bubala! Do you know your Doda has been waiting here for a half an hour? You should give her a key. And Audrey, it's Audrey, right? Come on over anytime. I might have some odd jobs for you, like babysitting. Do you like babysitting?"

I take the key from around my neck and stick it in the lock. "I've never done it."

She waves a hand at me. "It's simple. You tell them what to do, and if they don't do it, feel free to smack them."

"Really?"

Aunt Maureen comes up behind me to hurry things along. "Oh, Mrs. Weiner, you're such a kidder. Thanks for keeping me company. I appreciate it."

Mrs. Weiner has mesmerized me. "Are you joking?"

She shrugs. "Of course. Oh, here are my angels now."

Two little dark-haired boys are beating each other up as they walk down the sidewalk. I've never seen that before. How do you punch someone while you're walking? They fight up the stairs and past their mother, who screams, "STOP FIGHTING!"

She flicks her cigarette butt over the front porch, grabs her angels by their shirt collars, and pushes them through the front door. "It was nice to meet you, Mrs. Novak. You too, Audrey," she says before she shuts the door. The yelling continues.

Aunt Maureen then pushes me through our front door, her cigarette hanging between her lips. "Bloody hell, I have to pee!" She rushes past me and wiggles her way down the hall, trying to keep her short legs together. "Oh, I forgot. Happy birthday!" She throws a bag on the floor before she disappears into the bathroom.

Inside the bag is a shoebox. She must have bought me new sneakers. I open the lid and push back the wrapping paper. Pink Mary Janes.

Oh, crap.

And they fit.

Shit.

Aunt Maureen comes out of the bathroom looking a lot less stressed. She opens the fridge and pours some of dad's tonic water in a small glass and sits in her favourite chair.

"So what do you think?"

"Thank you for the shoes. They're very nice."

"Aren't they something? The only pink pair left at Brown's. I was delirious when I saw them."

That's the word I was looking for. *Deranged* would also apply.

"Now, what can I make you for lunch? I don't imagine your father left anything for you."

"Yes, he did." I open the pantry and take out a jar of peanut butter, and then slide up the curved front of the metal breadbox and take the last two pieces of bread from the bag.

"I despair," Aunt Maureen sighs before lighting another cigarette.

"I can share. Would you like an open-faced peanut-butter sandwich? They're all the rage. There's even grape jelly to go with it."

"Where do you come up with such drivel? Pass me that box of Ritz."

After I pour chocolate milk into a glass, we sit together and munch away. I'd rather be reading, but while I've got her here, I can snoop.

"Moo, when you say you grew up in a tenement, is that true?"

She nods her head and gazes out though the glassed-in back porch to the clothesline that's attached to the edge of our narrow back deck. It runs across the paved alley twenty feet off the ground, where it's tied to the single maple tree out in the scraggly backyard. She points at the few items on the line. "Even your socks have holes. Has your dad ever talked about it?"

"Not really. Only when I ask, and then he doesn't say much."

Maureen puts her hand inside the Ritz box and takes two. "I'm not surprised. He has a lot of bad memories. He's the oldest. I don't remember most of it."

"Why are his memories bad?"

"Our father. He once beat Jack up for taking the last slice of bread."

I look at my plate. Now I'm not hungry.

"My sister told me that our father slammed the piano lid down on his fingers when he was five because our grandmother was teaching him how to play. Dad thought it was sissy."

When I stare at my sandwich, I think Maureen realizes she's said too much.

"It was all a very long time ago and your father is a happy man now, because he has you."

"Sometimes he just pretends to be happy."

Maureen takes a long puff. She's thinking about what to say. I don't want her to say anything.

"I've been invited to lunch with a friend tomorrow. She lives at the top of the street in the first house."

"The white one? Are they rich?"

"No, Greek."

"Make sure you wear your new shoes. That way they might invite you back."

Mercifully, I have to go back to school, so Maureen pats my head and leaves.

I don't have the energy to take my bike, so I follow the Weiner angels as they scuffle their way back up the street ahead of me.

Most of the afternoon I stare out the window. Dark clouds gather and our classroom gets very gloomy. Montreal is known for its fierce thunder-and-lightning storms. Dad always opened the sliding door of our apartment balcony to stand and watch, listening to the rain. Now that we have a more protected covered front porch, I sat on his lap last week on a folding chair to scan the sky for lightning bolts as we counted between the rumbles of thunder to see how fast the storm was drifting away. The woman who lives in the upstairs duplex on our side (we don't know her name yet) gave us a disapproving look when she happened to open her door to put out her milk bottles.

"That's dangerous," she said.

"Thank you for your concern," Dad replied.

She shut the door in a hurry.

I'm resting my chin on my hand, watching the black clouds gather and the trees on the street bend with the wind. You can feel the energy right through the windows. What if *la fenêtre* blows in? I'd be cut to pieces with shards of glass. There would be no way to identify me, except for my curly hair.

There's a sharp poke in my spine. I turn around and my adorable Norwegian points his pen towards the front of the class and nods his head for me to look forward, so I swivel back and there's Mrs. Fuller, standing with one hand in the air, just about to throw a piece of chalk in my direction.

"There's no need to hurl that missile, Mrs. Fuller. I hear you."

She squints her eyes at me. "You will stay after class and write on the board, *I will not be rude to my teacher* one hundred times."

I don't care. It will give me more ammunition when I speak to the principal about her behaviour.

It might be my imagination, but as everyone leaves for the day, the boys who surround me give me a few admiring glances before they disappear. This fortifies me somewhat.

"Erase the boards, please," says Mrs. Fuller, "and then proceed. I have work to do."

Erasing a chalkboard is very relaxing. Enjoyable, almost. But trying to write a sentence in a straight line isn't easy. My cursive skills are admirable when I start, but by sentence forty-seven, they've deteriorated noticeably.

My wrist is sore after a while, but the thought of my father's handwriting keeps me going. It's absolutely beautiful. I have no idea how such a clumsy man has the ability to use a fountain pen with such finesse. It's almost as if he loves words so much that he makes a special effort to make them look their best. I'll never be able to write like him, which is why I save every scrap of his writing I can find. The tin box in my closet has many grocery lists and phone messages in it. And I treasure the few notes he's written to me. *My girl is offbeat, astute, scintillating, quirky, and mine.*

That's how I knew there was no Santa. When I was five years old, there was a brown tag tied on the handle of the case holding my small record player. It read, *To Audrey, Love Santa Claus.*

There's no way Kris Kringle wrote that, unless he's the world's best forger.

I'm at the end of this assignment. To make sure, I count my sentences. There are ninety-nine.

"That's enough, Audrey. You may go."

"I have to finish it. I have one more."

"I said go. It's getting late and it looks bad out there."

No way.

I quickly write, *I will not be rude to my teacher* in the only space left at the bottom right-hand corner of the board.

She gives me an exasperated sigh. "You are a stubborn little girl."

I place the chalk on the ledge of the board. "Yes. I am."

I'm drenched walking home and nearly get blown over a few times. All the lights are on in every house on the block except ours— and Mr. Murder's place across the street. The duplex looks lonely and it matches my mood.

Dad gets home at the usual time with a big birthday cake in a box.

"That wasn't necessary."

He smirks. "It's all for me."

I take our TV dinners out of the oven when he emerges from the bathroom after washing the dirt of the day off his face and hands. We sit together and peel away the tinfoil, uncovering the treasured soggy fried chicken underneath.

Time to play our game.

"So, what did I have for lunch?" He grins.

"Probably chicken, knowing you."

"No. I knew we were having chicken tonight."

"Tomato soup and a grilled cheese sandwich."

"Nope."

"Were you at a meeting?"

"Yep."

"Escargot and Dover sole. And two Manhattans."

"You're a genius."

"Dad?"

"Mmm?"

"We're out of bread."

"I'll get some after supper and bring you back a treat. Do you want a candy necklace?"

"I'm not five."

"You used to like them."

"A hundred years ago."

"Let's have cake first."

He brings back two boxes of Creamsicles, two loaves of white bread, chocolate milk, Cap'n Crunch, peanut butter, Ritz crackers, dish soap, cheese slices, and maple-walnut ice cream, along with a small box of Mackintosh's Toffee for me and a package of Liquorice Allsorts that he immediately sticks in the top drawer of his desk.

I decide to have a hot bath, since I'm still chilly from my walk home in the rainstorm. Before the water drains away, I realize I have a sore throat, so I gargle with salt and water and crawl into bed with my Collier's Encyclopedia. I'm on book R-S-T. Dad bought me the set a few years ago.

I'm trying to read, but Beethoven is coming from Dad's record player in his study and I end up listening to that. It's hard to believe that Beethoven still wrote music after he went deaf.

Dad's typing stops, and he appears in the doorway of my room holding three big yellow coconut Allsorts in the palm of his hand. He sits beside me as I pop them in my mouth one by one.

"You're in bed early. Are you feeling okay?"

"Just a bit of a sore throat. Although this helps." I eat the last piece.

Dad takes a small box out of his pocket. "Happy birthday, Princess."

"You already bought me a cake and Creamsicles. I'm good." He holds it out until I take it. "Thank you, Daddio." It's a silver necklace with a tiny typewriter charm. "This is delightful! I adore it!"

"Figured a wordsmith such as yourself might get a kick out of it."

"I'm never taking it off."

He helps me put it around my neck.

"Dad?"

"Um-hum?"

"Would you play the piano for me? I think it would make me feel better."

"Sure."

We go into the living room, me wrapped in a blanket, and I sit on the piano bench beside him as he plays "Moonlight Sonata" by Beethoven and my favourite, "Clair de Lune" by Claude Debussy.

Chapter Two

The storm must have become a hurricane, because I'm flying down the street with endless debris and all the rooftops have disappeared. The Weiner angels are still fighting in what's left of their bedroom. This is going to be a disaster. Dad's not that great with a hammer.

Someone grabs me by the arm and I'm suddenly in my bed.

"Audrey? Audrey? You've slept in."

When I open my eyes, Dad is there, looking mildly concerned. "You okay?"

My throat still feels scratchy, but then I remember my lunch date with the rich Greek. "I'm fine."

Dad feels my forehead. "It's not like you to sleep in. You look a little flushed. Maybe I'd better stay home." He looks at his watch. "Or perhaps Maureen can come over."

I throw back the blankets. "Dad, stop being a worrywart. I feel great."

"All right. Your cereal is in the bowl. I have to leave."

I'm already on my way to the bathroom. "Do you have everything?"

"Think so. Don't worry about supper. My friend Lucie is making a casserole for us."

I stop and turn around. "A female? How interesting."

"I do know quite a few women, and some of them are friends."

"How friendly is this one?"

"Friendly enough to make us dinner, so I'm not passing that up. Stay out of trouble, missy."

When he leaves, I go to the kitchen and pour the cereal back in the box because I have no appetite. Then I get under a hot shower and gargle again with salt water before I pick out a white blouse that's only a little pink from when I put red socks in the wash with it. My navy blue boxy tunic covers most of it, and I decide to wear my sash in a bow. That's as girly as I'm ever going to get. At least these stupid pink shoes look new. I end up putting on a headband to get my hair off my face, which is scrubbed. I even use some of dad's mouthwash. My new necklace adds an air of sophistication.

As I'm biking to school I remember I forgot to do my math homework. Oh, brother. Mrs. Fuller better not make me stay in at lunchtime to do it. Luckily there's a spot left for my bike, and I take my math book out of my bookbag and crouch down with my back against the brick wall to try and finish up the seven equations I have left.

Gloria comes running up to me. "Hi! I'll meet you here at lunchtime and we can walk over to my house together. We're having eggplant moussaka."

"Wonderful. Thanks."

Off she goes. I've never heard of eggplant or moose-caca. I hope I'm hungry by then, but mainly I want to see her house. And her mother.

This morning, I'm standing in my row, singing "O Canada" with the rest of my classmates. And I manage to finish the last three math problems while Mrs. Fuller dithers by her desk. I'm not exactly sure if they're right, but at least they're done. Math is not my strong suit. Neither is French. I am absolutely hopeless at French. It's like a foreign language.

But I love English. Anything to do with reading and books. Dad always took me to the library in Westmount. It's a castle. I miss it, so I write down in my notebook, *Find local library.*

Mrs. Fuller makes us go up to the board to do our math homework. Naturally she starts with me, since I'm in the first seat. I hate when this happens. Now everyone will see my idiotic pink Mary Janes. As I write out the first equation—$37=2+7y$—I feel dizzy, so I put down $y=6$ so I can get back to my seat.

"WRONG," Mrs. Fuller announces to everyone, unnecessarily.

My Norwegian is next. His answer is correct, and Mrs. Fuller gives him a delighted smile. She's probably in love with him herself. It seems flaxen-haired attractive boys can do no wrong. It would be interesting if he turned into a murderer, but I doubt he will. I saw his mother at the playground gate handing him a textbook, and she's absolutely beautiful. It's against the law for women like that to give birth to bad people.

At recess all I want to do is put my head down on my desk, but you-know-who shoos me out of the room before she disappears into the teachers' lounge with her box of chocolate-covered raisins. She eats them every day, so I've written that down. It could be why she has indigestion. Once I'm outside I lean against the chain-link fence and close my eyes.

"Are you asleep?"

My eyes pop open and there's the girl Mrs. Brown pointed out yesterday, Jane Andrews. Her hair is straight, glossy brown, and cut in a pageboy. A hairdresser would have done that, it's so perfect.

"No. The sun is in my eyes."

"I'm Jane." She holds out her hand to shake mine, which is rather startling. Dad does it all the time, but he doesn't make me do it because he knows I hate touching adults I don't know.

This is different, however. She's my age, so I shake her hand. "I'm Audrey."

"Yes, I know. Everyone knows who you are because you're new here. As soon as another new student shows up, you'll be forgotten and left alone."

"That will be a relief."

She smiles. "Mrs. Brown says you might be interested in joining Girl Guides. We only have three weeks left this year. We stop for the summer, but if you'd like to come and see what it's about, I'd be glad to take you this Monday."

"Do you have to be a member of the United Church to go? My dad's a Catholic, although he never darkens the door of a church. He doesn't trust priests."

"No. It doesn't matter. We only use their basement for our meetings. But you can always come to the United Church with me if you're interested. My dad is a warden and my mother is on every church committee imaginable. Dad says the place would fall apart without her."

How interesting. She sounds like a formidable woman. I'd like to see her in action. "Sounds fun. Thanks, Jane."

She passes over a piece of folded paper. "That's my phone number. What's yours?"

By the time I relay this information, the recess bell is going off. We wave goodbye to each other because she is in the other grade seven class. It's too bad she's not in mine. I like her. She's easy to talk to.

I spend what seems like hours listening to the mind-numbing details of life in Tudor England. The only fact that stays with me is that King Henry VIII was definitely a serial killer. Several headless queens can vouch for that.

Finally, the lunch buzzer goes off, and I'm feeling better as I run down the stairs and out the door to wait for Gloria. She's coming, still bouncing that damn ball of hers. I wish she'd hurry up. An hour for lunch is not long enough for a real investigation.

We join up and walk down the sidewalk together. She's not a great conversationalist. Maybe that's because she's keeping her eye on the ball. She even bounces it across the crosswalk. A car actually honks at her.

We hurry through her front door and Gloria hollers, "We're here!"

The first thing I notice is how colourful everything is. There's even a huge woven cloth hanging on the wall like a picture. I never knew you could put fabric on a wall. It's stunning.

A very pretty woman with black hair and big brown eyes comes towards me, her long skirt and loose blouse flowing as she moves. She looks like an actress. Much prettier than poor old Gloria, but I understand that when you're twelve, you still have several years to grow into your looks, so there is hope for both of us.

I get the shock of my life when Gloria's mother reaches down and takes my face in her hands. "Welcome, Audrey. It's so nice to meet you. I'm Mrs. Papadopoulos." She kisses me on both cheeks.

I'm so stunned, I don't say anything at first, and then I find my voice. "Thank you for inviting me. Most people don't like strangers in their house."

She gives me a big grin. "Oh dear. You don't know many Greeks! We love having people in our houses. Come along, girls. We'll wash our hands first."

This place is so nice. Chock full of stuff, with family photographs on every surface. How can they possibly know this many people?

I assume we're going into the kitchen, but Mrs. Papa—that's all I can remember—steers us into a separate dining room with an enormous table already set with every dish imaginable. The only time I remember seeing a table that looked like this was at a fancy restaurant.

There are already five people sitting there. Gloria's mother introduces them. "This is my husband, Mr. Papadopoulos, my mother, Mrs. Christodoulopoulos, and our sons, George, Nicolas, and Philip."

"Welcome to our home," the father says. He's wearing a white dress shirt with no tie and the top two buttons undone. I like this look. The boys nod but obviously want to get on with the meal. It's the grandmother who unnerves me a little. She's in a long black shapeless dress and wearing a black head scarf that covers up all her hair. There are several gold chains around her neck with a crucifix on the biggest one, and at least five bracelets on each of her wrists. She's giving me an evil eye and keeps making the sign of the cross before kissing the crucifix. Maybe she sees the real me.

Fascinating.

I reach for the water glass in front of me because I still have a tickle in my throat, but they lean forward, close their eyes, and pray, so I quickly withdraw my arm and follow suit.

"Glory to the Father and the Son and the Holy Spirit, now and forever and to the ages of ages. Amen. Lord, have mercy. Lord, have mercy. Lord, have mercy. Our Father, who art in heaven, hallowed be your name. Your kingdom come, your will be done, on earth as it is in heaven. Give us this day our daily bread, and forgive us our trespasses, as we forgive those who trespass against us. And lead us not into temptation, but deliver us from evil. For yours is the kingdom and the power and the glory, of the Father and the Son and the Holy Spirit, now and forever and to the ages of ages. Amen. Christ our God, bless the food and drink of your servants, for you are holy always, now and forever and to the ages of ages. Amen."

Wow.

The next several minutes are taken up with getting lunch in front of everyone. Nothing is recognizable and even the smells are unfamiliar. Gloria's mom hands me a plate groaning with food. "Please, eat up, Audrey. We need to put some weight on you."

"Thank you." I hope I can eat this moose dish. There's a slice of tomato on a piece of lettuce off to the side that I recognize, so I'll start with that.

Gloria hasn't said a word. She's too busy stuffing her face.

"Now, tell me, Audrey," says her mom. "Where did your family live before you came to this street?"

"In Westmount."

The parents look at each other in surprise. "Really? Where in Westmount?"

"The dodgy end. That's what Dad says."

The father chuckles. "So not with the Molsons and Bronfmans?"

"No, sir. I believe they're rich, like you."

Now Gloria's father slaps the table, he's laughing so hard. "Oh my! You are a funny girl!"

Everyone is smiling at me except the grandmother. Are all grand-mothers like this? It would not surprise me if she took that bony finger of hers and drew it across her neck as a warning. Maybe I won't get out of here alive.

Now I'm bombarded with questions.

"What does your father do?"

"He's a writer."

They look interested. "Does he write books?"

"He's been trying to write his own for twelve years." Now that I've said it out loud, it's rather depressing.

"Your poor mother must work then."

"No."

"I must go and say hello to her some day." Gloria's mother smiles. "Show her around the neighbourhood."

"I don't have one."

"You don't have what?"

"A mother."

Gloria's mom gives me a stricken look. "Oh, dear heart. Everyone has a mother, even if she's not with you."

"I've never thought of it like that. This is excellent, by the way. What's in it? I'll have to make it for my dad." Anything to get her off this topic. And the dear woman realizes what I'm doing, for which I'm grateful, and proceeds to list off the ingredients.

Then the boys yell over each other to tell their father about their day. Gloria is content to keep eating. At one point she bounces her ball under the table and her mother shakes her head, so Gloria puts it in her lap.

While this is going on, I keep picking at my meal, but I'm not sure what I'm eating. It is tasty, but I'm not that hungry. Finally, Gloria's mom takes my plate and shakes her head. "My children eat me out of house and home."

The grandmother finally speaks, but I have no idea what she says.

"Mama, enough. I think Audrey will like dessert."

Imagine having dessert for lunch. She brings out something called baklava and it's delicious. I make sure to eat every bite so the grandmother doesn't stab me with her butter knife, and then I take out my notebook and lick the end of my pencil. I've seen detectives do that.

"Is the sea off the coast of Greece as blue as it appears in pictures?"

The parents blink at me with surprise. Gloria giggles and her brother Philip twirls his pointer finger next to his temple. His mother slaps down his hand without looking at him.

"Why, yes," Mr. Papa says. "It's the most beautiful water in the world. I miss it. The St. Lawrence River looks like shoe polish by comparison."

"It must be warm, since your climate is Mediterranean."

"Yes, again."

"And why are all your buildings white? Who started that trend?"

Now he looks a little confused. The grandmother raises her hands to the heavens and seems annoyed.

Gloria's mother checks her watch. "I'm sorry, Audrey. I'm afraid it's time to go back to school. But we really enjoyed having you here. It's always nice to meet new friends."

"Please come again," Gloria's dad says. "I will show you pictures of Greece."

"That would be simply wonderful, sir. Thank you very much." My notebook and stub of a pencil return to my pocket. I'm about to scrape back my chair when they all bow their heads once again. Astonishing.

"We thank you, Christ our God, for you have satisfied us with earthly gifts. Do not deprive us of your heavenly kingdom, but as you, O Saviour, came among your disciples and gave them peace, come among us also and save us."

We kids assemble at the door after. Their mom holds their faces and kisses them in turn one by one before they are released to the outside world. I'm the last.

"Thank you again, Mrs. Papa…"

She holds my hand, leans down to kiss my cheek, and whispers, "My name is Sofia. If you ever need anything, Audrey, you can always come to me. You don't have to tell Gloria."

Her wonderfully soft brown eyes look into mine. My mouth opens to say something, but nothing comes out, so I simply nod my head and run after the others. As Gloria bounces her ball back to school, I have to ask. "What did your grandmother say?"

"'We left Greece so our children could have food and you waste it.'"

"Oh, dear. She doesn't like me."

"Don't worry. She doesn't like anyone."

"Does she wear black all the time?"

"Only since our grandfather died eight years ago."

"Gosh. She must have loved him very much."

"No, I don't think so."

We arrive in the schoolyard. "Thanks for inviting me, Gloria. Your mother is so nice."

"She's okay. See ya." Gloria races to the school wall to throw her ball against it.

She's an odd girl. Peculiar. Lucky.

—

When I get home after school, I shut the front door, open the inside glass door of the tiny vestibule, and decide to kick off my hateful Mary Janes and see if I can get them to the kitchen floor. It's at the other end of our narrow, straight hallway, so it will be quite a feat. They will have to sail past the french doors of the living room, Dad's bedroom and the study on the right, and the table, chair, coat rack, basement door, closet, and bathroom on the left, just to hit the target. It would be unrealistic to expect them to turn a sharp right at the kitchen table and go through the door to my little bedroom, but you never know. Maybe they'll even land in the kitchen sink staring me in the face at the very back of the house. There might be dirty cold water in the sink, but I usually don't have that kind of luck.

I rock back and forth like Jane Andrews waiting for her turn at jump rope, and then let go with a mighty kick of my right leg. My pink shoe hits the ceiling a foot away from me, rattles the light fixture, and lands two inches away from my big toe. I know this because I have a hole in my sock.

"Goddammit."

I'm no fool. I've learned my lesson, so I reach down and take my left shoe off and hurl it as hard as I can with my pitching arm. It reaches the kitchen all right. It knocks Aunt Maureen's favourite glass ashtray off the table and breaks it in half.

I grab my holey sock, pull it off my foot, and march up the hallway to throw it in the garbage pail under the kitchen sink. Then I go into the bathroom, pull out the overflowing clothes hamper, and drag it into the kitchen to dump the clothes on the floor and root through them.

Those Papa kids looked like they came out of an Eaton's catalogue. Even Gloria's socks were snow white. You can bet none of them have holes in their socks or stained underwear or undershirts. My father always looks very professional in his suits. His shirts are always clean and ironed because he takes them to a dry cleaner. Why aren't my things taken to a dry cleaner?

Why do I always have to wear inky clothes? Jane Andrews goes to a hairdresser. Her mother obviously takes her there. She thinks she's important enough to make the effort. I bet Jane and Gloria have never heard of open-faced peanut butter sandwiches.

There's only one pair of shorts that doesn't have some kind of mark on it. Everything else is grubby, so I take all the clothes in my arms, open the back door, and throw them off the balcony and onto the driveway below.

"HEY!"

They have dropped onto the head of one of the Weiner boys, who has been riding his bike around in circles below.

"Sorry," I yell down at him.

I didn't notice Mrs. Weiner leaning over the railing smoking her cigarette. "Sorry, Mrs. Weiner. I didn't mean to hit him."

"He'll live. Having a bad day?"

I shrug. She pulls open two lawn chairs that are leaning by her door. "Come and sit. I'll get you a drink."

That usually means water, so I sit and wait, but she's inside for a few minutes. Maybe she's forgotten. Then she comes out with what looks like a milkshake.

"Drink that up. It's a special elixir my husband just discovered. He's too fat and he's on Weight Watchers, but he found this recipe and says it tastes just like a vanilla milkshake."

"Thank you." I take a sip. "This is very good."

She takes a puff and smirks, smoke coming out of her nostrils. "That's because I put lots of sugar in it. Why should a poor man who works all day in a junkyard come home and live on cottage cheese and pineapple? It's not right."

"Goodness. It must be very hard to lift junk. Does he have to wear industrial-strength gloves?"

She makes a squawking noise. "Oh my. That's hilarious. No, he owns the junkyard. He wouldn't be caught dead handling rusty metal. He sits on his ass in a trailer and talks into two phones. That's why he's fat. It's a very lucrative business, because we Jews stick together."

Out comes my notebook and pencil. "Do all Jews stick together? Is this a standard practice?"

The moment I know I love Mrs. Weiner is when she doesn't bat an eyelash at this question. She pauses to consider it seriously.

"On the whole, I would say yes. We have a troubled history, we Jews. Take the war, for example. We rely on each other to survive."

I scribble down this information. "That makes perfect sense. Birds of a feather and all that. You look out for your own. I bet turtles take care of other turtles."

"Well, Jewish turtles have had to be clever and hardworking because the non-turtles block us from working in a lot of jobs, and some of the turtles make a lot of money, and then some non-turtles are jealous of this ability and call us names."

"What kind of names?"

"Not nice ones."

"That's awful. I'd never do that."

"You think you'd never do that, but sometimes we make mistakes."

"MA! MA! WATCH THIS!!"

The angel riding his bike below us gathers speed and thrusts his front wheel off the pavement and into the air for three seconds and then drops back down. "DID YOU SEE, MA?"

"YEAH! DON'T BREAK THAT BIKE OR I'LL BREAK YOUR NECK!" she yells back. "David is very insecure. Always afraid Michael is going to get ahead of him."

"How old are they?"

"Six."

"They're twins? They don't look alike. They're not even the same height."

"They're fraternal. And that's the problem. Michael is twelve minutes older and has always been bigger and never lets David forget it."

"That's too bad."

Mrs. Weiner gives me a slow smile as she taps the ash off the end of her cigarette. "They probably need to see a shrink, but brothers fight. Ever heard of Cain and Abel?"

"Vaguely. Something to do with the Bible, which I don't know a lot about. Didn't one kill the other?"

She nods. "If you like stories, read the Bible. There's stuff in there that would curl your toenails. Now, tell me. Why have you thrown out all your clothes?"

I put my notebook down and drink my fattening milkshake.

"You don't have to talk about it if you don't want to. It's none of my business, but it will go nowhere. My mouth is a steel trap."

I haven't known Mrs. Weiner long, but I'd say she's deluding herself if she thinks that's true. Still, she means well.

"It's hard to keep clothes clean."

She nods. "You need to be disciplined. Come with me."

She makes me follow her into her house, which looks exactly like our place except it's cozy and there are pots boiling on the stove and what smells like fresh bread in the oven. We go down the stairs to her laundry room.

"This is where the magic happens. Every Monday and Thursday, pick up the dirty clothes your thoughtless children and lazy husband leave all over the floor and put them in the clothes hamper. Then take the hamper down here and separate the clothes into a white and dark pile. You can't mix them, otherwise everything comes out a dingy grey. Your new underwear will look like you've been digging in a coal mine."

She points to a row of bottles and boxes on shelves above her washing machine. "When you do a white wash, you add bleach to your detergent. That will make the whites really white. Sometimes you have to soak your clothes before you wash them. Like those socks you had hanging on your clothesline. You'll never get the grime off if you don't. Same with underwear. You might even have to scrub them with a washboard." She takes one down off the shelf for me to look at. "A great investment. Found in any hardware store. For stains on white sheets or tablecloths, leave them on the clothesline and the sun will bleach them."

"I don't think we own a tablecloth."

"Throw out underwear every four to six months. Throw out socks that have no heels. Throw away blouses with cigarette burns."

"I don't smoke."

"Good girl. Nasty habit. And always get rid of T-shirts that have stains under the arms. Boys don't like girls who stink."

"I don't care what boys think."

"You will."

"What do you do if you hate your shoes?"

"Buy new ones."

"Thank you, Mrs. Weiner. You've been very helpful."

We go back upstairs and out on the deck. David and Michael are wrestling under the maple tree. Mrs. Weiner puts her fingers in her mouth and gives a shrill whistle. They look up.

"You boys pick up that pile of clothes and bring it here."

They whine about it, but do as they're told. Now the pile is between us as we sit on our chairs. She sorts through it and tells me which clothes are salvageable and which ones belong in the trash. "While we're here, go get the clothes in your drawers and closet. Might as well purge the lot."

It takes thirty minutes for us to finish. Mrs. Weiner goes into her kitchen and gets a large garbage bag to gather up the clothes that are either dirty, worn out, or too small for me.

"You've been such a great help, Mrs. Weiner. I feel much better now. I'm making progress. I'm in recovery."

"You sound like an alcoholic. This was just a clothing intervention. Glad I could help. I love kids." She leans over the railing at her boys who are hitting each other with sticks. "DON'T MAKE ME COME DOWN THERE AND HIT YOU WITH THOSE! HURRY UP! SUPPER'S ALMOST READY!"

I take my remaining clothes downstairs and make two stacks in front of the washing machine. No time like the present. In the junk drawer there's a battered tin jar with money in it in case I have an emergency. I'd say having no clothes is an emergency, so I take a five-dollar bill and stuff it in my pocket, then put on my holey sneakers, lock the front door, and get on my bike. This is when I bump into Dad getting out of his MG, or his dinky toy, as Aunt Maureen calls it. His female friend is having a hard time keeping her short skirt from riding up her legs while she emerges from the car holding a CorningWare dish, her purse, and a wrapped gift.

Dad looks at me with surprise. "Where are you going?"

"To the corner store to buy Cold Water All, Rinso with Colour Bleach, Borax, and Downy Fabric Softener."

"Jesus Christ, it's almost suppertime." His friend has managed to make it to his side. "And I want you to meet Lucie Girouard. Lucie, this is my daughter, Audrey."

Lucie's hands are full, so luckily she can't shake mine, but she leans forward in that way some people do when they want to pat a cute dog. "Oh, it's so lovely to meet you, Audrey. Your dad has told me so much about you."

"Nice to meet you too. Sorry, I have to go. I'll be right back."

As I leave them behind, I know I don't like her. There's no reason for it, and it's a snap decision, but I usually trust myself on these things. As I bike past Gloria's house, I see her mother, Sofia, in the kitchen window. She must be making dinner. She sees me, smiles, and waves, so I wave back. Now, why can't he bring home someone like that?

When I buy my items, I put the paper bag in the basket of my bike. There's enough money left over to buy a Creamsicle, so I take my time riding home, sucking on the orangey loveliness. The store is only three blocks way. There's a park with some tennis courts beyond a metal fence on one side of the street. A group of older boys race around a bench, probably up to no good, and then I take a closer look and see Pamela and her chesty friend sitting in the middle, laughing and carrying on. These are high school boys, and for some vague reason I'm nervous of them. Pamela looks in my direction, so I bike away. What would it be like to be her? Does her mother know where she is? Does she care?

I'm still chewing on the Creamsicle stick when I come in. Dad is by the kitchen sink and turns around at the sound of the front door banging shut. "You took your time. Supper is on the table."

"I'll be right there. I just have to do something first."

He growls. "For the love of..." Then he remembers he has a guest.

Downstairs, I put my dark wash in first, since there's more of it, and read the instructions on the boxes. Tomorrow I plan on buying a washboard to scrub my whites before I soak them. When I hang my bleached whites out on the line, I want Mrs. Weiner to see that her efforts have not been in vain.

"GODDAMMIT, AUDREY!"

When I sit at the kitchen table, I can feel my father's annoyance with me. Suits me fine. I'm annoyed with him, wearing his dry-cleaned shirt.

Lucie takes my plate and doles out a spoonful of what looks like dog food and macaroni. This is my kitchen. Why is she serving me?

"I do hope you like it, Audrey. Most kids like a casserole."

"I prefer TV dinners."

Dad glares at me.

Lucie's fake laugh tinkles down around us. "Is that all you feed this child, Jack? You naughty boy!"

Dad glares at her.

It's always riveting to see uncomfortable adults. Luckily, I'm a kid and don't have to help.

"Want to play our game?" Dad asks me.

"No."

"Oh! What game is this?" Lucie smiles. "Sounds fun. Can I play?"

Through mental telepathy and a kick to his shin, I warn my father not to reveal our secret. It's *our* silly game. No one else's. He remains clueless.

"Audrey guesses what I have for lunch every day."

Lucie takes a bite of her dog food and then claps her hands. "What fun!" she says with her mouth full. After she swallows, she continues. "Let me try. Did you have a Caesar salad?"

"No."

"A smoked meat on rye?"

Dad's neck gets redder by the minute. "No."

"What about a fresh bagel with cream cheese, smoked salmon, capers, and red onions?"

"No."

I decide to put him out of his misery. It's Friday. "You had an egg salad sandwich on whole wheat with two dill pickles."

"Yes!" He gives me a grateful look, but that's as much as I'm going to do for him.

"And do we guess what Audrey had for lunch?" Lucie asks.

"Oh, that's easy," Dad grins. "A peanut butter sandwich."

My hatred knows no bounds. "As a matter of fact, I had eggplant moussaka"—I looked up the spelling in school—"and baklava. It was delicious."

Lucie makes a face. "I've never heard of that."

"You wouldn't have. It's Greek. One of the oldest civilizations in the world."

Lucie looks down at her plate and Dad looks up from his. I clear my throat. "I'm sorry, Lucie. That was rude. I'd never heard of it before today either, but if you ever go to a Greek restaurant, be sure to order both dishes. I don't think you'll be disappointed."

Dad looks down at his plate and Lucie looks back up from hers. "Thank you, Audrey. I definitely will. Maybe we could all go together?"

When neither Dad nor I say anything, she quickly reaches down by her feet and picks up the gift she brought with her. "I thought you might like this, Audrey. Your dad tells me you love to read."

Now I'm ashamed of myself. Why do adults do that? Just when you want to despise them, they do something nice.

Then I open it. A French–English Dictionary. "Your dad says you're having a hard time with French. I'm French. It helps to have something like this to do your homework."

"That's very kind of you. Thank you very much."

Lucie seems pleased. Dad doesn't look in my direction.

"If you'll excuse me, I must finish doing my wash."

"But you've hardly eaten a thing," Lucie cries.

"I'm sorry, but that huge lunch today ruined my appetite. It was nice to meet you. Thank you again for my book." I grab the dictionary, bolt from the table, and head down to the safety of our washer and dryer.

I stay there leafing through my new dictionary, waiting for the spin cycle to stop.

stupid—*stupide*

father—*père*
idiot—*idiot*
harlot—*prostituée*

I take out my trusty notebook. The *Women I Admire* notebook is upstairs but I don't want to sidle past a woman I don't admire to get it.

Sofia Papadopoulos is a woman who sees you and treats you like a real person and not just a kid. I will aspire to be like her when I grow up.

Sharon Weiner notices a problem and deals with it. She's no-nonsense and forthright. And very funny.

Eventually, I hear Dad and Lucie leave. He obviously has to drive her home. By the time he gets back, my dark wash is out of the dryer and in my drawers and closet. I'm in bed chewing on my toffee and reading *Charlotte's Web*, which I do often.

His footsteps coming up the hallway sound slow, like he's really not interested in seeing me. And he isn't. He stops in his study first. I hear him open his top drawer. No doubt he's chewing on a few Allsorts while he thinks.

My door is partly open. Out of the corner of my eye, I see him walk over to the cupboard, grab a glass, and fill it with water. Then he takes a spoonful of powdered Eno and stirs it in before drinking. He says it helps his indigestion, and it must because he always belches afterwards. Maybe I should try it.

He comes to my door and knocks on it softly. "May I come in?"

"Sure."

He usually sits right down on the bed, but tonight, he stands by my bureau and fiddles with my stuff.

"Sounds like you had a good day. You didn't tell me you were invited out for lunch."

"I forgot. I mentioned it to Aunt Maureen. She told me to wear the new pink shoes she bought for me, because they're rich, and that way they'd invite me back."

"And are they rich?"

"I don't think so, but they live in that nice white house at the top of the street."

"Very nice. I know the one. And you liked them?"

"Yes. They're pleasant. Delightful. Charming. Gloria's mother said I could come over whenever I want. The only one who made me nervous was the grandmother. She was dressed head to toe in black. Kind of looks like a nun. She might have put a curse on me. A hex."

"A malediction. I doubt it, but Greek grandmothers are forces to be reckoned with. I've known a few in my time. The world would be a much better place if we listened to them."

He goes over to my window and looks out. "You should close your blind so people can't see in."

"Unless our neighbours are twenty feet tall, I don't think they can."

"I'm staring into the kitchen of that house across the yard. It looks like the woman is angry. She's pointing a wooden spoon at someone."

"Her husband. He comes home late every night."

Dad whips around. "You really are a Nosy Parker."

"I'm not nosy. I'm curious."

He sits on the end of my bed. "And I'm curious about your behaviour with Lucie."

"I apologized."

"Yes, you did. Thank you. But I got the feeling you were angry with her for some reason."

"I don't like her, but I wasn't cross with her. I was vexed with you."

"Good word. Explain."

"You take your clothes to the dry cleaners. My clothes are crap."

"Crap? Find a better description."

"Worn out, dishevelled, ill-fitting, stained crap. Mrs. Weiner spent all afternoon with me, explaining how to wash clothes so I don't have to look like a guttersnipe. Because that's how I felt when I came home from the Greek family. They look pristine. Their parents care for them. I feel like an afterthought, despite my fabulous necklace. I'm walking around with holes in my shoes, so poor Aunt Maureen thinks she's doing me a favour and buys me an expensive pair I hate. She doesn't have that kind of money to throw around. All I want is a new pair of sneakers."

"Why didn't you ask me? You know you can have whatever you want."

I throw *Charlotte's Web* at his head. "Because I wanted you to *notice* that I needed a new pair of shoes! Do you ever look at me? The only time you see me is when I'm handing you your coffee in the morning, and even then, you're in a rush. You say I'm not an orphan. Well, I sure felt like one today when Gloria's mother said if I ever needed anything, I could come to her. She'd known me thirty minutes and could see I look neglected."

"Audrey...I'm so..."

"Don't talk to me. And don't ask me to like Lucie. I don't care if you want to have a girlfriend, but don't ever bring home someone who calls you a naughty boy. That's disgusting. I have to go to sleep. I've had a long day. Goodnight."

Once more I throw the covers over my head and escape to my world under the blankets where no one can reach me.

Dad gets up, turns out my light, and quietly closes the door.

Chapter Three

When I open my eyes, I can tell it's Saturday. My bedroom door is still closed and there's no radio blaring from the bathroom. My throat is much better, and when I look at my alarm clock, I do a double-take. It's nine-thirty! I never sleep in this late.

What's the reason? With my hands behind my head, I ponder this. Yesterday I had good food, did a lot of exercise with Mrs. Weiner, bending, stretching, and lugging laundry and had—I look at the clock again—twelve and a half hours of sleep! Whatever bug I might have had has been well and truly vanquished. I'm ready to face the day.

And then I remember my conversation with Dad, and my heart feels hollow. It wasn't very nice to throw a book at him. A stuffed animal, maybe, but he loves books. *Charlotte's Web* is on my bureau, so he must have taken it off the floor and placed it there before he left my room. He'd never leave a book lying on the floor.

I'm unsure what to do, so I lie there on my bed until ten. This is what teenagers do. How boring. It occurs to me that I really need to pee, so I throw back my sheets, jump out of bed, and yank the bedroom door open.

And scream.

Aunt Maureen and Dad are sitting at the kitchen table wearing sunglasses and Hawaiian shirts. They look like the Cuban Mafia.

My hand reaches for my throat. "What are you two idiots doing?"

Dad waves tickets in my face. "We're spending the whole weekend at Expo!"

"Are you serious?" I screech before hopping up and down.

Aunt Maureen excitedly points at three shoeboxes on the table. "And you can't walk around Expo without a new pair of sneakers. Take your pick. Black, white, or navy blue."

Fifteen minutes later, we're on the bus heading to Atwater Station, because I refused to waste time eating breakfast, so now I'm crunching on an apple and staring at my new black sneakers. I've also got a blue zippered bag with the Expo 67 logo on it that Dad picked up this morning when he bought our tickets at the drugstore. The tickets are called passports and will be stamped when we go into the different pavilions, as if we're visiting a foreign country, which is thrilling.

"How much were the tickets?" I ask Dad.

"Two dollars and fifty cents a day. One twenty-five for you."

"This is so great."

He smiles at me and then he looks out the bus window.

Being on a bus with Dad is a novelty. He looks strange sitting on a bus, like he doesn't belong. Aunt Maureen, on the other hand, looks like she lives here. I've been taking buses by myself for years. Most city kids do. Although probably not Jane or Gloria, unless their mothers are with them. But now that I have a bike, I don't need the bus as often. I was a little sad when I waved goodbye to Henri for the last time. He was the bus driver on the route to my other school. A very nice man. Always a big *"Bonjour, mademoiselle!"* when I stepped up to put my ticket in the slot. He looked and sounded like the actor Maurice Chevalier. I wonder if he ever thinks of me. According to my notes he always took a tartan thermos to work, and I used to wonder if he had a Scottish family connection. The day I saw him eat a shortbread cookie, I deduced my theory was correct.

After the bus, the metro, and the Expo Express train, we arrive at this world exhibition and it's completely overwhelming. I've never seen this many people in my life, and it's a little scary. Daunting is a more appropriate word. The pavilions don't seem real. There are so many huge flags flapping in the wind that they make a loud racket if you stand beside them. Everywhere you go there are pretty hostesses wearing uniforms. Their skirts are really short. You can go to them if you get lost or need to know where the bathrooms are.

Dad thinks we should get on the monorail first to get the lay of the land. A great plan, because I can pretend to be Judy Jetson flying up in the air looking at the view below. We pick out the pavilions we'd like to see, but everything is so vast we quickly realize we'll never see everything this weekend.

"Don't despair," Dad says. "We have all summer to come back."

That makes me breathe a little easier. So, this isn't just a two-day apology. Maybe I really did get through to him.

By Sunday night Aunt Maureen gives us a weary wave and steps off the bus in front of her place to go soak her aching feet. We get off the bus at the top of our street and limp home to soak ours.

"Never wear new shoes and walk four hundred miles on asphalt," I groan.

"How's the blister?"

"Bigger than a peach pit."

The blister breaks in the tub. I did help it along, against Aunt Maureen's instructions. How can you not? It's so tempting to burst a bubble on your own body, but now it's leaking like a sieve, and really tender, so I put a hand towel under my foot as I lie in my bed with a new notebook and a freshly sharpened pencil.

My impressions of Expo 67, Montreal, Quebec

First of all, this guy passed out a hard candy ball as we stood in line to get into the USSR pavilion. It looked like one of those multi-coloured marbles. It was very tasty and as you sucked it, the taste changed, and then changed again. There must have been eight flavours. Ten minutes later he went by once more and I grabbed another one. The line was long, so the third time he passed us, he purposely kept his tray away from me.

"Can you buy these anywhere?" I asked him.

"Nyet."

So much for the USSR pavilion theme, "Everything in the name of man, for the good of man."

The United States pavilion is an enormous globe twenty stories high made of plastic and glass. There are escalators everywhere and a space capsule hanging in midair. It's gleaming, impressive, and modern. Dad said it looked very American, whatever that means. And I suppose that's the whole point if your country has a pavilion at a world's fair, so they get an A+.

Canada's pavilion is an inverted pyramid structure nine stories tall and tells the story of man in the environment of Canada. It has a People Tree, a huge reproduction of a maple tree. The leaves are hundreds of coloured pictures of Canadians at work and play. I wonder if you had to pay someone to be included.

The Israeli pavilion was all about man's struggle against the desert, and the Netherlands was about man's struggle with the ocean. Obviously, we humans are constantly struggling to live on this planet.

One of the pretty hostesses told Dad to head over to the Czech pavilion for its World of Children puppet show, and she was right! They were doing Brothers Grimm and Hans Christian Andersen. Kids in Czechoslovakia are reading the same books I am. Neat.

La Ronde is the fairground at Expo, but Aunt Maureen refused to go on any of the rides. She sat on a bench and ate ice cream while Dad took me on the Gyrotron, another giant pyramid. We were whisked up high and you think you're in space, then it plunges into the bowels of the earth where a monster rises up from a fury of molten lava. I spent the entire time under Dad's armpit. Thank God Aunt Maureen didn't go on it. She'd have had a heart attack.

I loved the kiosks. I bought a Mexican sombrero with little red balls hanging off the brim and an Indian jewellery box with tiny bits of mirror and embroidery on it, since I now have my necklace to put in it, but I'm never taking my necklace off, so that was kind of silly. A Peruvian change purse, and blue pencils stamped with Expo 67 logos were my next purchase, but my favourite souvenir is my matryoshka dolls. They're wooden. One doll is inside another one until you get to a little itty bitty one. Normally I hate dolls, but these are perfect because you don't have to do anything with them.

Aunt Maureen thought Habitat 67 looked like Chinese takeout containers in a garbage can. Dad said they are concrete modular units arranged on top of each other and that she doesn't appreciate artistic vision. I think Aunt Maureen's right. They're exactly like some kid knocked over a box of Legos.

Dad comes in to inspect my heel. "That looks sore."

"It is."

He has a large square Band-Aid in his hand and starts to open it.

"Where did you get that? We don't have Band-Aids."

"Which is a travesty I plan on remedying this week, along with procuring other essential kid-friendly items. I borrowed this from Mrs. Weiner."

"I hope she doesn't expect it back."

Dad smirks. "Smartass." He puts it gently against the back of my heel and presses it firmly in place around the edges. "How's that?"

"Good."

"While I was over getting the Band-Aid, I thanked Mrs. Weiner for her kindness. She's a little eccentric but obviously has a heart of gold. Always gather people like that around you. She also said that she'd be happy to take you and Aunt Maureen shopping in her 'big-ass Cadillac DeVille.'"

"Nice."

"I wonder what Mr. Weiner does, if he drives a Caddy."

"He makes a ton of money selling junk."

"What kind of junk?"

"Junk-junk. She says it's a very lucrative business because Jews stick together."

"Oh! Something else." He leaves and comes back with a brand-new washboard. "She said this is for you."

"Perfect. I'm getting up at six tomorrow to do my whites and put them on the line before I go to school. And by the way, I'm going to a Girl Guide meeting at six tomorrow evening with a new friend, Jane Andrews."

"You're settling into this neighbourhood, Audrey. I'm so pleased. Maybe we made the right move after all."

"Maybe we did. Goodnight, Daddio."

"Sweet dreams."

I only hear about twenty seconds of Bach's "The Well-Tempered Clavier" from Dad's study before I sleep like the dead.

———

My alarm clock goes off at six and I jump out of bed, grab my washboard, and head to the laundry room. Dad's bedroom door is still shut.

This is very exciting. I fill the laundry tub with hot water, detergent, and bleach and throw everything in to soak. Then I run back upstairs to give myself a sponge bath and wolf down some Cap'n Crunch. When I open the fridge there's an egg sandwich on a plate covered with cling wrap. Dad's writing is on a small piece of paper. *For your lunch.* There's a May West cake in its wrapper and an orange beside it too.

"Christ almighty."

After my breakfast, I rush back downstairs and take the washboard and scrub everything within an inch of its life, like Mrs. Weiner told me to. It's not as easy as it appears. Your knuckles get sore against the bumpy surface of the washboard and my hands are quite red and itchy by the time I put everything in the wash. While I wait for the washer to finish I do my homework at the kitchen table. With the excitement of Expo, I'd forgotten all about it. Dad's bedroom door opens and he grunts at me from the hall before he disappears into the bathroom and turns on the shower.

When the wash is done, I put everything in the laundry basket and drag it outside to hang on the line. It's such a nice time of day. The sky is sort of pinky and soft and the street is quiet, although I can hear Mrs. Weiner shout at David and Michael through the back door that if they don't eat their waffles, they won't get any supper.

Somehow, I doubt that. If she can't stand the thought of depriving her husband of sugar when he's on a diet, she'd have a nervous breakdown over not feeding her kids their dinner.

Looking at my whites sway in the breeze is very satisfying. Mrs. Weiner told me to put the bigger items, like blouses and sweaters, first, followed by T-shirts and undershirts, underwear, and then socks. And always put the socks in pairs, but hang them separately, so they'll be sure to dry. To my mind everything looks very, very white but very, very long. They'll probably shrink back to normal once the sun gets at them. I dust off my hands in satisfaction.

Jane and I meet at recess and make our plans. She says she'll bike to my house, since she knows where it is, once I pointed it out.

"Be ready by five thirty," she says. "That will give us plenty of time. I always like to be there early."

"Why's that?"

"I'm not sure. My mother is always early for everything, so I guess it comes naturally. Is your mother like that?"

After all these years, you'd think that when people ask about my mother, it would get easier to say something, but it never does. Do I just say no and leave it be? She'll ask me again at some point, and then it will seem odd that I didn't mention it. I like Jane. There's a good chance we'll become close friends, so I don't want to get off on the wrong foot.

"I don't have a mom."

She actually gasps. I've had a lot of responses over the years, from pitying and stricken looks to total silence, but she seems thoroughly flummoxed.

"How can you not have a mother?"

"People die, Jane."

Her head shakes. "Oh. Of course. I'm sorry. I should've thought of that."

Maybe Jane is not as bright as I thought she was.

It's obvious she's totally rattled by this conversation, and she seems anxious to get away from me, no doubt embarrassed by her reaction.

"I'll see you at five thirty," she mutters and gives me a wave before hurrying off.

"Yeah, see ya," I say to her back.

I hate acknowledging I have a dead mother. It sours my mood every time. But when the lunch bell goes off, I remember I have an egg sandwich in the fridge at home, and this pleases me to no end. My stomach even growls at the thought of it.

When I arrive home the front door is ajar. A shock of electricity goes through my skeleton. I immediately swivel to look across the street and see if Mr. Murder is crouched between the parked cars, ready to batter me with his crutch. Of course he's not. He's already in my house.

I'm unsure how to proceed, and then I remember that I'm a spy, and spies do not flinch in the face of danger, because details could be missed. It runs through my brain that Mrs. Weiner is home, because Michael and David are pulling each other's hair by their father's shiny black Cadillac DeVille. If I have to scream, she'll come running.

I tiptoe up the steps and listen before I proceed to slowly open the door a little wider.

"Hello?" I whisper. Like he's going to answer me. Be brave. "Is anyone in here?"

"Only me!"

"Jesus, Mary, and Joseph." My hand bangs the front door open. "Aunt Maureen! What are you doing here?"

"Your father gave me a key and told me to make you supper because you're going out with a friend to Girl Guides, which I think is wonderful, by the way."

"You left the front door open! I thought the assassin across the street was in here waiting to kill me."

She pokes her head out of the steamy kitchen. "There's an assassin on this street? Why would your father move here, if that's the case?"

I grumble up the hallway. "He might not be one. Why are you here at noon when I'm not going to eat until five?"

"It takes several hours to make a pot roast." She reaches for her cigarettes and lights one.

"I'd be happy with a hot dog, which I could've made myself and saved you the bother of coming over here."

"Your father says he wants you to start eating better."

As I open the fridge and reach for the sandwich he made for me, I realize I've created a monster.

She looks around. "Where's the ashtray?"

"I broke it."

"Hey! That was a nice ashtray. How did you manage that?"

"You don't want to know."

Aunt Maureen heads to the pantry. "Never fear. I have the solution."

While I eat my egg sandwich, May West, and orange, she opens a can of sardines, pours out the oil, eats them bones and all, and uses the empty tin as her ashtray.

"Don't throw this out," she says. "What's wrong with your hands?"

"Nothing. I just bleached my whites this morning. Oh! I totally forgot. I have to see if my wash is dry."

As I scurry past her at the sink where she's peeling carrots, she shouts, "I hope you wore gloves. Bleach will burn your skin."

This was something Mrs. Weiner forgot to mention, and now that I have this information, it explains a lot. My teacher told me this morning that if I didn't stop scratching my hands, she was going to send me to the school nurse to see if I had scabies. I didn't bother to point out that if I did, I'd be scratching my scalp.

My dreamy Norwegian passed me a small tube of hand cream when Mrs. Fuller was writing about the governor-general on the blackboard. My love for this individual is deep. One day I might attempt an actual conversation, but he's on the left side of the schoolyard, and I'm on the right. Our paths may never cross.

Hallelujah! Everything is dry, but then again, my socks are about a foot long. How did that happen? I knock on Mrs. Weiner's back door. She opens it, pink-sponge curlers covering every inch of her head.

"Bubala. What can I do for you? Would you like another milkshake?" She throws her head back. "Frank! Make another milkshake!"

Her husband's name is Frank Weiner. This is too good to be true.

"It's my socks." I hold them up for her to inspect. "I scrubbed them on the washboard like you said, but they seem to have grown."

She looks over at my wash with dismay. "Audrey!" Then she pushes past me and hauls my clothes off the line, yanking them closer with the clothesline pulley. "What did you do? How long did you scrub?" The clothes are now in a pile by her feet, so she picks up a T-shirt and holds it up to my chest. It's down past my knees.

Aunt Maureen comes out to see what's going on. "Hi, Mrs. Weiner. Lovely day."

"NO! It's a TERRIBLE day. I feel awful. I told Audrey to scrub her clothes on a washboard, but I didn't think she'd scrub the life right out of them. Look at this!" She picks up a pair of underwear. "These would fit you!"

Aunt Maureen looks mildly insulted. "Hardly."

"Audrey, when I said scrub, I meant gently. You're not on a farm raising hogs."

"Listen, Mrs. Weiner," Aunt Maureen jumps to my defense. "When someone tells you to scrub something, you assume they mean to really scrub something. Did you tell her to be gentle? And did you tell her to wear gloves while she used bleach? NO! Look at her hands! Her father will be livid."

Now Mrs. Weiner drops my underwear and yells, "OY VEY!" She grabs my hands and holds them to her cheek. "Bubala! I'm so sorry. Me and my big mouth. Everything is ruined! Ruined. I apologize, Mrs. Novak...I'm sorry, I don't know your first name?"

"Maureen."

"You're right, Maureen. I'm Sharon, by the way."

The two of them shake hands in front of me.

"I had no business sticking my nose in." Then Mrs. Weiner looks at me. "I told your father last night that I'd be happy to take you and your Aunt Maureen shopping. We'll go to the Jewish wholesale district. Never shop retail! It's a complete racket! I will pay for the clothes I've ruined. Will you let me do that for you? We'll go this Saturday."

"Do you have enough underwear until then?" Aunt Maureen asks me.

"I'm fine!" I want them to stop talking. This is so embarrassing. And then Mr. Frank Weiner shows up on the porch with a vanilla milkshake. He's a very large, cheery looking man with a small mustache. He's actually the spitting image of the fat guy from Laurel and Hardy. I like him instantly.

"One vanilla milkshake for our new neighbour, as requested." He hands it to me. "Nice to meet you, Audrey. Sharon tells me you're going to be our new babysitter. The last seven quit."

"FRANK!"

I press my lips together so I don't laugh out loud.

"You'll find this is a very nice milkshake. I can't get over how good it is."

"Thank you."

Then the boys come out and pinch each other senseless. There are so many of us on this little platform of wood that if we don't get off it soon, we'll be on the concrete driveway in a pile of broken bones.

It's only after we agree to go shopping and let Mrs. Weiner pay for everything that the Weiner family heads back into their house. Aunt Maureen picks up my clothes and says she'll use them for rags, because you can never have enough white rags. I follow her into the house sipping the milkshake.

It's terrible. No sugar at all.

———

The serious-looking woman standing as straight as a stick in this church basement says, "Company! Left face! Quick march into your horseshoe formation."

It's not clear if I'm included in this, but Jane waves her hand discreetly and I follow behind her, not exactly marching, because if you don't usually march it feels awkward and silly. Once we're in this somewhat crooked horseshoe, the woman at the front says, "We will now recite the Guide Promise."

Twenty-four girls give a three-finger salute and say together, "On my honour, I promise that I will do my best to do my duty to God, the

Queen, and my country, to help other people at all times, and to obey the Guide Law."

It's over before I have a chance to get my fingers into the proper formation.

Then she says, "What is the Guide Law?"

Once again, they repeat as one, "A Guide's honour is to be trusted. A Guide is loyal. A Guide's duty is to be useful and to help others. A Guide is a friend to all and a sister to every other Guide. A Guide is courteous. A Guide is a friend to animals. A Guide obeys orders. A Guide smiles and sings under all difficulties. A Guide is thrifty. A Guide is pure in thought, in word and in deed."

This might be a cult after all.

"Patrol leaders!"

Jane and three other girls march away from us. Where are they going?

"Company, fall in."

The girls scatter into four groups of six each, and once again, Jane is waving her wrist at me to come and join her.

Now we sit in one corner of the room with Jane in the centre, while the other groups sit in the other three corners of the space. It's like having your own gang. There are bulletin boards with clippings and decorations on the walls surrounding each circle. Jane smiles at me. "This is Audrey, everyone. She's here for these last few weeks to see what it's all about. Audrey, this is my troop. I am the patrol leader, and Wanda here is my patrol second. I have a whistle." She takes it out of her pocket and puts it around her neck.

I'm impressed.

Jane points to the emblem sewn on her shirt's left pocket. "We are the Bluebells. Over there are the Sunflowers, Violets, and Forget-me-nots."

"No Dandelions?"

No one laughs. Jane gives me a tolerant smile and opens a tuck box. It looks exactly like my father's wooden shoeshine kit. "This is our patrol box, with our attendance book, where we keep our dues, rope, and paper supplies. When you are a leader, you're responsible for this."

I only hear one thing. "What are the ropes for? Do you hang people who don't pay their dues?"

Jane pretends she doesn't hear me, so I quickly realize she takes her responsibility very seriously and I shouldn't be making light of it. But the fun has gone for me. Still, this is an interesting opportunity to learn about this organization, so I take out my notepad.

"Dues are five cents a week," Jane says. Her troop takes their money out of little change purses they have attached to their belts on their blue uniforms. I'm rather intrigued by these uniforms. They almost look like those worn by nursing sisters during the war, but I only know that because I saw a picture of nurses by a Jeep in my encyclopedia.

"I'm sorry, I didn't realize I needed money," I mumble to Jane.

She takes out another nickel from her purse. "Don't worry. You can pay me back."

Thank goodness she's forgiven me for my flippant remarks.

Over the next hour and a half, I learn that the older leaders are called Brown Owls, Tawny Owls, Snowy Owls, Barn Owls, and on down the line. There are two leaders here; one is a Guide captain and the other a lieutenant. When they come over to our little group, Jane and I stand up and she introduces them to me. The captain, who led the group in the Guide Promise and Guide Law, holds out her hand to shake mine. I hate that, but when I reach out, she says, "Guides do not shake hands with their right arm."

"Very interesting. And why is that?"

She perks up. It appears she likes questions.

"While the exact origin of the Guide and Scouts' left-handed hand-shake is unknown, many attribute it to Ashanti warriors, whom Scouting founder Lord Robert Baden-Powell met long ago in Africa. It is said that when Lord Baden-Powell entered Kumasi, a city in the Ashanti Region of South Ghana, he was met by a great chief. He saluted the chief and then offered his right hand as a sign of greeting and friendship. The chief transferred his shield that was in his left hand, shielding his heart, to his right hand and offered his left hand to shake. He explained by saying, 'In our land only the bravest of the brave shake hands with the left hand, because to do so we must drop our shield and our protection.'"

"Fabulous."

"It is, rather. Welcome, Audrey. I think you'll find the Girl Guides an asset to someone with an inquisitive mind." The captain and her smiley lieutenant drift off to another group. Wanda leans over to me. "She likes you. That almost never happens."

Jane frowns. "Hush, Wanda. You know perfectly well you have to earn the captain's affection. She can't be all ooey-gooey over everyone the minute they walk through the door."

Jane is a bit of prig. But I still like her.

The girls tell me all about the badges you can earn and show me their sashes with the badges sewn on. There's a badge that has a cup of tea on it, an actual iron, and one with a horse. There's even a pick and axe! I wonder what you have to do to earn that.

"Is there a badge with a clothesline on it?" I whisper to Wanda. "I hope to earn that one someday."

"I don't think so. But I'm not as knowledgeable as Jane. She's the PL."

"PL stands for patrol leader, right? And you're the patrol second. Are you a PS?"

"Not sure. Jane only picked me to encourage me to stay. I almost stopped coming after my sister quit."

"Really?" I take out my pencil and notice that the girls have a small pencil hanging off their elastic belts. I need to become a Girl Guide to get one of these marvellous items. "And why did your sister quit?"

"When you're a Brownie, you 'fly up' to Guides. She thought that meant she would actually fly. When they just led her by the hand past an old toadstool, she burst into tears and never came back."

"I don't blame her. That must have been a great disappointment."

"My mother was furious with her. She's a member of the Trefoil Guild."

"And what's a Trefoil Guild?"

"Just a bunch of old Brownies and Guides. Some of them never get over this stage of their lives."

I think I like Wanda too.

Now it's time for word games and puzzles and lessons on how to make a fire, even though we don't have wood or matches. Jane says not to worry, it's just a reminder. Then they start the actual games, like Duck, Duck, Goose, only you have to recite the Guide Law while you're running around, after which all four patrols sit in a big circle and sing campfire songs and hold hands. Then we sing and clap our hands. Then we sing and swing our hands.

Frankly, I'm totally worn out by the time the captain tells us she'll see us next week.

Both Jane and I are rather quiet as we ride our bikes. It is now dusk, and the street lights are coming on. Jane lives a couple of blocks away from the church, so it seems only a minute before she stops her bike and stands astride it. "This is my house."

I stop too. "It's lovely." A large, two-storey, dark red brick house with white shutters, a rounded oak door flanked by two black carriage lamps, and a huge pot of greenery on the front patio. "It looks like a magazine cover."

"Tell me mother that. She'll love you forever." Then she hesitates. "Audrey, I'm sorry about today. I didn't mean to sound so stupid when I asked about your mom."

"That's okay."

"I'm very sad that you don't have a mother."

"Sometimes I am too."

"I told Mom about you and she said I should invite you to church on Sunday and then you can come over and have lunch with us. We always have roast beef with roast potatoes, Yorkshire pudding, and gravy."

Not a clue what Yorkshire pudding is, but it's about time I find out. "That would be nice. Thanks, Jane."

"Did you like Guides?"

When I hesitate, she notices. "If you don't want to come back, that's okay."

"I did like it. I'd like to get the uniform and earn badges. I'm just not used to so many voices all at once. Dad and I are pretty quiet at home. I better go before it gets dark. I'll see you at school tomorrow."

"Bye, Audrey."

As I pedal down the street and pass the tennis courts, there's Pamela on the bench with two boys. I'm not sure why I always have a funny feeling when I see her there. Maybe she doesn't have a home. Maybe she sleeps on that bench. How awful. I should get to know her better and find out for myself. A Guide's duty is to be useful and to help others.

As I glide along, I try to imagine whether my mother would've let me have friends over for supper. Or if she would let me be out at dusk with older boys. I need to find out more about her before I can make these judgements. Dad thinks he's covered all the information I need to know about my mother, but he is dead wrong. Incorrect. Mistaken.

When I pull up to our place, it's starting to spit rain, so I decide to put my bike in the garage. The door is at the back of the duplex, to the side of our deck. Dad has an old MG in here that he's not working on. He says he will one day, but he never does. I didn't even know he had one because it was in storage somewhere, and this is why he was so excited about the duplex. A garage of his own. Now this 1936 hunk of metal sits nice and cozy in here, and his new MG is out in the street. That doesn't make a lot of sense, but he says I know nothing about cars.

That can be easily remedied.

I open the inside door from the garage into the very old basement part of this house. It's my favourite place. Very spooky, dark, with lots of cobwebs and cubbyholes and pipes, with a tiny door that has a small dirty window at the top and opens at the side of the building into the driveway, once you walk up three steps. This little entrance-way is absolutely perfect for spying and saving my bacon. On more than one occasion, I've run away from Jacques, the boy next door who called me a bad name, and dashed in through this portal, only to see him zoom by on his bike looking for me. Dad keeps tools down here on a battered piece of thick lumber that serves as a bench. The stuff is amazing, and not his. He only had a hammer and a bunch of screwdrivers in the storage locker at our apartment. The old couple we bought the place from said Dad could have all their tools because they couldn't take them where they were going, which made me curious about where they were going. Heaven? Hell?

If there are ghosts, and I'm not yet convinced there are, this is where they'd hide out, and they'd be quite content with the arrangement.

Once you navigate this maze, you go through another door into the downstairs portion of our dwelling. The laundry room/bathroom is down here, but we only use the toilet and sink. The rusty metal shower has never been used since Dad tried it. All I heard from upstairs was a screech and then "Jumpin' Jesus! This piece of shit is as cold as ice!"

I suppose you'd call this floor the den. There's a hodgepodge of furniture, an old sofa I lie on, and Dad's favourite La-Z-Boy recliner with stuffing coming out of the arms. Aunt Maureen said he couldn't put that miserable chair in the living room upstairs because it would bring down the tone of the place. He growled and left it here along with his old television set so he can watch *Hockey Night in Canada*. I'm thankful because I get to be upstairs with the new television to watch *Johnny Jellybean and his Squawk Box* at noon. By the time I troop upstairs and walk down the hall towards the sound of Dad's typewriter, I'm fading. I stop in his doorway. "Hi."

He looks startled and quickly removes the pipe he has clamped between his teeth. "Oh! You're home. I didn't hear you come in."

"I came through the garage."

He pushes his glasses up to his forehead. "Did you have a nice time?"

"I think."

He opens the top drawer and takes out the Allsorts. "Explain."

I cross the room, put a candy in my mouth, and sigh as I lean against his desk. "I know in my heart that Girl Guides is a very worthwhile organization and some kids love everything about it. My friend Jane, for one."

"But?"

"I'm not sure it's for me."

"Why not?"

"They make such a racket."

He puts back his head and expels a great puff of air from deep in his chest that's his version of a laugh. "You are just like me, Audrey.

You can't stand noise. But give it a chance before you throw in the towel. Like anything else, you have to give it time."

"Yeah, I suppose. I'm going to read in the tub and then go to bed."

"Okay. Goodnight, honey."

I'm in the hall when I hear him say quietly, "You're just like your mother too."

When I poke my head back in, he's staring away from me, towards the window. "She was a free spirit."

And then he realizes he said it out loud, so he quickly puts his glasses back on his nose, throws the candy in the drawer, and starts typing.

He always does that.

I write down *free spirit* in my notebook.

Chapter Four

On Wednesday I wake up and Dad isn't here. I knew he wouldn't be. He told me he had an early meeting, and I vaguely remember him kissing me on the head through my blankets before he left, but it's still odd to walk around by myself in my pyjamas, so I put on the bathroom radio for company.

"This is the *CBC News*. The time now is seven o'clock, Eastern Standard Time."

While I dry off from my shower, despairing over my hairy legs, I hear this news item.

"Millions of rats moving in a block fifty miles wide and one hundred and fifty miles long may reach the town of Marree, four hundred miles north of Adelaide, South Australia, an official said Wednesday."

"Eww." Shuddering, I quickly turn off the knob on the radio. Animals are my favourite things in the world, but a hundred and fifty miles of anything walking in your direction would be unsettling. Unnerving. Alarming.

I've always wanted a dog or a cat, but Dad said we weren't allowed one in the apartment. But then the church next to our apartment caught fire and all the tenants had to run across the street to the fire station for safety. (Yes, there was a fire station on our street and the church still burned to the ground.) That's when I noticed people guiltily holding small cats, dogs, birds, lizards, and fish bowls under their coats. Even the super had the turtle wrapped up in a blanket. I folded my arms and glared at my father.

"I can't help it if we're the only ones who obey the rules," he said.

I didn't speak to him for a week, and then he got annoyed. "Goddammit, Audrey. I don't think it's fair to keep a dog in a small apartment all day when no one is home. How would you like to be kept in solitary confinement?"

Once I looked that up, I had to agree, but other people do it and their dogs seem happy enough. There's a bulldog named Rollie who lives on the end of our street by the high school, and his owner is a five-year-old kid who walks him three times a day. Rollie is bow-legged and he waddles. The first time I met him I fantasized about kidnapping him, but the kid is cute and he likes to talk, so I wouldn't want him to be sad. He told me Rollie farts.

"He farted when the Rabbi came over."

"No kidding."

"Rollie doesn't care."

Rollie stared up at me with his big googly eyes and his wide-open mouth that splits his face in half, his tongue hanging down to the sidewalk.

"If you ever need a dog walker, I'm available."

"Thanks." Then he and Rollie kept going.

On the table is a box of Raisin Bran and a bowl. This makes a nice change. I reach into the fridge for the chocolate milk and my momentary happiness disappears. There's no sandwich for me. Well, that lasted, didn't it? I slam the door shut.

Then I bang the front door shut on my way to school. I'm biking past Jacques's house and see him kneeling on the ground tying his shoelace. I sail by him and then sail over the front of my bike and hit my face on the pavement after he thrusts a stick in the spokes of my front wheel.

I'm completely dazed and not sure what's happened. By the time I lift my head, Jacques has disappeared. It feels like my teeth are loose. I put my hand up and there's blood. I need to get off this street. I'm not sure if anyone saw me. I'm in a fog when I run back up our front steps and fumble with the key to open the door.

When I look in the mirror, I have a bloodied fat lip, scrapes all over my face with tiny pieces of gravel still stuck to them, and I'm bleeding from my forearms, palms, knees, and shins. I sit on the toilet and my body cries, even though I don't want to. I don't like it. It makes the air seem thick and too much to manage.

But after a while I stop. Dad told me once that whatever I'm feeling, it will always stop at some point, so don't panic and just wait it out.

It takes some time to clean myself up. There's no way I'm calling Dad. His meeting is so important he forgot to make me a sandwich, so I can't possibly bother him. Aunt Maureen would be more of a hindrance than a help, fussing around me like a fruit fly. But I'd love to see Mrs. Weiner take a baseball bat to my friendly neighbour. She'd beat him until he was flat.

Now I'm very late for school, but I have to go because we have a history test. Maybe that's what I'll do. Cut Jacques's head off like Henry VIII always did when he was annoyed with people.

When I show up at my classroom door, Mrs. Fuller takes one look at me and comes straight over from the front of the board and pulls me away from the door, so the kids don't keep gawking at me. "What happened, Audrey?"

"A boy put a stick in my bike wheel."

"Someone from this school?"

"No. I think he goes to the French school."

"We're going to the nurse right now and get you checked over." She puts her arm around my shoulders and walks beside me down the hall. It feels nice.

Suddenly I like Mrs. Fuller. She smiles at me as she leaves me with the nurse. "Take your time. Only come back when you feel ready. I should call your parents."

"No! Dad has an important meeting and my mother is unavailable." She gives me a curious look.

I thought I'd cleaned myself up pretty well, but obviously not. The nurse takes her time to disinfect all my cuts and scrapes.

"You're lucky you don't need stitches in this lip," she says, taping a piece of gauze over it. "Only have things like soup for the next few days. Your mouth and teeth are going to be sore. Here's an aspirin. Can you swallow pills?"

"Yes."

Turns out I can't. I make a mess and cough up the pill and the water. She takes two spoons and crushes another aspirin into powder and adds sugar to it and makes me eat it and then drink some water. I'm interested about the fact that she keeps sugar in here.

She tells me to lie down for half an hour and I doze off, but the recess bell rings and as always sends a shockwave across my skin. I feel better, so I tell the nurse I'm fine and I'd like to go. She knows I have a history test after recess and says she'll give me a note to postpone it, but I tell her I'd rather not. Who knows how long these dates will stay in my brain?

When I get outside, a mob of girls including Gloria and Jane come over to check out my injuries. Even Pamela hangs around. When I tell them what happened, Pamela tsks and says, "The little bastard." This makes me feel better.

After a few minutes the girls wander off because I'm having a hard time talking, so I just stand there and stare into space. That's when a girl plows into me, running after a soccer ball. I know she didn't mean it, but she's so intent on running after it she doesn't even look back to see if I'm okay.

The injustice of it all overwhelms me. On today of all days. Aren't I sore enough?

"Fuzzy Wuzzy!" I hiss under my breath.

She's a Black girl.

She doesn't hear me, she's smiling and calling to her friends. But *I* heard me. Where did that come from so effortlessly? Didn't I just say to Mrs. Weiner that I'd never call people bad names? I don't know what to do or whether I should apologize for something she didn't hear in the first place, so I walk away.

This is the worst day of my life.

In the middle of writing the history test, I feel another poke in my back. I turn around and my Norwegian passes me a tissue and jerks his head towards my arm. It's bleeding again, so I take the Kleenex and nod, pressing it against my skin. He goes back to his test, and so do I.

Mrs. Fuller comes over to collect our papers. She says to me quietly, "I think you should stay home this afternoon, Audrey. Do the questions on page fifty-nine of your science book. That's what we'll be going over in class."

"Thank you, Mrs. Fuller."

Why did I ever think she was mean? I should tear up my notes on Mrs. Fuller. Other than throwing chalk, she's an upstanding citizen who loves poetry, especially "High Flight" by John Gillespie Magee and "The Wreck of the Hesperus" by Longfellow. She will be the latest addition in my admiration notebook. The simple act of putting her arm around me to keep me safe when I felt very alone meant a lot.

I'm nearing my house when I see Jacques kneeling on the sidewalk by a car bumper. He glances in my direction and then takes off down his driveway. When I get closer to where he was, I look down and see a small kitten with wire wrapped around its neck. I can't believe it. Instantly I grab the dear little thing and twist the wire away, holding it under my sweater to keep it warm as I run to the house.

Thirty minutes later, the cat, whom I have named Sally-Anne after the Salvation Army, is cuddled in a soft towel on my bed, sleeping contentedly after finishing off a bowl of warm milk. She's safe. Then I walk outside and creep along the back of our duplex and see Jacques working on his bike. His little sister with the rotten baby teeth is sucking on a jawbreaker, sitting on their back steps. That can't be helped.

I'm on him before he even looks up, and I hit him as many times as I can before he really starts to hit back. His sister never stops sucking.

Pretty soon we're both out of breath, so we stand there and look at each other. I don't know what else to do, so I walk away. He doesn't come after me.

My father is so incensed when he gets home and hears what happened, he immediately says I can keep Sally-Anne and he'll personally run out and buy kitty litter and cat food. Then he says I'm not going back to school on Thursday or Friday because I need to recover and he wants Aunt Maureen to take me to the doctor to make sure I don't have a concussion. Then he says he's going to buy us a pizza for supper after he goes over to the little shit's house and gives his father a piece of his mind.

"I can't have pizza, Dad. The nurse said to only have soup for the next few days."

"I'll find pizza soup." And then he adds, "I was in such a rush this morning, I accidently put your tuna sandwich in my briefcase. I only realized it after it started to stink."

Dad must have called Aunt Maureen, because I'm in bed with Sally-Anne when she comes bursting through my bedroom door.

"I can't believe it!" She sits next to me and holds my face to examine it closely. "Who does this to a person?"

"Dad went over to talk to his father."

"And?"

"The guy told Dad to get off his porch."

She crosses her arms. "You see. That's the mentality of some people. The kid's probably been dragged up by his hair. His old man no doubt beats him. That's why some kids are cruel."

"Dad isn't cruel. And you should see his little sister's teeth. They never brush them."

"Well, there you have it. And this is the other victim?"

Sally-Anne is purring in my arms, her grey-and-white head snuggled into my elbow. "Isn't she sweet?"

"She is now. But they grow into mountain lions who eat you out of house and home." She gets off the bed. "I'm going to make some soup."

"Now?"

"The nurse said soup, you get soup."

I'm feeling pretty tired. Dad comes back in and suggests I go to bed. He says he'll take Sally-Anne so she doesn't wake me up tonight.

"No! I want her. I'm not going to be able to sleep anyway."

"You must be sore."

"It's not that." I look down and rub my cat's soft fur for courage. "Something happened today, besides the bike thing."

"Explain."

I tell him the awful thing I said about the girl at my school. "It was a lousy thing to say."

"Can you think of another word?"

"Prejudiced. Demeaning."

"Better. Kids sometimes say mean things, but I don't ever want you to insult someone for who they are. It's the lowest form of behaviour."

"It was a bad day."

"One I know you will never repeat."

"No. I won't. I promise."

And I mean it. I'm supposed to be a nice person, but I said something nasty very easily just because I was hurt and angry. Doing something nasty seems to be Jacques's way of dealing with hurt and anger. He and I are not so different, which is appalling to me. Maybe I should keep a record of his father's behaviour on his behalf. He's likely not thought about doing that. The police might need it someday.

The next morning, instead of going to school, Aunt Maureen drags me to the doctor's office in her rattle-trap of a car. All I do is fret about Sally-Anne.

"Cats sleep twenty-three-and-a-half hours a day! She won't even know you're gone."

We're at a red light and I think my aunt needs a new muffler. "I'm a new mother. That's what mothers do, isn't it? Worry?"

"Some do. Want some gum?" She takes a dirty half a stick of Wrigley's Doublemint gum out of her pocket and passes it to me.

"No thanks. My mouth is sore and bandaged, remember?"

"Oh, yeah." She unpeels the foil and pops it in her own mouth.

"Was your mother a worrier?" I ask.

"There were too many of us to worry about."

"What happened to her?"

"She died on the living room chesterfield when she was in her forties."

"Was she sick?"

"She died of overwork. She just lay down and died because she was too tired to live."

The light turns green and we jerk forward. Then the car backfires and a puff of black smoke trails behind us.

"That's so sad. I didn't know that people could die from being tired."

"Too tired to live. There's a difference. People give up."

"Did my mother give up?"

She doesn't say anything. Typical of my relatives. Always a cone of silence like on *Get Smart* when the discussion turns to my mother. Little do they know that the more they don't say, the more I'm going to find out why they are so reluctant to talk about her. This compulsion comes in waves. Sometimes it's too overwhelming for me, so I let it go because it makes my life easier. Other days, it's all I can do to not jump out of my skin.

Then she says, "Yes. She did."

I open my mouth to ask more, but she shuts me up. "Okay, we're here."

I've been going to Dr. McTavish since I was a baby. He's an absent-minded elderly pediatrician and I think it's about time I graduated. His equally absentminded elderly sister runs his office, and between the two of them, they can never find a thing. But the mothers who come to his practice love him and will forgive him anything because he makes house calls.

But they aren't the ones stuck in their underwear being weighed by the sister. A three-year-old might not mind, but this twelve-year-old does, and I'm not having it. Aunt Maureen sits on a little chair pushed in the corner of his office while I sit on white paper on the examining table. The sister comes in holding my chart. No one knows what her name is.

"Strip to your underwear, please, and get on the scale."

"I don't need to be weighed. I'm just here to see if I have a concussion."

Aunt Maureen looks like she's swallowed her gum. The sister lifts her head, her grey hair coming out of her frazzled-looking bun, and peers at me over the glasses perched on the end of her nose. "That matters not a whit."

"I'm not undressing."

"Fine." She closes my chart and walks out, slamming the door behind her.

"Audrey!"

"Why am I still coming to a baby doctor? It's embarrassing."

66

Then Dr. McTavish comes in, and he is like an old, worn-out mountain goat, so I can't stay mad at him. He doesn't have a problem with me sitting in my clothes. Maybe it's just his sister I don't like.

"Well, well, well," he says. "Looks like you lost the fight."

It turns out I don't have a concussion, and he pats my head and gives me a lollipop and a tongue depressor on the way out.

———

On Saturday morning, I'm still loath to leave Sally-Anne and go shopping with Aunt Maureen and Mrs. Weiner, but Dad says she can sleep in the candy drawer of his desk, so I settle her in with a hand towel and she is quite cozy. For a while. She's now running up and down everything, hanging on to curtains with her claws.

Aunt Maureen shows up at nine. We're not leaving until ten, so she's excited about the prospects of doing something different for a change. She actually says, "This is exciting."

She stirs boiling hot water into a cup of instant coffee. "I've never been to the Jewish wholesalers. Would you like some hot chocolate?"

"No, thanks."

She turns her head towards Dad's study. "Jack? Do you want some coffee?"

"Sure! Two creams, two sugars. One cream for Sally-Anne."

I smile. He likes my little puff of fur.

At ten on the dot, we hear a car horn blaring outside, as if there's a wedding going on. I push aside the curtains in the living room window to see Mrs. Weiner behind the wheel of her Cadillac DeVille frantically waving at me.

"She can't come to the door like a normal person?" Aunt Maureen mutters. As we scurry to get on our shoes, she says, "Get a sweater. There's a breeze."

"Bye, Dad! Bye, Sally-Anne!"

"Have fun!" Dad yells down the hallway.

Aunt Maureen gets in the front passenger seat and I crawl into the back. This car is so enormous it's like entering a swimming pool.

Of course, I'm used to the MG. Not that I go in it often, just when Dad takes me to Ruby Foo's for dinner as a special treat.

"Hello, ladies! Are we ready for an adventure?! My gawd! What happened to you, Audrey? You look like you had a run-in with a cheese grater!"

"Jacques made me fall off my bike."

"That little shit. He doesn't dare come near my boys. I chased him down the street once with a pan shovel."

Before we can respond, there's a loud banging on Mrs. Weiner's side of the car. David and Michael are pounding each other and the car, wailing for their mother. The car has honest-to-God electric windows, which I've never seen before. They lower with an even hum. Mrs. Weiner smacks her kids back like a lion tamer.

"DON'T MAKE ME GET OUT OF THIS CAR! I SWEAR TO GOD!"

She starts honking the horn again and Mr. Weiner opens his front door and waves happily at his family.

"FRANK! COME AND GET THE BOYS!"

"When are you coming home, Mommy?" they whine together.

"WHEN I'M GOOD AND READY. NOW BE GOOD BOYS AND I'LL BRING YOU BACK A TREAT. FRANK!"

The happy Frank comes over to the side of the car and sticks his head in the window. "Hello, Maureen and Audrey. I hope you have nice day."

"Thank you," we say in unison.

He kisses Mrs. Weiner's red lips and she gives him three kisses back, and then he picks up his sons, one in each enormous arm, and throws them over his shoulders. They are still kicking and screaming.

"Goodbye, honey!" She waves out her car window and doesn't even look behind her to see if there's a car coming before she veers into the street, almost knocking her husband off his feet.

She never stops talking the entire way to Mount Royal, which is just as well, since Aunt Maureen and I are too frightened to open our mouths. The woman drives like a maniac. She speeds up when she sees a yellow light and most of the time it's red before her big-ass car goes through the intersection. She careens between lanes of traffic like a game of pinball and lays on the horn every ten seconds.

"Montreal drivers! Can you believe it? They're a danger to society."

I'm so glad I have a sweater on, since Mrs. Weiner has the air conditioning on full blast.

"It's a Saturday morning," Aunt Maureen gulps with her hand on the dashboard to keep herself upright. "Do you think we'll find a parking space?"

"Parking, schmarking!" Mrs. Weiner laughs with a wave of her hand. "Don't worry."

We pull up to a street with cars along both sides, bumper to bumper.

"There's the store we want," Mrs. Weiner points.

"Oh dear," tsks Aunt Maureen. "This doesn't look promising."

Mrs. Weiner pulls up to a car by the store's front door and parks alongside it. "You'll have to crawl out on my side, Maureen. You too, Audrey."

Aunt Maureen is totally flustered. "You can't double-park! You'll get a ticket!"

"So what?"

"But what if the person who owns this car has to get out?"

"They can damn well wait. You worry too much, Maureen."

This is better than going to the movies.

The store is packed when we go in. Women who look exactly like Mrs. Weiner, with teased hair piled high or smoothed down and curled into one gigantic flip at their necks. The younger ones are wearing sleeveless mock-turtlenecks, patterned capri pants, and flats. The older ones look like Gloria's grandmother, only their shapeless dresses and head scarves are brightly coloured.

This is like nothing I've ever seen, and I'm sure, by the look on Aunt Maureen's face, she's never experienced it either. The clothes are in big bins and the shoppers stand together and pick their way through them, grabbing items they want and tossing others aside as need be.

All of these ladies are animated, unlike the hushed tones in Ogilvy's department store. They are having much more fun while they shop, laugh, and argue with each other. After ten minutes my ears are ringing. My aunt and I stand aside as Mrs. Weiner takes charge. She grabs everything at once and tells us to follow her over to the dressing rooms. There's a lineup and half of the women don't even wait to go behind the curtain. Since I've never seen an older woman's body in any stage of undress, my eyes bug out of my head. I didn't know that breasts could reach a woman's navel, or that aprons of extra flesh lived happily around hips.

Mrs. Weiner pushes her way through the crowd. "Make way! We have a very sad girl on our hands. Look at this poor child's face. Her father beats her up! I'm buying her a present to make her feel better, but we don't have much time. He might have followed us here."

The crowd parts and we sneak behind the nearest curtain. Aunt Maureen looks shell-shocked. Mrs. Weiner tweaks her cheek. "You have to go after what you want, Maureen. Life is not going to hand it to you on a plate."

Mrs. Weiner keeps going back into the store to drag more things into the dressing room.

"This is too much. I don't need all this."

"Listen, bubala. This will be my only chance to buy clothes for a girl. Let me have my fun. And by the way, you don't need undershirts anymore. You need bras. Doesn't she, Maureen?"

Aunt Moo turns bright red. "I never had daughters. I don't know."

"You've got eyes, and tits, I presume. Look at the girl. She might be skinny, but those little marbles are going to flower soon, and she'll want them securely in her shirt before September, when those little bastards in high school rub themselves all over her. Lock and load them away, I say."

Words keep bubbling to the surface. *Mortification. Humiliation. Shame.* And that's before she makes me try on a training bra.

I think Mrs. Weiner realizes that we seem to be traumatized, as I stand trembling with my back to her, covering my buds, and Aunt Maureen has turned into a statue, staring at the dressing room curtains.

She hands it to me. "Don't worry, Audrey. I'm not going to look."

I have no idea how these straps work. "What am I actually training my breasts to do?"

"To become still and invisible for as long as possible."

She ends up showing me how to attach the hooks and eyes, and when I see myself in the mirror, I'm surprised at how powerful I feel.

"I look like a grown-up."

"You look beautiful," Mrs. Weiner smiles. "Doesn't she, Maureen?"

Aunt Maureen turns around and her face softens. "She does."

———

It's Sunday morning, and I'm wearing brand new underwear, my training bra under my new Peter Pan white blouse, a navy pleated skirt, and white ankle socks with my pink Mary Janes, because I'm going to church and having Yorkshire pudding.

Dad and Sally-Anne think I look very smart. He gives me a nickel so I can pay back Jane for my Guide dues, and he hands me two quarters for the church collection plate.

"You have to pay to go to church?"

"Sort of."

"And put your money on a plate? Doesn't it just slide off?"

"It's called a plate, but it has sides. Just do what everyone else does. When they stand, you stand, when they sing, you sing, when they recite the Lord's Prayer, you do the same."

I sit at the kitchen table and put the money in my Peruvian change purse. "Do I have to believe what they're saying?"

"No."

"So why say it?"

Dad eats his toast and offers a small piece to Sally-Anne, who nibbles at it. "It's not possible for me to explain church before you go. I'm realizing we should have a conversation about it at some point, and perhaps I could've made more of an effort to take you, if only so you can experience for yourself the mysteries of the world we live in. I for one do not believe in Heaven and Hell. They can be found right here on Earth."

"You don't believe you go to God when you die?"

"God is not an old man in the sky. God is the energy that makes up this entire universe. It's you and me and Sally-Anne and the trees outside and the oceans and the winds and the mountains and that spider making its web in the window. Living things. People are not the boss of this planet, even though they think they are. We're just some of the creatures who live here. Churches were formed to make people behave. But churches aren't all bad. They bring comfort to some. Lonely people want to believe in something bigger than themselves. It's filled with good folks who mean well, but like everywhere else, it can have some not-so-good people too. Don't get sucked into thinking that everything you hear in church is gospel. Make up your own mind."

I pat the pocket of my skirt. "I have my trusty notebook and pencil with me. I'll jot down my impressions."

"You do that. Never rely on someone else's opinion. Not even mine."

It's quite windy this morning as I bike to Jane's house. At one point I have to stop riding and button up my sweater. The sky is a pewter grey. This has been a very rainy spring, but because of it the leaves on the trees and grass are really *green* green. They look brand new. Young and fresh. I like noticing things like this. When we learned in school that plants have a life cycle too, everything became more real for me. Now I watch the leaves on our maple tree out back and I've named some of them. (Three of the cutest are Snipp, Snapp, and Snurr.)

When we first moved here in April, the buds were opening. These were the babies. Right now, they're teenagers, and by the time I go to high school in September, they'll be Dad's age and their colours will change like his did. But I'm not looking forward to October and November. I don't want them to die.

By the time I pull up to Jane's house, I know my hair is not quite as neat as it was when I left, but at least the gauze is off my lip, and my wounds aren't quite so livid. My stupid bike won't stand up, so I lay it down by the side of their walkway and reach up beside their very impressive oak door and ring the doorbell.

When the door opens, it's like walking into an episode of *The Donna Reed Show*. This immaculate family with perfect hair, perfect clothes, and perfect faces grin like idiots as I stand there. Donna Reed herself comes forward and pulls me in.

"Hello, Audrey! Come and meet the family."

No wonder this woman runs the church. She seems to be running the show here. "This is my husband, Mr. Andrews."

What is it with adults always wanting to shake your hand?

"Hello, Audrey. Welcome to our home."

Despite the handshaking thing, I really like Mr. Andrews. He's tall and good-looking in a matinee idol kind of way. Not like Dad with his shorter, grumpier Julius Caesar persona.

Mrs. Andrews then draws her handsome, tall son forward. He's got the biggest Adam's apple I've ever seen. "And this is Peter."

He at least keeps his hands to his side. "Hello."

"And this is our baby, Dixie."

Well, she's as cute as a button. Dixie hops up and down. "I'm in kindergarten!"

"And do you like it?" I ask.

"I LOVE MRS. BROWN!"

"I love her too."

Jane is in the background waiting impatiently. I'm sure she's thinking, *This is my friend, why don't you all back off*, so I make a point of smiling at her. "Hi, Jane. It's good to see you."

She opens her mouth to reply, but her mother takes me by the shoulders and steers me into their very formal living room. "We're not leaving for a few minutes yet. Would you like some lemonade, dear?"

"Sure."

Mrs. Andrews snaps a finger at Jane. "Get us some lemonade, sweetheart."

Jane makes a face and disappears. The men in the family seem to have evaporated as well. Only Dixie remains, hopping in the centre of the room, holding the skirt of her dress over her head.

"Watch me jump!"

I watch her jump. "Very good jumping."

Then she throws herself on the plush carpet and does three somersaults. "See?!"

Her mother has had enough. "Dixie, dear. Stop messing up your Sunday outfit."

Dixie stops and picks her nose. Mrs. Andrews gets up and takes her away but comes right back. "She's excited to have company."

"Well, that's very sweet of her."

Mrs. Andrews is as nice looking as her husband. She could definitely be on television, she's so tall and slender, and there's not a hair out of place. Now I know where Jane gets it.

Poor old Jane comes back with a couple of glasses of lemonade and gives one to me and one to her mother. She sits in the chair across from us. "How are you feeling?"

"Yes!" cries Mrs. Andrews. "How are you feeling, dear? Jane told me all about that wicked boy. He needs to be punished."

"I'm better. I have a cat now."

"A cat!" Mrs. Andrews smiles.

"I'd love a cat," Jane says.

"I'm allergic to cats," Mrs. Andrews tells me.

"You're allergic to everything," Jane mutters.

My sip of lemonade hides my grin, sort of. Jane sees what I'm doing, looks away, and smiles.

"I don't think Jane will ever forgive me for being allergic to dogs and cats, but it's not like one has any choice in the matter."

"I've seen pictures of you growing up with dogs and cats all over your bed!"

Mrs. Andrews purses her lips. "That's very true, but you can develop allergies when you get older, as I've explained before. Now, enough about us. I want to hear all about Audrey. Jane tells me you don't have a mother. That's just awful! What happened to her?"

"Mother!"

"She died."

Mrs. Andrews waits for me to say more, but I don't. I know it's killing her, but she can hardly ask how.

Still, I throw her a bone. "When does church start, Mrs. Andrews? I've never been to church."

The shocked look I expect arrives right on cue.

"Really? Never?"

"No. My father doesn't believe in religion."

"And what does he believe in? Communism?"

"That's a good question. I'll ask him when I get home."

Jane gets up. "Want to see my room?"

"Sure."

We race up the stairs and Jane shuts her bedroom door behind us. "Oh, Audrey. I love you. No one has ever handled my mother like that."

"She means well."

"Ya think?"

I'm a little dazzled by Jane's room, to be honest. I've never seen a canopied bed before. Only in the Eaton's catalogue. "Wow. This is quite a room. Your ruffled curtains match your ruffled bedspread."

"It's much too girly and fussy. Dixie loves it, but I don't."

Then I spy a white Princess phone on the end table by her bed. "You have your own *phone*?! In your *room*? Imagine that. Our only phone is in the kitchen. It's got a long cord so I could always take it into my room, but the door won't close properly then, and no one calls me anyway."

"I'll call you."

Mrs. Andrew's voice floats up the stairs. "Girls! Time for church."

I know that St. John's United Church is a nice-looking brick building with red doors, but I've only been to the basement for Guides, and we went in a separate entrance. Walking in through the church doors and seeing the interior is quite awe-inspiring, with its vaulted ceiling and stained glass windows.

The solid wood pews are filled with families who nod to one another as we sit in our seats near the front. People are looking at me wondering who I am. I'm glad I have on my locked-and-loaded bra. One wouldn't want to jiggle up the aisle in front of all these eyes. I'm forever in Mrs. Weiner's debt.

There are little shelves on the back of the pews with prayer books and hymn books leaning side by side waiting to be picked up. It's a place to put our pamphlets too. Two old men in suits handed them to us. I fold mine into my pocket to examine later. And then there are even tinier protrusions every so often with two holes drilled in them. When I point at them, Jane whispers in my ear, "That's where you put your grape juice shot glass when we take Communion."

"We get grape juice? Aunt Maureen told me to expect wine and stale bread. I was looking forward to the wine."

"No, we're United. We never do anything that interesting."

Church is kind of boring. Old guys get up and talk a lot. But I like the choir and the organ music. It's nice to sing along, even though I don't know the tunes. Hearing voices singing and reciting together makes you feel a part of something. I can understand that people would feel less lonely here.

But then the reverend ruins it for me by telling us to greet our neighbours. We have to turn around in our pews and shake hands with other strangers, saying "Peace be with you."

What is it with the grown-up obsession with handshaking? Don't people realize that other humans wipe and scratch their bums, pick their noses, and pick out their earwax with their fingernails? Who wants to touch that? Why can't North Americans just bow to each other like some of the Asians do? It makes much more sense and is completely civilized.

Organ music pipes us out of the church. Everyone has to wait along the aisles for the minister to shake our stupid hands before we're allowed to escape. Poor old Dixie is about to lose her mind. Her mother ran out of little boxes of Sun-Maid raisins twenty minutes ago.

Then I realize that most of the women, and quite a few of the young girls, are wearing short white gloves. Okay! I'm going to get myself a pair if I ever come back here. That would solve the germ situation.

Mrs. Andrews puts her hands on my shoulders and stands behind me. "Reverend Haliburton, this is Audrey Parker, a friend of Jane's from school. It's her first time in church."

The reverend quickly reaches out with both hands and grasps mine in a very firm grip. Almost to the point of pain. "We're very glad you came, Audrey. New sheep are always welcome to our flock."

For a second, I thought he said "fuck."

Then I hear Mrs. Andrews whisper over my head. "She doesn't have a mother."

Motherless children seem to be a pet project for some people. Mrs. Andrews obviously takes the role of mother seriously, and I'm giving her the benefit of the doubt that she's trying to include me in her circle. To help me in some way. But I'm almost feeling like a stray dog at the pound.

Still, she is going to make me a Yorkshire pudding, so I remain grateful.

Jane and I have fun on the swing set in their hedged-in back garden while her mother puts on her full apron and roars around her kitchen with seventeen pots and pans. I see her through the patio doors. She's a lesson in precision and concentration.

Dixie insists on hanging off the rings between our swings, and we keep getting kicked in the face.

"Dixie! Go away!"

She sticks out her tongue. "You can't make me! You can't make me!"

"You little creep!"

"I'm going to tell Mommy!" Dixie runs off to spill the beans to her mother.

Jane laughs. "I knew that would get rid of her."

"You're lucky you have a little sister."

"Maybe."

"Do you ever babysit her?"

"Sure. I took a babysitting course."

I'm still swinging back and forth looking at the sky. "So, twelve is not too young?"

"Are you a responsible twelve-year-old?" Jane laughs.

"Who knows! I think my neighbour Mrs. Weiner wants me to babysit her boys, but I'm nervous about it."

"The Weiner wieners?! Those little creeps are a menace! I wouldn't touch them with a ten-foot pole!"

"It's so odd. Mr. and Mrs. Weiner are the nicest couple in the world. And I have a feeling that as generous as she is, and as desperate as they are, I'd probably make a fortune."

"Well, that's true."

"She actually told me that if they don't do what I say, I can smack them."

"Then I'd definitely do it. I've wanted to smack them since they started kindergarten."

It's amazing to see other people's rituals. Whereas Dad and I don't own a tablecloth, Mrs. Andrews obviously irons hers, and she has actual napkin rings for her cloth napkins. She brings out a huge platter and places this enormous prime rib roast in front of Mr. Andrews.

Is that all his?

He then takes a carving knife and slides it back and forth across something that looks like a metal nail file. After that he carves the meat at the table, just like the Grinch in Whoville.

"Our guest is always served first." He smiles as he passes me over a big slice of meat, but it's rather thin. As he goes along, his slices get thicker and thicker. This roast is so good I'm dying to have more, but since everyone is declaring how full they are, I don't dare say I want another piece. It would make me seem greedy.

The best thing about our lunch is the Yorkshire pudding. I thought it would come in a bowl, but it's like this little bun, and when you cut into it with your fork and knife it's hollow, and at first I think, *Well, that's not fair,* but I look around and everyone else's is hollow too, so it seems that's the way they're made. They're really delicious with gravy.

All in all, it's been a really nice time. I thank her parents very much for the lovely meal.

"You're more than welcome to come back any time," Mrs. Andrews says. "Perhaps you'd like to come for leftovers tomorrow before you and Jane go to Girl Guides."

Jane clasps her hands together. "Oh, please! That will be fun."

"I'll ask my dad and let you know."

I'm feeling a little guilty that I haven't seen much of him or Sally-Anne this weekend. It's almost three o'clock in the afternoon when I wave goodbye and head home. Aunt Maureen was right about moving here. My social life has improved a hundred percent.

But I've made up my mind. I need to find out more about my mother, and quickly. If I'm making friends left, right, and centre, I require a more interesting story to tell the Mrs. Andrewses of the world. Just saying I have a dead mom is not working for me. I'd like to say something else about her, like maybe she was a writer too, or went to the Olympics or was a fabulous cook. Something that makes her come to life. Then I won't feel so abnormal. It's not easy being an oddity.

With this decision made, I'm humming as I glide my bike along our driveway and lean it up against the garage, to take the curved stairs two at a time before I burst through the back door and into the kitchen.

"I'm home!"

No one answers me.

"Anyone here?"

Then I hear a faint, odd noise coming from Dad's study and hurry to his open door.

I can't take in what I'm seeing. Dad is sitting in his chair and Sally-Anne is lying on the desk in front of him. He's breathing into her mouth, and keeps doing it over and over again.

"What's wrong? Daddy? What's wrong?"

He looks up at me and a sob escapes his lips. "I'm sorry. I came in and she had the cord from the window blind around her neck."

"Is she dead?"

"I've been trying to make her breathe for an hour. I'm so sorry."

I go over and pick her up in my arms and take her to my room. As I sit on my bed hugging her lifeless body, my father is crying. That's a sound I've never heard before.

And I never, ever want to hear it again.

Chapter Five

My nose is completely blocked as I sit with Dad and Aunt Maureen at the kitchen table. Sally-Anne is wrapped inside my Christmas stocking, because it's the prettiest thing I own and just the perfect size. Dad places her in my sneaker shoebox lined with a towel, so it looks like we've tucked her into bed. Because we only had Sally-Anne for a few days and didn't have time to get her a toy, I place my Ponytail Barbie in a red swimsuit beside her to keep her company, the one Aunt Maureen bought it for me before I could tell her I hate dolls.

Then I add a can of tuna.

"She doesn't need that," Aunt Maureen sniffs.

"Who cares?! I want her to have it!" I yell.

"It's okay, Audrey," Dad says. "You can put it in."

It's now suppertime, but none of us can eat. Aunt Maureen came over as soon as Dad called her. She was teary and she doesn't even like cats.

"We should bury her under the maple tree," Dad suggests. "That way you can see her when you look out your bedroom window."

"I'm not burying her tonight. She's sleeping with me."

"Oh, Audrey," Aunt Maureen sighs. "You can't sleep with a dead cat."

"She's hardly dead! She was alive a few hours ago. She doesn't stink! She's not rotting away! She's absolutely perfect, except for the fact that she's not breathing. How can you be here one minute and not the next? That stupid kid puts a wire around her throat and I save her only to have a cord get wrapped around her neck in this supposedly safe house and now she's dead anyway. Why was God so insistent that she die with something around her neck? Somebody explain that to me!"

"Life is unfair," Dad says. "Most of us can never understand it."

"Is this how you felt when my mother died?"

When he doesn't say anything, I slap my hand on the table. "Oh, here we go! I ask a question about my mother and you two clam up. Do you know how pathetic that is? I'm not a kid anymore. I don't need to be protected from the truth."

"This is exactly how it feels, Audrey. When you suffer a loss of any kind, not just death. Your heart breaks. And you think your life will never be the same. But it gets better. I promise you."

"But I will always miss this damn cat! I will always miss her! That is never going away! I will miss her until I die!"

"And that is allowed. You are allowed to miss her forever. I know I'll never forget her."

Aunt Maureen nods up and down. "And I'll never forget her either, even though I only knew her for forty-five minutes."

I'm so distraught, I have to pace. That's when I remember something.

"I have to call Jane. Her mother wanted me to come for dinner tomorrow before we went to Guides, but there's no way I'm ever going to Guides again. I don't even want to go to school. I can't wait for this school year to be over. I don't want to do anything or go anywhere or eat at someone else's house. My cat died because I wasn't here looking after her. I wanted to eat Yorkshire pudding and poor Sally-Anne was in a new place, and probably confused. I should've been here. And you should've been more careful, Dad!"

"Yes, you're right. I should have been watching her more closely. Would you like me to call Jane's mother?"

"Yes, please. And I didn't mean that. It wasn't your responsibility. It was mine. Only mine."

I take the shoebox off the table and go into my room and shut the door, but then I open it. "And I will never eat Yorkshire pudding again. Just so you know."

———

Dad stays home with me the next day and says I don't have to go to school. His guilt is enormous, obviously, but I'm grateful, because I didn't get any sleep. It's hard to hug a shoebox. And I hate crying, but it seems like my face leaked all night with a will of its own.

Perhaps the safest thing to do is never love anything again. If this is what it's like to grow up, who needs it? All I know is that I never want to be a mother. So that means I have to become a nun. At least nuns get to drink wine.

Dad comes into my room to tell me that he's dug a hole under the tree, but there's no hurry. I nod and hug the shoebox tighter, so he leaves.

Finally, at two o'clock, I know I have to do this. I've finished the eulogy. You have to write one when somebody dies. My really old cousin Stu wrote one for his dad, my Uncle Jerry. And Sally-Anne wants to rest. She actually told me. She wants to snuggle in the earth and says she'll keep an eye out for murderers and con men, and signal me from the tree if she sees anything suspicious.

Dad and I walk outside and over to the little grave. Mrs. Weiner comes out and stands on her back deck, holding a plate of something. She gives me a sad wave. The older British gentleman who lives to the left of us and tinkers in his garage looks out, wiping his hands on a dirty rag. He touches his cap when I glance at him. People must have seen Dad dig the hole and asked him what he was doing. But I'm glad the neighbourhood kids are still in school. The last thing I need is the twins strangling each other during this ceremony.

Aunt Maureen comes flying down the driveway on her short legs. Dad must have called her. For someone who has a problem with her always showing up at our house, he certainly summons her a lot.

I place the box in the hole and open my folded piece of paper.

"Sally-Anne, you were my first pet and I'll always love you the best."

I have at least five paragraphs to go, but my throat closes over, so I shake my head at Dad to let him know I have nothing else to say.

Aunt Maureen and I watch as he covers the box with dirt and pats it down flat. That's when it hits me.

"I don't have any flowers!" I shout.

"FLOWERS? YOU WANT FLOWERS?" Mrs. Weiner cries from the balcony. "I'VE GOT FLOWERS!"

She puts her plate down on one of her folding chairs and disappears into the house, only to come back twenty seconds later with a bouquet of two dozen long-stemmed red roses. She rushes down her back steps and hurries over to us.

"Here, bubala! Flowers for your kitten."

"I can't take these, Mrs. Weiner. They're too nice."

"Look, they've done their job. It was our wedding anniversary yesterday and now they're going to sit on my coffee table and gather dust. Take them before the boys find out they have thorns."

Now Sally-Anne has beautiful red roses that cost a fortune on her grave. Mrs. Weiner follows us up the back stairs and makes us take the plate.

"Just something I baked this morning, hamantaschen cookies, so you can have a little nibble. No doubt you don't feel like eating. Make sure you have some hot tea with plenty of sugar for the shock. If you need anything, Audrey, I'm always here."

It's too much. I want to tell her something but I don't know how, so my mouth hangs open. She bends over and cups my chin. "You'll be all right. I felt just like this when I chopped the head off my first chicken."

An hour later, Jane shows up at my door. School is over. She takes a cookie tin out of her book bag. "Mom made these for you. We're very sorry about your cat."

"Thank you. Would you like to see her grave?"

"Okay."

She's impressed by the lovely flowers. "Wow. Did you buy these?"

"Mrs. Weiner gave them to me. Would you like to see my room?"

"Sure."

Jane is surprised my bedroom is off the kitchen. "It's really small. Why didn't you take a bigger room?"

"My dad is a writer. He needs a study, and I'm a kid and don't need much."

"I wish my mother thought like that. I'm always drowning in stuff that she thinks I want."

"She loves you."

"She loves stuff."

We sit on my bed. "When you get your own house, don't put anything in it," I suggest.

"That would drive my mother crazy."

I look at Jane's very clean face. "You talk about your mother a lot." She looks like she's going to cry, which is horrifying. "I'm sorry, I didn't mean that as an insult."

"I know. She just makes me tired sometimes. You don't have a mother, so I shouldn't complain. When you said you and your father are quiet at home, I thought you were lucky. I don't talk to my dad very often because Mom is always in the room."

"And I think you're lucky because you have a brother and sister and a tablecloth."

"Are you coming to school tomorrow?"

"Yeah, I've missed three days now."

Jane nods. "We only have a few weeks left of elementary school. I'm nervous about grade eight. Everyone looks so grown-up in high school." She looks around my room, but there's not much to see. "I guess I better go."

"Sorry I'm not coming to Guides tonight."

"That's okay. See ya. I'm sorry about your cat."

For those few minutes talking in my room I forgot about Sally-Anne, and when I realize this, a wave of guilt crashes over me. I told myself I'd never forget her, and here I am, yakking away as if she isn't dead. I look in my bureau mirror.

"You are an awful person."

Dad and I eat cookies for supper. The oatmeal raisins from Mrs. Andrews are familiar, but Mrs. Weiner's hamantaschen cookies look like three-cornered hats and are stuffed with apricot, prune, and poppy seed fillings.

"These are delicious. Why aren't we Jewish?"

We watch a little television, and at one point Dad pats the space beside him on the chesterfield and I go over and snuggle under his arm. We don't talk at first because there's nothing to say. It's been such a long and lonely day for both of us.

I trace the veins that run along his gnarled hands. The hands that dug a grave and filled it in again. They're bumpy and blue, his thin skin looking like that of an onion but with brown spots and fine grey hair on the swollen knuckles.

"How do you write so well, with hands like these? How do you play the piano?"

"Beats me."

"Does typing on a typewriter make these bones more noticeable? I can't see mine."

He looks at his. "Hands don't hide your age. Think of how much we do with our hands in the run of a day. I'm sure that's why they look worn out. But it probably didn't help that I used to box in the navy."

"You were a boxer?"

"Yep."

"You were in the navy?"

"Yep."

"How did I not know this?"

Dad shrugs. "It was a long time ago."

"Dad, we seriously have to set aside some time so you can fill me in on your life. It's ridiculous that I know so little about you. We live together."

"All right."

A thought occurs to me. "Were you a spy in the navy? Is that where I get my inquisitive nature?"

"You're just a Nosy Parker. And if I had been a spy, I wouldn't tell you. Spies keep their mouths shut, remember? If they didn't, they'd be dead."

"Of course. So it's best if I don't tell people I'm a spy."

"Exactly."

"That way the one-legged murderer across the street won't kill me."

He gives me a look. "What gave you the idea that the guy across the street is a murderer?"

"He's only got one leg. Someone managed to chop it off as he was killing them."

"Jesus, Audrey. No doubt he was in the war and lost his leg in battle. He's probably a hero."

"But he comes home late at night in a taxi and looks suspicious, and never turns on a light."

"He might suffer from depression. A lot of soldiers do. Their lives were ruined by what they saw and what they were asked to do. And I'll tell you one thing, missy. Spies don't jump to ridiculous conclusions. They gather evidence. Before you go around accusing this man of murder, do your homework. For that matter, go up and talk to him. If he is a recluse, maybe you could be helpful and run a few errands for him. Use your noggin, kid."

"Aww, jeez. Now I feel bad." Substandard. Deficient.

And then we hear this terrible racket on the front porch and something banging and Aunt Maureen yells, "Open the damn door!"

The two of us rush into the hallway and Dad pulls the door aside. Aunt Maureen is trying to hold on to a big box that's moving on its own, with terrible screeching and hissing coming from it.

"Outta my way!" she roars by us and dumps the box on the floor, grabbing her chest. "God, I hate cats!" she wheezes.

A gigantic orange paw appears from the gap at the top, razor-sharp claws looking for something to shred.

"What the hell is this?" Dad shouts. "What are you doing?"

"It's Jerry's damn cat. Audrey wants a cat; she can have this one."

"Maureen! Have you no sense? You can't just bring any old cat in here and expect Audrey to love it. And obviously this cat doesn't think much of the arrangement either."

"Look, I thought it might make Audrey happy. Who knew the damn animal would completely freak out?"

"You can turn around and take him back home. Now!"

"No, wait!" I shout. "Can I see him first?"

As if the cat knows what I said, he squeezes his head up from between the narrow space of the cardboard flaps and glares at us, wild-eyed and furious. Then uses all his strength to push his way out of the box completely.

He's almost as big as Rollie and has plush, orange-striped angora fur and a tail that is almost as wide as it is long. He honestly looks like a lion, except his mane kept growing and it's now covering his entire body.

I clap my hands. "He's gorgeous."

Aunt Maureen points at him. "This is Tom. Say hi, Tom."

Tom growls deep in his throat, stands on his hind legs, and charges at us with his front paws swinging. We run into the living room and slam the French doors shut. Tom prowls back and forth in front of them like a jail warden, daring us to come out and fight like cats. His eerie whine is scary. But he's the most beautiful creature I've ever seen.

"Oh, Dad! Can we keep him?"

"Keep him?! Christ almighty! We'll be lucky if we don't starve to death in here."

Aunt Maureen seems contrite. "I just wanted to help." She lights a cigarette and Dad puts his hand out. "My nerves are shot. Give me one of those."

"Dad, you don't smoke cigarettes."

"I do now."

"Can I have one?"

"NO!"

By the time they throw their butts in the fireplace, Tom has decided he's bored looking at us and starts to sniff around. When he moves through the door to downstairs, Dad carefully opens the French doors, tiptoes across the hall, and slams it shut. The beast is contained for now.

Aunt Maureen heads to the front door. "You have a kitty-litter box. I'll get his food and brush-and-comb set. Jerry brushed him four times a day. He said you had to because he's a Norwegian forest cat."

"Norwegian?!" I'm going to swoon.

"Stop right there!" Dad shouts at her. "I'm not having this wild ani-mal in my house! He could claw Audrey's eyes out, and I'm not having it, do you hear me?"

"Oh, please, Dad! He's just upset at the moment. He doesn't know where he is. We can keep the kitty litter, food, and water behind this door for a few days, and when he calms down, we can let him out. Can we at least try it? Isn't it worth a shot?"

"Tom spends most of his day outside," Aunt Maureen adds helpfully. "He hates being cooped up."

"My only pet died on your watch, Dad. Don't you want to make it up to me?"

My father points at me. "Now you're not being fair."

I know. I'm hoping the tactic will work.

"Daddy. Please. It's been such a hard week, what with my almost concussion, my loose teeth, my scabby wounds. And just hours ago I attended my first funeral. I need something to live for."

"For Christ's sake! You're not a spy. You're headed straight for the stage, you miserable kid."

And he storms up the hall and slams his study door behind him.

Aunt Maureen and I grin at each other.

"It totally worked."

"You're a genius, Audrey."

Dad turns on his record player to an ear-splitting level and plays Mozart's *Don Giovanni*, Act II.

———

My father doesn't forgive me easily, so I stay out of his way. His cursing goes through the roof and his growling is only matched by Tom's.

Poor Tom has been locked away for a week, because he's as stubborn as Dad. I sneak downstairs to change his litter and food and water, always ready to bolt back up if he chases me, but he's never around. I realize his favourite spot to sit is the windowsill, which is level with our front lawn.

He spends his days staring at the world from behind a pane of glass. I did that to him. He gazes at me with undisguised resentment and I feel totally wretched. Both Dad and Tom hate me.

This is the eighth day and I'm home for lunch eating a peanut butter sandwich, since my father said I could make my own damn sandwiches, when I realize I can't take it anymore. I go downstairs and luckily Tom's at his food dish. I quickly hop on a chair and reach up to slide open the basement window. I have to wrench the mesh screen ajar as well.

Tom sniffs the fresh air.

"I'm sorry, Tom. Aunt Maureen had no right to take you from your home, especially when you are no doubt grieving for Uncle Jerry, and I had no right to keep you prisoner down here. I'd take you back to your house if you'd let me, but you'd likely bite my face off, so if you could please just leave by the window and find your own way home. You only live two blocks from here. I'm sure you know the neighbourhood. I'll tell Aunt Maureen to expect you."

No sooner are the words out of my mouth than he takes a flying leap from his food dish, lands on Dad's Laz-Z-Boy then the arm of the sofa, and whooshes past my head and right out the window. He doesn't even stop when he hits the grass, just streaks down the sidewalk like a flash of lightning.

I call Aunt Maureen. "Tom is on his way home. I let him go. He's so unhappy here and I can't stand it."

"Well, shit."

"How come you don't like Tom? He's a beautiful cat."

"Jerry loved that cat more than me. And quite frankly, he's more attractive than I am. Okay, I'll be over tomorrow to pick up his stuff. It was worth a try."

Now I need to make amends to my father, so I bike to the store and buy us a couple of frozen TV dinners and Jos Louis Vachon cakes for dessert.

When I hear him come through the front door after work, I yell, "Hi! How was your day?"

"Fine."

He still sounds grumpy.

"I'm making TV dinners."

"Good," he grunts and then disappears into the bathroom to wash his face and hands.

We sit at the table and eat. When Dad doesn't say anything, I pipe up.

"Well, I had a good day. Mrs. Fuller threw a piece of chalk at Derek, the kid who sits beside me, but it landed on my Norwegian instead and when I turned around to see if he was okay, he said, 'Did it leave a mark?'"

"And this was a good day why?"

"He's never spoken to me before."

"And did it leave a mark?"

"Not really. And Mrs. Fuller did apologize to him."

"Why has he never spoken to you before, if he sits at the desk behind you?"

"He's too beautiful to talk."

Dad shakes his head ever so slightly, and I can see the edge of his mouth twitch, like he's trying not to grin.

"I'm so sorry, Dad. I was wrong to bully you into taking Tom. It made you unhappy and Tom unhappy, and in the end, it made me unhappy. I let him go. He's probably back at Aunt Maureen's now."

"How did you get him out?"

"The downstairs window."

Dad wipes a paper napkin across his mouth. "Well, thank you. I was very nervous with that cat in here, and I didn't appreciate the way you blackmailed me into taking him."

"You're right, that wasn't very nice. That why I bought you a Vachon cake."

The next morning, I'm sitting on the toilet when I hear Dad yell from the kitchen: "That son of a bitch!"

I try to stop peeing so I can go see what's wrong, but that never works, so I impatiently wait for it to stop, wipe myself, and pull up my pyjama bottoms as I open the door. "What's wrong?"

He points out the back-porch window. "Look who's sitting on the railing."

Tom, in all his leonine glory, is perched there, staring at us. I clasp my hands. "Oh, Tom!"

"He can't come in."

"I know. I'm just glad he came for a visit. That means he knows where we live."

"Just our luck."

Tom watches us get ready for work and school. When Dad heads out the front door, Tom jumps down off the railing and runs to the front porch to watch Dad get in his car and drive away. He's still there when I come out and lock the door, so I sit beside him on the top step.

"Thanks for coming by."

He rubs his face on my leg, so I reach over to pat his huge head. "You are so beautiful. It's because you're Norwegian. Even their cats are too good to be true."

When I bike away, he wanders back down the street.

Now that my Norwegian and I have a relationship, there's no time like the present to get to know him better. I turn around in my seat before class starts.

"We have a cat—well, we share a cat with my aunt, and he was really my uncle's but he died, so we had him for week—"

"You had your dead uncle for a week?"

"NO. The cat. But the fascinating thing is, Tom's a Norwegian too."

"Your uncle Tom?"

I think I liked it better when this beautiful boy didn't talk.

"Please turn around, Audrey," Mrs. Fuller says. "Everyone, open to page 160 in your geography books."

I face the front and sigh. My crush is over. It was fun while it lasted.

———

The last day of elementary school is upon us. We're getting our report cards this morning, and I'm nervous about my French grade. Jane and Gloria are feeling wistful because they've been going to this school since they were five. I've only been here for a few months, so my loyalty hasn't had a chance to firm up.

Yana, the chubby Polish girl whose coat hook I'm always stealing, is crying by the fence, so I wander over to her. "Don't be sad. You're going to the high school next year."

"No, I'm not."

"Why?"

"I'm dying."

This knocks the wind out of me. "Oh my gosh! I'm so sorry! Is it a massive pulmonary embolism? That's what happened to my uncle."

"I've got blood in my underpants."

Pamela happens to be leaning on the fence beside us, picking polish off her nails. "You're not dying. You've got your period."

I've heard about this, but it hasn't happened to me yet.

"What's a period?" Yana asks.

Pamela does her famous eye roll. "Doesn't your mother tell you anything?"

Yana shakes her head. "She doesn't speak English."

"Do you speak Polish?" I ask her.

Now she nods.

"Then ask her in Polish what a period is and I'm sure she'll tell you."

"Okay," Yana sniffs.

"Go to the nurse's office and ask her for a pad," Pamela adds. "They're called sanitary napkins. She'll give you a few for now. Then get your mom to buy you some, because this is going to happen every month for the rest of your life."

"It is?" I'm astonished. "I thought it was a one-time deal."

"How is it possible that you two know so little? When you get your period, that means you can have a baby if a boy sticks his penis in you. That's how babies are made."

Yana moans, covers her mouth, and looks like she's going to be sick, so she rushes off, presumably to the nurse's office.

"A boy sticks his penis where?" I want to know.

"Between your legs."

"I don't know what a penis looks like, so I'll have to be vigilant. There's no way I'm putting anything between my legs unless it's a horse."

Pamela snorts. "I like you."

"Thanks."

"Maybe we can hang around this summer. I'm not going anywhere. My parents are getting a divorce."

"Oh. That must make you sad."

Pamela shrugs.

"I only have one parent, so it can be done," I assure her.

"Dad left. He didn't even say goodbye."

"Well, that was shitty. Unkind. Thoughtless."

"Hey! He's still my dad."

"Apologies."

The school bell rings, so we head into Mrs. Fuller's class for the last time. She hands out our report cards and I hold my breath as I slide it out of the brown envelope.

English 98

History 90

Mathematics 57

Science 85

French 50

Physical Education 95

Summary: Audrey is a bright and inquisitive child, but she needs to apply herself when it comes to French and Math. I was happy to have her in my class.

Whew. I passed French by the skin of my teeth. All in all, not a bad report. It's what I expected, anyway.

Everyone is talking to each other, happy in the knowledge that we have the whole summer ahead of us. Even Mrs. Fuller looks cheery. She motions me up to her desk.

"Audrey, I called your father when you had your bike accident to see how you were getting along, and in the course of that conversation he mentioned he is raising you by himself, and instantly a lot of things fell into place. I grew up without a mother, and it can be very hard, especially at this time of your life, when many things are changing, and fathers aren't always aware of the issues young girls face. But I am confident that you will succeed in whatever you do, because you're right. You are a stubborn girl. And that is an asset as far as I'm concerned. I wish you all the best."

Now I'm sorry that I'm leaving this class. "I'll miss you, Mrs. Fuller."

"No, you won't. Now go."

A lot of parents are milling around the schoolyard. They laugh and chat while they wait for their kids to come out. It's a party atmosphere. Mrs. Weiner waves and I wave back. The kids in kindergarten stream outside, all of them holding a cellophane bag tied with a ribbon, full of candy and crayons and stickers. That Mrs. Brown is so sweet.

Gloria comes up to me. "I'm allowed to invite some girls back to the house for a tea party in the backyard. Would you like to come?"

"Sure! Thanks, Gloria."

"Come over at eleven. I have to ask some more people." And she takes off. That's when I notice Jane standing alone looking at her report card, so I go over to her.

"Hi, Jane. You look unhappy. Did you fail or something?"

She passes me her report card, so I open it: 98 or 99 in all her subjects.

"Wow! I didn't know you were this smart."

"They're not 100s."

"So what?"

"My brother only gets 100s. My mother will be disappointed."

It's beginning to dawn on me that Jane is headed for an ulcer.

"If it helps, tell your mother I got a 50 in French and a 57 in Math."

"It won't help."

"Why don't you come to Gloria's tea party? I'll ask her. I'm sure she won't mind."

"Nah, I don't feel like it. I'll see you later." She starts to walk away and then turns around. "I forgot to mention that every summer, I go to church camp for a week in the Laurentians and Mom wondered if you'd like to go. She said she'd tell your dad the details. It does cost money. Remember Wanda, my patrol second? She goes too. It's something to think about."

"I'll consider it. Thanks, Jane. I'll call you tomorrow on your Princess phone."

She gives me a smirk and keeps walking.

Unbelievably there's no need to hang around, so I run towards the gate, but with the sun in my eyes I end up crashing headlong into my Norwegian, so hard he has to steady me with his hands momentarily.

"Watch where you're going!"

"I'm sorry."

He nods. "That's okay. Have a good summer, Audrey."

He knows my name. He actually touched me.

"You too, Nicholai."

Now the phrase *walking on air* suddenly makes sense to me. I'm floating down the street in front of the school when I run into Mrs. Weiner, who is attempting to stop her boys from stabbing each other with pencils.

"You look happy." She smiles. "Did you get a good report card?"

"Pretty good. But I only got a 50 in French."

"I know a woman. Remind me to give you her number."

"Why do I need a woman?"

"She's a tutor. Call her in September. Now that school's over, can you babysit for us tonight? We'll only be a couple of hours."

Michael and David are now kicking each other's shins as their mother resolutely marches them along.

"I'll have to ask my dad."

"Of course."

Suddenly I spy something down the street that makes me break into the biggest smile. "Look! There's Tom. He's waiting on the step. He's my friend."

"What a handsome fellow. He'll help you get over your kitten."

We happen to be walking by Jacques's house and both Mrs. Weiner and I notice him watching Tom from his front yard. She lets go of her boys, walks over, and grabs him by the shirt. "If you ever touch this girl again, or that cat, I'll beat the living shit out of you. Do you hear me? I can see you day and night from my window, so I'll be watching you. And I'm not afraid of your punk-ass father either. My Frank will knock him out cold. Have you got that, you little bastard?"

The kid nods furiously. When she pushes him away, he runs up his steps and into his house.

"What time shall I come over, Mrs. Weiner?"
She wrinkles her nose with delight.

Chapter Six

Tom and I sit under the maple tree, and I tell him about Sally-Anne as the white clouds float overhead on this last day of grade seven. It's hitting me now that I won't see Nicholai tomorrow, and I can't believe I don't know where he lives. Why didn't I follow him home at some point? I'm a pretty useless spy.

Tom also seems interested in the tea party with Gloria. Her mom made delicious sandwiches without crusts. She put them on flowered napkins and we drank Kool-Aid and iced tea out of real china cups, like we were important. Fortunately, her grandmother stayed in the kitchen cutting up slices of watermelon. Her dad came out with a photo album, and he and I sat on patio chairs to look at pictures of what he called "the old country." But then another man came outside wearing sunglasses and Mr. Papa jumped up, happy to see him, and they kissed each other on the cheeks and then on the mouth. I'd never seen that before, but it must be normal for Gloria and her family, because no one batted an eye.

Fascinating. I take out my notebook and jot down this observation. *Men can show affection for each other by kissing on the mouth. It's no big deal and so much better than a boring old handshake. Not that I'd want to do it. I won't be going to New Zealand any time soon either. The Maori press their noses together to greet each other. Their cold and flu infection rates must be through the roof.*

Just then the old English gentleman who likes to mess with tools comes out of his garage and walks over to us.

"How do." He nods and touches his cap with his hand. He did that at Sally-Anne's funeral.

"Hello."

"Tristan Moore. At your service."

"Audrey Parker. And this is Tom."

"Good to meet you both. I'm sorry about your cat. Your dad told me. I didn't want to interfere on the day."

"Thank you. It was quite a blow."

"Just wanted to see this magnificent chap. My Edie loved cats." He holds out his fingers and Tom gets up and rubs his enormous face into Mr. Moore's open hand. "Oh my, what a lovely chappie you are."

"He likes you."

"Oh, aye."

"He's my Aunt Maureen's cat."

"Oh, aye?"

"Dad says you're British."

"Oh, aye." This has to mean "Oh, yes" in British.

"Do you not have your Edie anymore?"

"Nay, child. I lost Edie ten years ago. A lovely woman. I miss her, but whenever I see a cat, I always think that's my Edie coming up to check on me."

"My mom's dead. I wonder if she checks up on me."

"I'm sure she does."

"Were you in the war?"

He straightens up and seems surprised by my question. "Oh, aye. The Great War."

"World War One?"

"Aye. The war to end all wars. But they were wrong. They always are."

"If you don't mind my asking, were you a spy?"

His old eyes twinkle. "Nay, child. You had to be educated for that. I was in the trenches."

I look up at the clouds. "If you got out of the trenches alive, I'd say you were very smart."

He smiles at me. "I knew a thing or two."

Just then Dad comes walking down the driveway with his briefcase. "Hello, Mr. Moore. Lovely day."

"Oh, aye. Just shootin' the breeze with your clever girl here and this glorious beast."

"He's a beast all right."

Tom rubs his face all over Dad's pant legs and purrs, as if to apologize for his past behaviour. Then he flops on his back, shows his belly, and begs to be scratched.

"He's changed his tune," Dad says.

"I think he loves men. That's why he loved Uncle Jerry more than Aunt Maureen."

"Nice chatting with you, Audrey. And you, Tom. I'll bid you all goodday."

We say goodbye to Mr. Moore and he touches his cap again and goes through his open garage door, but Tom is not finished with him and follows him, his bushy tail swishing back and forth, to jump on Mr. Moore's workbench and nose around.

"You're early."

Dad nods. "Thought you might like to go to a restaurant tonight to celebrate the end of the school year. Your choice."

I jump up off the grass. "Thanks, Dad. That's very thoughtful. Could we go now? I have to be back to babysit for the Weiners at six."

"Are you old enough to babysit little kids?"

"I'm twelve! Jane babysits her sister all the time. And it's not like I'm looking after them in the wilderness. You are next door if I need help."

"I'm not great with little kids. They scare me."

"I'm getting paid, Dad."

He perks up. "Hey, that's true. Okay, just let me get cleaned up."

We head over to the stairs and he puts his arm around my shoulder. "Hey, Audrey?"

"Yeah?"

"Don't grow up too fast."

We hop in Dad's MG and take off down the highway. He reminds me of a secret agent, shoving the gearshift around. When "Paperback Writer" comes on the radio, we sing along with the Beatles at the top of our lungs. Since the car top is down, a few people look over at us at red lights and smile.

"Where are we going?" Dad asks.

"Orange Julep!"

"You're a cheap date."

"I love that place!"

Orange Julep is a huge orange building shaped exactly like an orange off Décarie Boulevard. It's been a Montreal icon for years. Their drinks taste like Creamsicles, my favourite. Dad lets me order a large. We also have a hot dog and fries.

It's been a great day so far.

As we sit in the car eating our meal and enjoying the sun, a woman with three kids trailing after her walks by holding a tray of food. She glances at us and gives us a quick smile and then does a double take.

"Jack?"

"Yes." Dad sounds uncertain. I don't think he knows this person.

"You don't remember me. Betty. I lived across the hall from you and Rosemary when our babies were a year old. This must be…"

"Audrey," I tell her. "You knew my mother?"

"Audrey! That's right. Well, the years do fly by. I have three kids now. How is Rosemary?"

Dad is struggling, so I say, "My mother is dead."

Betty looks stricken. Her kids aren't sure what to make of this conversation. "My God, I'm so sorry."

"What was my mother like?" I ask her. Dad keeps staring at the gas pedal, so he's going to be no help. "I don't remember her."

Poor old Betty is unsure what to do or say. "She was lovely, Audrey. Always chatty and happy. You look just like her."

"I do?"

"Your hair. It's the same. I remember I was sorry when your parents moved out. It's always nice for a young mother to have a friend with a child the same age. Rosemary and I discovered we both went to Montreal West High School, but we didn't know each other there. A small world." She gives Dad a concerned look. "I'm sorry I interrupted your meal. And I'm very sorry to hear about Rosemary."

"Thank you," says Dad. "I'm sorry, we have to go. Audrey is babysitting tonight."

"Of course. Goodbye then." She and her kids walk away.

Dad starts the car and puts it in reverse.

"Wait! I wanted to talk to her!"

"A parking lot is no place to carry on a conversation. And her supper was getting cold."

"Dad! She knew my mother."

"Audrey, please understand. It's hard to tell people your mother isn't here anymore. I hate it and needed to leave. I'm very sorry."

I sit back in my seat. Too often I forget that dad lost her too. All I can do is take my notebook out and write down everything this Betty said. Why didn't I get her last name?!

———

Poor Dad. He doesn't want me to grow up too fast, but my hair turns grey after only two hours with the Weiner twins.

I can't quite believe that Mr. and Mrs. Weiner have let these two live for as long as they have. They deserve a medal.

Mrs. Weiner puts the fear of God into them as she is leaving. "I WANT NO FUNNY BUSINESS, DO YOU HEAR ME? YOU LISTEN TO AUDREY AND DO WHAT SHE SAYS. SHE HAS MY PERMISSION TO LOCK YOU IN YOUR ROOM IF YOU DON'T BEHAVE."

They look at me with hatred. Great. Thanks, Mrs. Weiner.

Then she kisses both of them like the adoring mother she is and they cry, hanging off her dress, and beg her to stay. Mr. Weiner gives a jolly chuckle and pulls them away. "Now, fellas. Let your mother go and I'll bring you home a treat."

Mrs. Weiner gives me a relieved wave as the two of them slam the front door, run down the steps, and make their escape. Their tires squeal as they pull away from the curb.

The boys grin at me.

"So, what shall we do?" I ask them. "Would you like to play a game? What about cards? Do you know Go Fish?"

They take off and lock themselves in the bathroom. I hear the water running into the tub full blast.

For the love of Pete. I've only been here for two seconds. Now I pound on the bathroom door. "Let me in! You stop that right now. Do you hear me?"

"You can't make us, pee-pee head!" They laugh and laugh. "PEE-PEE HEAD!" they shout even louder, in case I didn't hear it the first time.

Think, Audrey. What would Tristan Moore do? He faced much worse in the trenches of the Great War. I saw pictures of it in my encyclopedia. Or Dad in the navy. He had to deal with water. There's no way I'm going home to ask him to help me. He'll never let me babysit again.

I'm not strong enough to bash the door in. Maybe I can pick the lock.

"DOO-DOO HEAD!" they screech. "POOP-BUM!!!"

That's good. At least I know they're still alive.

And then I remember David calling out to his mother to watch him on his bike. What do little kids hate more than anything? No one paying attention to them. I go out to the living room and turn on the television so loud that even they'd be able to hear it over the running water. I sit on Mrs. Weiner's plastic-wrapped settee and put my feet up on her coffee table and wait.

It's a game of chicken. How long does it take for a tub to overflow? Sweat starts to form on my upper lip. The only thing saving my sanity is that I can still hear them in there, so it hasn't occurred to them to drown each other, which is a very real possibility with these two. Then I start to laugh and laugh, as if the show I'm watching is hilarious, which it isn't. It's *Reach for The Top*.

And Mother of God, it works. The water stops and the door opens. I completely ignore them when they come in, looking to see what's so funny. When they realize they've been duped, they go to their room and slam the door. It boggles my mind that the Weiners allow them to sleep together.

But my plan backfires, because now it's too quiet. I shut the television off and listen. Not a sound. That can't be good. It's almost worse, so I creep down the hallway and quickly open the door. Michael has a pillow over David's face. The shock of it stuns me. I run over and grab it from him. David is actually purple, and gasps for air.

"You little creep!" I grab Michael and jam the pillow over his face and press down on it hard. "How do you like it? Think this is funny, do you?" I'm so mad I could very well kill him, so I pull the pillow away and he looks at me with real fright.

I frighten myself. Maybe the incident at Orange Julep upset me more than I realized.

"Both of you get in the living room, now!"

They weep as they sit on the sofa and stare at me. "Don't either of you move a muscle."

We look at each other for an hour. I really have to pee, but I don't dare. Fortunately, by hour two, their thumbs are in their mouths and they're asleep. The show-off in me would love to put them in their beds so their parents can see what a competent sitter I am, but I don't dare, in case they wake up.

Besides, I know the truth. I'm a lousy babysitter. I could've smothered that kid.

And I got five bucks for it.

———

It annoys me that Dad feels the need to ask Aunt Maureen to keep an eye on me. My freedom is important, as I want to track down the clues this Betty told me about my mom. My plan is to take a bus to Montreal West High School and ask to see their yearbooks. With schools closed for the summer I'll have to put it off for now, but at least it's start.

Still, I don't want Aunt Maureen breathing down my neck, and I tell Dad if I'm old enough to babysit, I'm old enough to not need a babysitter myself.

"I don't care, Audrey. You're only twelve, and I can't have you roaming the streets alone for two months while school's out."

"I've roamed the streets for years!"

"You most certainly have not. Not in the summer. I paid good money to have people watch you when we lived in the apartment."

"Oh, like the woman who made me fry bacon when I was too young to use the stove? And had me brush her hair and rub her feet for hours. Did you know that?"

"No! Why didn't you tell me?"

"I was five! What did I know?"

"Look, I'm not asking you to stay in all day. Maureen will be here in case you need her, to make lunch and whatnot. She might as well sit and knit here while she watches her soaps on television. That's all she does at her place."

"She lives two streets away. I could go to her if I want something."

"Goddammit! That's enough. I'm not discussing it. End of story."

He retreats to his study, so I stick out my tongue.

But in the end, that's how Tom ends up living with us. When he sees Aunt Maureen come in every morning, he follows her. Mind you, he does spend most of the day outside, but he shows up for snacks and drinks from the water dish. Then he discovers the top of the fridge and the upper cupboards and sits there like a Buddha, eyes closing in the heat.

One morning Dad shouts and points at the ceiling. "Judas Priest! What's that monster doing up there?"

I peek out my bedroom door. "He's here because Aunt Maureen is here. You wanted this arrangement, remember?"

"I made no mention of Tom. He was not part of the bargain."

"What bargain? I happen to like this cat, and he's not doing anyone any harm, and you're not here all day anyway, so what difference does it make to you? Goddammit, Dad! That's enough. I'm not discussing this any further. Tom stays because he makes me happy. End of story."

I shut my door and wait. Dad growls, but that's it. When I reappear, Dad is in his study and Tom is snoozing in a sunbeam.

———

The days of summer melt into each other. My memories are jumbled together and I can't tell you when or in what order they occurred.

Pamela wants me to go to La Ronde with her and her friends on a Saturday, and I ask Dad.

"Will there be an adult with them?"

"I doubt it. Her father left her without saying goodbye."

"Will there be boys?"

"Probably. She only seems to have boys for friends."

"Over my dead body."

I have to stop being so honest.

Dad takes me to Expo on the weekends. He even buys me a Kodak Instamatic camera with flashcubes so I can take pictures of neat stuff. Aunt Maureen doesn't bother coming. "I've had it with learning about the world. I'm too old to care." So we take Jane and Gloria with us once, and that's when I learn that my father is a real bore. I never noticed how often he stops to light his pipe, and he reads every display on every floor of every pavilion. It's obvious Jane and Gloria are impatient with this, and it also doesn't help that Jane and Gloria don't like each other very much. They are completely different people, and Gloria's habit of taking that damn ball everywhere she goes really gets on Jane's nerves. I'm not crazy about it either, but it's a stress reliever for Gloria, and that's something Jane could use big time. It's upsetting when two friends you like don't like each other. Now I wonder who I can live without.

To be truthful, I prefer Jane, but there's no way I'm giving up Gloria's mother, and Gloria makes me laugh sometimes because she's clueless about so many things. It's because she never has to think for herself, but that's not her fault. Her family adore her and make her life easy. And lately I've noticed that her brothers are cute, so I'm not falling out with Gloria anytime soon. Although the day she told me that grandmothers crochet spiderwebs at night, I considered it.

Dad and I go to Expo by ourselves after the adventure with the girls, and in every picture, I'm wearing the same stupid red coat. We love the Automat at La Ronde. Endless snacks in a wall of vending machines.

"Don't you wish we had one of these at home, Dad?"

He's not listening. He's reading a poster about foods of the world.

Jane and I spend a lot of days riding around the neighbourhood following the ice cream truck. I'm almost certain the guy who drives it is a spy. I mean, it's the perfect cover for scouting out locations without being seen. Jane isn't convinced, but she likes it when we hide clues. We write down the addresses he's been to and what time of day to see if there's a pattern, and then bury the pieces of paper under rocks and shrubs and in the cracks of foundations, in case he captures and frisks us. But most of the time we forget where we hid them.

And after a while the guy gets annoyed with us. "What's up with you two idiots? I see you everywhere, but you're too cheap to buy anything? Don't waste my time!"

"Fine. I'll have a maple walnut cone, please. What would you like, Jane?"

"Maple walnut?! We got chocolate, vanilla, and strawberry. This ain't no Steinberg's Supermarket here!"

I buy two chocolate cones. And hand him a tip. That shuts him up.

"I don't think I can eat this." Jane frowns while holding her cone. She hates it when people get mad at her.

"Don't mind him, Jane. We're never going to see him again anyway, because he's obviously not a spy. Spies blend into the background. They don't cause a scene."

It's just as well that the ice cream truck gig is up. Jacques makes it his business to follow us around and he finds quite a few of our notes, which he waves in our faces as he zips by on his bike, his middle finger always up in the air.

"What is that boy's problem?" Jane asks me.

"His father is nasty. *Méchant.* Let's spy on him."

We do for a few days, but spying on fathers is not easy. They work. Still, we write down that he never talks to his kids when he comes home. He ignores them. One day he pulls Jacques up the front steps by his arm and marches him into the house. That doesn't bode well. And he swears a lot, but so does my dad.

I'm not exactly innocent in this regard either.

Sometimes I go over and talk to Rollie. When the thought of dognapping him becomes too intense, it's a way to relieve my yearning. He's always on his front porch with his owner, Avi, who's a very interesting person, even though he's only five years old.

"Do you know a lot about bulldogs, Avi?"

"Everything."

"Like what?"

"They were bred to fight bulls."

"Poor bulls. Poor dogs."

"Don't let them near water. Because of the shape of their bodies, they have a hard time in water."

"I didn't know that."

"They are very protective of their owners. No one can mess with me."

"You're lucky."

It's while I spend time patting Rollie that I meet Maria, Avi's next-door neighbour. She's Italian and goes to the Catholic school, so that's why I've never met her before. Maria has a younger brother who never talks.

"Never?"

"Never," she says.

"How old is he?"

"Seven."

"Wow. How do you know what he wants?"

"He cries or hits. Mama knows what he wants."

"How does he manage in school, then?"

"You're nosy. Wanna come up and see my trolls?"

Her mother is pleasingly plump and wears an apron all day, and it turns out she makes the finest spaghetti and meatballs in the world. Unsurpassed. Her dad keeps trying to give me vegetables out of his garden. It's like a jungle out there, and he's very proud of it. I've also seen him smack his sons on the back of the head, so it must be a sign of affection, but he doesn't do it to the kid who doesn't talk.

That summer I have to re-think my strategy of spying on my neighbours. One night while I watch the world through my mother's opera glasses, I see a man looking at me. That's when I realize I only have my bra and underwear on, and it makes me feel funny. It's probably an accident, but I need evidence, so I stand in the window the next night with my bra on and there he is again, this time with a pair of binoculars.

I reach up and pull my blind down. Whereas I spy to gather information, this guy is spying on my trained breasts. That blind remains down all summer, even though it gets really hot in my bedroom. Dad buys me a fan.

The best day is when Tom chases Jacques up the maple tree and he has to sit on a branch for twenty minutes, because Tom makes that weird noise in his throat and stares at him from the bottom of the tree, his tail slashing back and forth the whole time. I take a picture from my bedroom window and don't even have to waste a flashcube because it's sunny out. My understanding of Jacques's situation doesn't mean I'll ever forgive him for his treatment of Sally-Anne. The fact that Tom corners him at the foot of her burial plot seems deliberate and very satisfying.

I learn all about Shabbat Laws. Shabbat is the Sabbath to Jewish people, like Jane's Sundays, only Shabbat takes place on Saturday. When I tell Aunt Maureen, she says Catholics are even more devoted. They go to church on Saturdays for confession and on Sundays for the Eucharist.

"I don't think it's a contest, Aunt Maureen."

On Shabbat I go over to Mrs. Weiner's to turn on and off her lights, stove, radio, and television because they're not allowed to handle electricity. Sometimes I write lists if she forgot to do it the night before, because she can't write. I take it to the store and buy a few groceries if she's run out, because she's not allowed to drive or go shopping.

"What if they don't have a veal chop? Do you want a pork chop instead?"

Mrs. Weiner looks horrified. "Never! Jews don't eat pork."

"No bacon? Fascinating. Why not?"

"We can only eat animals that chew their cud and have cloven hooves. That rules out pigs."

Out comes my handy notepad. My pencil is poised for further information. "Anything else you can't eat?"

"Shellfish. Nothing that doesn't have a fin or a scale."

I scribble this down, along with the pig tale. "You can't eat a lobster? My dad's favourite."

"Dirty scavengers eating garbage off the bottom of the ocean floor? No, thank you."

"I think I should be Jewish. I don't like lobster either."

"I'll introduce you to some nice Jewish boys when you're older."

Mrs. Weiner hates not using the telephone on Shabbat, so she and Aunt Maureen often sit on the back step to smoke and gossip, even though we don't need Aunt Maureen on weekends. I'm glad she has a friend. She's a lonely person. Forsaken, maybe? Not quite. But I do ask her about it one day. "Why don't you hang around with your own family?"

She turns around from spreading mustard on my ham sandwich. "That's not a very nice thing to say."

"Sorry, I didn't mean it that way. Why don't any of your brothers and sisters come and see you and Dad? I must have cousins and I don't know them, except for your two, and they were always too old to bother with me."

"We're not close. Some families aren't. Once our mother died there was nothing keeping us together."

"Was your father still alive?"

"He died soon after. He wasn't someone you could rely on anyway."

"Why did you and Dad end up being friends?"

"I'm the baby. Your dad always had a soft spot for me. He left when I was young to join the navy. He needed to get away from our old man, but he always stayed in touch, which meant a lot to me."

We eat our sandwiches and Tom wanders in so I give him a few pieces of ham. Aunt Maureen makes a cup of tea and has a smoke.

"How come there's no pictures of Dad when he was little?"

"He probably has a few. You should ask him. Families didn't used to have access to cameras the way they do now. But there's one picture of our grandfather John when he came over from Scotland. Your dad looks a lot like him, and he's named after him. Jack is your dad's nickname. We called him Jackie when he was young. Our grandfather sang in the church choir and had a beautiful voice, and our grandmother played the piano. That's where your dad's love of music comes from."

"If it's in my blood, I should play the piano. How much do lessons cost?"

"Beats me. Your dad plays by ear. He never had a music lesson in his life."

"What do you mean, 'by ear'?"

"He hears a tune and can play it, just by listening to it. He can't read a note of music."

This piece of information impresses me so much that when Dad comes home from work, I hug him.

"What's this for?" he smiles.

"Nothing."

He kept playing the piano even though his father tried to stop him. Dad is stubborn too. That's where I get it from.

My father says I can go with Jane to camp for a week, but when Mrs. Andrews sends me home with a list of everything I need, he reads it and blows up. "Christ! If nuclear war breaks out while you're gone, at least I know you'll survive."

I'm worried. "Is it too much? Will you be able to pack it all in the MG?"

"Not in a million years. I'll ask Mrs. Andrews if they can take you. Didn't you say they own an enormous station wagon? Maureen will have to put all this shit together."

Mrs. Andrews kindly says I can come with them and I can't wait until Jane's parents drop us off. It's an actual camp, like you see in the movies. Cabins in amongst trees and a lake and a mess hall. There are even canoes! That's as Canadian as you can get. I hope to take a picture of a beaver as well. A big wooden sign overhead reads *Whispering Pines*. Not very imaginative, but you can't have everything.

When Mr. Andrews drives away and leaves Jane and I standing there with her mother, I'm confused. "Why is your mother still here?"

"She's the camp leader."

Here I was thinking poor Jane has a whole week to herself without her mother breathing down her neck, and it turns out that she runs the stupid place.

Mrs. Andrews is a very nice woman, but she likes everything to be perfect, and that has to be exhausting. I know Jane is worn out. I can see it in her face.

And soon I'm dog-tired, because Mrs. Andrews is under our cabin window every morning at 5:15 A.M. banging a pot with a wooden spoon, yelling, "Rise and shine! Praise the Lord for this blessed day!"

For the most part, it's wonderful. The swimming and canoeing and scavenger hunts are my favourite activities, but doing crafts bores me to tears. Wanda and I agree on that.

"What is the fascination with Popsicle sticks?" She and I are trying to glue a bunch together to create a bird feeder. Jane's already on her second and her first one is painted.

"And pipe cleaners," Wanda tsks.

"I hate cutting felt. The scissors they give us are useless."

Jane puts down her black marker so she can glare at us properly. "Will you two quit bellyaching? You'd think you were being asked to build a log cabin. It's just a birdhouse."

I hold up my construction and three tacky sticks slowly give way and fall on my lap. "No bird is going to find sanctuary in this particular shelter."

Jane shakes her head. "You're pathetic."

We're eating Rice Krispies out of little cereal boxes at breakfast when Mrs. Andrews announces we're going to put on a play. Okay! This should be fun. She hands out our parts.

It's about Jesus and God. I have to wear a tinfoil halo because I'm an angel, apparently, which I feel is lousy casting.

I put up my hand. "Does it have to a religious theme? Can't we perform a musical like *The King and I* or *Seven Brides for Seven Brothers*?"

Mrs. Andrews looks slightly annoyed. "The show is tomorrow, Audrey. It's not Broadway and we are a church camp, remember."

It isn't a memorable production, except when Wanda trips over the mop handle Jane was using as a staff and nearly twists her ankle.

The best part of the week is sitting around a campfire at night, listening to the fire crackle and watching the sparks rise up like fireflies into the black starry night. The toasted marshmallows are pretty spectacular too.

There's only one bizarre thing that happens. A couple of nights before we leave I'm coming back from the outhouse and see Mrs.

Andrews kissing our swimming instructor on the mouth behind the mess hall. And it isn't a "Mr. Papa and his friend" kiss. It reminds me of when George and Mary kiss for the first time in *It's a Wonderful Life*.

When I pull the covers over my head in my bunk bed, I'm upset. Poor Jane. Always trying to please her mother. Mrs. Andrews goes to church and wants Jane to be perfect, but Mrs. Andrews clearly isn't without fault. Aren't adults better than that? The fact that maybe they aren't is disconcerting. Who can you count on, then?

Out comes my notebook and pencil. I hold my flashlight under the covers and write:

Monday, July 24, 1967. Approximately nine-thirty, EST. Mrs. Andrews and Terry Bathing Trunks are kissing behind the mess hall, quite close to the outhouse, which doesn't strike me as a romantic place for passion. Mrs. Andrews is married and has no business kissing her employee. He's also much younger than she is and a total show-off. No one needs to walk around in a bathing suit all day, even if he is teaching kids how to swim. I must protect Jane.

The next day I pretend to drown. This Terry character doesn't seem to notice. It's not until I yell, "Hey you! I'm drowning!" that he rushes over. Several other kids hear me and they're coming too. I only have a few moments. As soon as he grabs my neck, I push him away and accidently spit water in his face. "You leave Mrs. Andrews alone or I'll write an incriminating letter and report you to Reverend Haliburton. I can do that. I'm a spy."

"Do you have pictures, James Bond? If not, it's your word against mine. And no one is going to believe someone who says they're drowning when they're not." He picks me up and carries me to shore. "I've got her! She's safe now!"

And he becomes a big hero.

I have a lot to learn.

When I don't say much on the drive home, Mrs. Andrews asks me if I'm feeling okay. I tell her I'm tired from having so much fun. Everyone laughs.

That makes me feel worse.

Dad and Aunt Maureen are there to greet me when we pull up in the station wagon. They help me out with my gear, and while Jane and I hug, Dad shakes hands with Mr. and Mrs. Andrews and thanks them again for giving me a lift and taking such good care of me. We wave goodbye from the sidewalk as they drive off down the street, Mr. Andrews giving a little honk of his horn.

When I step into the house, Tom is there to greet me, his purring motor running. I pick him up and bury my face in his fur.

Dad says, "Boy, did we ever miss you! Didn't we, Maureen?"

"It was awful! Don't ever go away again."

I put Tom down and hug my father and his little sister around their waists at the same time. They squeeze me back.

"I think someone missed us too," Dad says over my head.

—

Jane asks me if I want to go to church with them again and come over for lunch, but I tell her no, because I don't see my dad during the week, so I want to be with him on the weekends, and she's fine with that. Then she asks me if I'd like to go for a swim in the pool at their tennis club, and I say yes.

Why am I punishing Jane for something her mother did?

It's easy enough to stay away from Mrs. Andrews at the pool, because she's busy laughing with the other mothers who wear sunglasses and tennis skirts while drinking wine at the patio tables by the courts. These women assume the lifeguards will save us if anything happens, but I'm nervous of Dixie splashing around the edge of the shallow end. Jane doesn't seem to notice, but to Mrs. Andrews credit, she does crane her neck often to see where Dixie is.

Maybe Mrs. Andrews is lonely. Jane did say her father works all the time. He's a stock broker. I looked it up. He deals with the stock market. I looked that up too. It seems dreadfully boring, so maybe she's bored too. And she's always nice to me. I decide to give her a break. After all, I did nearly smother Michael, so I'm nothing to write home about either.

But it's occurred to me that I haven't put her in my Admiration notebook. I can't quite do it for some reason. I'll have to ponder this.

When Mrs. Weiner asks me to babysit again, I agree, because she's so thrilled with my success last time.

"I don't know what you did with those boys, but they had a great time. I didn't hear a peep out of them, and they usually complain bitterly about babysitters."

"They're nice kids."

And surprisingly, we do have a good time. Fear is an amazing motivator. We play Go Fish and then with their dinkies, and I scoop ice cream for them. It dawns on them that I'm not a crazed demon, and I do my best to make it up to them.

When it's time for bed, I tell them to brush their teeth.

"You have to put the toothpaste on our brushes," David says. "That's what Mommy does."

"Okay." I find the rolled-up tube of toothpaste in the medicine cabinet and put a dab on both their brushes. They push each other at the sink. I'm starting to realize that this is how they play. They have to touch each other all the time, just to make sure the other one is still there. Do all babysitters grow fond of their charges? Even the brats?

The boys brush their teeth and their mouths get very foamy.

"This is yucky!" Michael tells me.

"It's fine."

David agrees. "This is pooh!"

"Never mind! Just do it."

We go back in their room and I read them a story I brought with me from one of my Junior Classics. Number 4, *Hero Tales*.

"This is about Roland and Oliver. "One summer afternoon rather more than eleven hundred years ago..."

"Eleven hundred years!" they shout together. "Wow!"

I read for quite a while. It seems they love books. Sometimes you have to get to know kids before you pass judgment on them. The fact that they love this story and ask me to bring more next time makes me feel very affectionate towards them. I can see why Mrs. Weiner lets them live.

When I go back to the bathroom to straighten up the towels and put the cap back on the toothpaste tube, I unroll the tube a little and realize I made them brush their teeth with their father's Brylcreem. I thought it was Gleem toothpaste.

Those poor kids.

One day I go over to Maria's house to show her my new troll with its sticking-up orange hair. Ever since Tom came into my life, orange has been my favourite colour. Since I was fascinated with Maria's collection, I bought the troll with my babysitting money. I call it Rollie. My policy is to hate dolls, but these things are so ugly they don't qualify. After an hour, our bums get sore from sitting on the floor and we end up on her bed. She starts to tickle me, so I tickle her back and we roll around laughing. Her older sister comes in and gives Maria a filthy look. For some reason I feel instantly guilty and jump off the bed.

The next day I realize I left Rollie over at Maria's, so I ring the doorbell and her sister answers. "What do you want?"

"Is Maria home?"

"No."

"I left my troll in her room."

"Too bad. Don't come over here anymore. You're not allowed to see Maria."

"Why not?"

"You know why not." And she goes to slam the door in my face, but I stick my foot in the way. "I don't know, actually, but regardless, I want my troll back and you better give it to me."

"Wait here."

My cheeks are burning. What did I do?

The sister comes back with my troll, so Maria must be home. She's the only one who knows what Rollie looks like. I reach out my hand to take him and the sister throws it behind my head and slams the door. I pick Rollie up and smooth his hair. When I go down the steps I look up and can see Maria in the window behind her curtain. She looks sad.

My feelings are terribly hurt. I don't want to tell Dad or Aunt Maureen because I'm ashamed. Gloria and Jane probably won't know what to do, so I go over to Pamela's place. I've been there a few times, but she never wants to do anything but watch television, so it's not much fun. Still, something tells me she's the person to ask.

When I tell her my situation, she rolls her eyes as usual. "Her sister thought you were trying to kiss each other. Some people are very uptight about sex."

"Sex? We weren't trying to kiss each other!"

She smirks at me. "Are you sure?"

"I'm not sure of anything at the moment. It was fun to be rolling around. But I thought sex was with boys?"

"Sex can be with anybody. You and I can have it."

"Gross. How do you know about all this, Pamela?"

She shrugs. I tell her about the man in the window with binoculars looking at me.

"Well, if you insist on sitting in your window in your underwear, why wouldn't he be looking? He's a man. Men like looking at girls. It's a fact."

"Not all of them."

"Oh, please! Don't kid yourself. They all love it, unless they're fruits."

"Fruits?"

"Guys who like other guys."

"There seem to be an awful lot of categories for sex. You must be an expert."

I worry about her. And then I worry about Dad. Ever since I told him not to bring Lucie back, he hasn't been with a woman. Maybe he's a fruit now.

One rainy day I find myself alone in the house. Aunt Maureen has a doctor's appointment. I finish *The Lion, the Witch and the Wardrobe* by C. S. Lewis. This is the seventh time I've read it. Every time I finish it, I sit back and wish I had brothers and sisters. Life would be much more amusing. Droll. Mirthful.

At least I have Tom for company. He's not around at the moment, but I know where he is. He's always in Dad's study now. He sits on Dad's lap. The first time I saw them together, I folded my arms across my chest and tapped my foot. Dad pretended not to know why I was annoyed.

"What? You've never seen a cat on someone's lap before?"

Tom purr-meowed at me.

"That's my cat."

"He's his own man. He decides where he wants to be."

Tom sits beside him on the piano bench when Dad plays Handel's "Water Music."

And here he is, curled up in a basket by Dad's bookcase. I've come in because I'm desperate for something to read, since I've gone through my entire Anne of Green Gables series this summer as well as every Nancy Drew, Trixie Belden, and Hardy Boys I own. But I don't want something that takes six weeks, and Dad's books are pretty heavy going. A whole set about the Second World War by Winston Churchill. Another set, *The Story of Civilization* by Will Durant. *A Study of History* by Arnold Toynbee and *Mankind's Mother Earth* by Arnold Toynbee. He likes that guy apparently. The only one that looks vaguely interesting is *The Indomitable Hornblower* by C. S. Forester. Who knows what it's about, but anything with the word *Hornblower* in it has to be terrific.

When I glance at the bottom shelf, there's a thick hardcover book called *Human Reproduction: An Illustrated Textbook.* I pick it up, blow off the dust, and open the pages.

I'm really not sure what I'm looking at. Diagrams of a man and a woman doing gymnastics together? This must be sex. It looks complicated and sort of creepy. But at least now I know what a penis looks like. Poor boys. Imagine having that hanging off you all day.

Is this really what you have to do to have a baby? My mother and father must have adopted me. I can't imagine Dad doing this with anyone, least of all Lucie.

But I am quite interested in the diagram that shows what's between a woman's legs, since I've never looked myself. I thought we only had two holes. One for bowel movements and the other for urine. So, this third opening is called a *vagina*, and that's where the penis goes in and where a baby comes out. I'm relieved to know that. It was worrying to think of a poor baby coming out with pee all over its face.

And this vagina is where the blood must come from every month. It talks about fallopian tubes and eggs. EGGS! I remember a girl in my old school telling me that mothers have eggs and fathers do something with them. I thought she meant like they make omelets. I'm really glad to be gathering facts. Poor old Yana was overcome because she knew nothing. I don't want to find myself in the same position, but maybe I'll be more interested in this when I'm thirteen. Right now, it's all a bit too much and I don't want to think about it. I put the book back and open up Dad's left-hand drawer to take a few Allsorts, but it's a new bag and Dad hates it when I tear the top off, so I open his middle drawer to get a pair of scissors and there's a magazine called *Playboy* and it has a woman on the cover with big breasts coming out of her bunny costume.

I don't think Dad's a fruit.

Chapter Seven

We only have a few more weeks of summer left before high school starts, and Jane and I are a little antsy about it. Gloria isn't bothered, but she's had fifty cousins playing in her backyard all summer, so she hasn't noticed anything. She's a lucky person. Blessed.

Aunt Maureen is making us grilled cheese sandwiches for lunch. We were over at the tennis club in the morning, swimming in the pool, and Mrs. Andrews wanted Jane to stay for her tennis lesson, but to my surprise, Jane put her foot down.

"Mom, I keep telling you I hate tennis."

"Who hates tennis? You're just being obstinate."

"I hate the tennis instructor."

"Antonio? He's a sweetheart."

"To you and your friends, maybe, but don't you know he hates kids?"

"Hates kids? Don't be ridiculous."

Why don't adults ever listen to us? I haven't been to the tennis club that many times this summer because there's a limit to how many times a member can bring a guest, and I'm only allowed in the pool, not the tennis courts, but even I can see from the sidelines that Antonio hates kids. I've seen him pinch them, grab them by the ear, wallop them on the backside with his racket, and once pull a little girl's pigtail so hard she cried.

"You can't make me stay. I'm going to Audrey's house."

Mrs. Andrews's nostrils become pinched. They always do when Jane ticks her off. "Your father pays good money for your tennis lessons, and it's selfish and rude to refuse."

Jane gets red in the face. I cross my fingers that she sticks up for herself.

"Mom, I have to go to Audrey's house today. Her aunt Maureen asked me to come for lunch because summer vacation is almost over and she wants to repay your kindness and hospitality to Audrey. She has ordered a special cake and everything. I was supposed to tell you and I forgot."

Mrs. Andrews blinks and seems surprised. "Oh. Is that right, Audrey?"

"Oh yes! We're having it catered and everything."

"Catered?"

I've gone too far. "Not *catered* catered. She's ordering sandwiches from a deli I like, because I thought Jane might like them too."

"Well, I suppose if she's gone to all that trouble...but I wish you'd told me, Jane. Now I have to tell Antonio you'll miss your last lesson."

"Tell him I'm sorry. I'll be home for dinner." And she kisses her mother's cheek.

"Well, all right, dear. You two have fun."

"Thanks, Mrs. Andrews," I say. "Aunt Maureen will be really happy."

Jane and I run across the pool's edge and the lifeguard blasts his whistle to warn us to slow down. When we get to the dressing room, we snort with laughter.

"I thought you were going to blow it with that catering remark!"

"Oh, me too! Sorry. I was so caught up with your ingenuity. You are definite spy material."

While we eat our grilled cheese, I tell Aunt Maureen about it. Jane kicks me under the table.

"Don't worry, Jane. Aunt Maureen loves stuff like this."

She cackles as she opens the fridge to pour us some Coke. "That was brilliant, Jane. Please feel free to use me any time. That Antonio sounds like a miserable worm."

"He never bothers with me because Mom is on the board of the tennis club, but it stinks that he knows who he can pick on."

"Sweetie, the world is full of people like him."

"Growing up is hard," Jane says.

Aunt Maureen sighs. "And when you get older, it gets even harder."

"This is supposed to be a party, Aunt Moo."

She livens up. "With cake, apparently. Let's bake one and eat the whole thing!"

———

Dad takes me to the Senneville Yacht Club, on the western tip of the island of Montreal, to go sailing with his friends. It takes us about forty minutes to get there.

"It's your last adventure before school starts."

I'm really excited. There are at least a hundred boats tied to the docks, all of their masts and wires clanking together in the wind, and it's very gusty today, which worries me. But the two men and the lady on the boat are happy about it.

"Great sailing today, Jack!"

Dad introduces me to Juliette, François, and Alain. François and Alain are much prettier than Juliette. They are very nice and make a big fuss over me. They tell me to put on a life jacket and Dad wears one too. The others laugh at him.

"Hey, I'm a father! If I drown, who's going to look after my kid?" he jokes back.

That's right. I never thought of that before. Now my stomach turns. And that's before we get the sails up.

Once we are out in the middle of the lake, I know with every fibre of my being that I hate sailing. I hate it with all the hatred I have in my hate locker.

Dad notices I'm very quiet as the boat tips sideways to the point of almost falling over into the choppy navy-blue water. He lurches over to me because the wind and the waves make it impossible to do anything else.

"It's okay, Audrey. This is what the boat is made to do. See how much faster we're going when it's like this?"

He sits down beside me and I crawl into his lap and hang onto his chest like a baby orangutan. "Make it stop."

"I promise you I'll keep you safe."

I'm old enough to know that I'm putting him in a bad position if I make a scene and become hysterical. It doesn't often happen that he takes a day off to do something for himself, and the fact that he wanted me with him makes me very happy. So, I decide to bite the bullet and pretend I'm not on this fucking boat and I keep my face plastered into his neck with my teeth clenched.

Dad has to carry me off the boat still wearing our life jackets because I haven't let him go yet. He takes me to a bench outside the yacht club while the others go inside. We rock together for a while until I loosen my grip. Eventually I lift my face and wipe slobber off my mouth and his neck with my jacket sleeve.

"Sorry."

"I'm sorry, Audrey."

And we say no more about it.

We go back to what turns out to be François and Alain's place. I thought Juliette was the housewife, but no. When the two men start cooking together in the kitchen, all four adults have a wine glass in their hand. Dad smiles at me drinking from my can of ginger ale as we sit on stools side by side.

"François and Alain are a couple."

"I know. A couple of fruits."

Dad spits out his wine. François and Alain spin around with their mouths open while Juliette puts her hand on her chest.

"That's what my friend told me to call two men who love each other."

They burst out laughing, and now I'm embarrassed.

"That's right," Alain says, once he's collected himself. "We've been each other's *dates* for twenty years now."

They laugh again, but then Dad puts his wineglass down. "We're making a joke, but to call a gay man a fruit is demeaning. Remember our talk about not insulting someone for who they are? That word applies in this situation."

"I'm very sorry. I had no idea."

"No harm done, *ma chérie*," François says as he passes me a dish of pretzels. "Dig in."

François and Alain have a dog named Missy. She's an Afghan and very, very beautiful. She doesn't look real, with her narrow face and long silky hair. She spends the whole time on her own chair and is clearly not interested in me going anywhere near her, which is disappointing. Give me Rollie any old day.

What we had for dinner is still a mystery to me. It's not something I'd want again, but Dad loved it. He's having such a great time. The four of them spend hours around the dining room table drinking bottles of wine while I curl up in a chair and read the *New Yorker* magazines on the coffee table, before that gets *très* boring, so I take out my notebook.

> *It's impossible to believe that humans willingly got into boats*
> *and sailed across the ocean to see what was beyond the horizon.*
> *Sailing is horrific. Dreadful. Harrowing. Vile. Never again.*
> *Men who love each other are called gay. To use the word*
> *fruit is insulting. I love the word gay. It's happy. Cheerful.*
> *Uplifting. And that certainly describes François and Alain. But*
> *unfortunately, not their dog. She has the personality of a potato.*

Dad lurches over to me like he did on the boat and puts his hand on my shoulder. "Honey, I've had too much wine and can't drive. We're going to have to stay here tonight. There's a spare room all made up for you at the top of the stairs. The bathroom is next to it."

"Okay."

He kisses the top of my head. "Thanks, kiddo."

They all yell "*Bonne nuit!*" from the dining room table.

I do mind, because who likes to sleep in clothes you've worn all day? But I try not to sulk. How often does he get to play with his friends? Wait. Am I the adult? Is he the kid? That can't be right. It's been a long and stressful day.

So, I go upstairs and look through the medicine cabinet for toothpaste to squeeze on my finger and wipe across my teeth, but I don't see any. This would be a good time for spying through bathroom drawers, but I'm too worn out. The sun and wind have knocked the stuffing out of me, so I go into the bedroom and pick one of the twin beds to lie down on. Because I'm in my clothes, I don't want to get under the covers, so I yank up a blanket that's folded at the bottom of the bed and drape it over myself. I'm asleep in minutes.

And then dying in the middle of the night. I'm having a hard time breathing. I sit straight up in bed and gasp, chest heaving. I know Dad told me not to panic in these situations, but I'm in the dark, in a house I don't know, and I can't get air into my lungs.

I stumble around and finally find the door and run down the hall and open the first door I see. Dad and Juliette are in a bed together sleeping. I pound his back and he jumps with fright, but as soon as he sees me, he grabs my arms. "What's wrong?"

"C...can't breathe."

He picks me up and runs downstairs and right out the front door. The minute the cool night air hits me, I can feel my lungs expand and I take a breath. It's more of a wheeze, but it feels so good. Dad rubs my back.

"Just slow breaths, Audrey. Easy does it."

And he's right. I slow down and the breaths come.

The other three are now outside and running around like chickens. Dad tells them to knock it off and they do.

The tightness eases and I can take big breaths of air. The wheezing has stopped as suddenly as it started.

Everyone wants to know what happened.

"I don't know. I lay down on the bed and pulled the blanket over my head and fell asleep. Then I woke up because I couldn't catch my breath."

Alain hits François on the arm. "I bet it was Missy's blanket! Were you on the bed by the door or the window?"

"The door."

"OH! *Mon Dieu*! She must be allergic to Missy's fur. I never thought to remove it."

"And you never shake it out, either!" François shouts.

"Fellas, calm down. It's no one's fault but mine. I had no business drinking so much wine last night. Let's get you home, Audrey."

I put my head on his shoulder. That sounds nice.

Dawn is breaking as we drive home. It's a peaceful time of day to be on the road. There's no traffic and Dad isn't yelling "Bonehead!" or "Meathead!" at other drivers. He gets very impatient with them. Dad is a great driver, although he goes a little fast. He says he has to, to get around the fatheads who cause accidents.

Tom sniffs me all over when I come in and then scurries away.

"He must smell Missy off me."

"Audrey, you take a shower and I'll shake your clothes out before we put them in the hamper. You don't want that dog hair on you. Then go back to bed for a couple of hours. That's where I'm going. Oh, my aching head."

We sleep until eleven. Aunt Maureen is reading the paper at the kitchen table when we shuffle out of our rooms. Dad stretches with his elbows over his shoulders, twisting his neck around, and then yawns, which is always a huge production. Most people just yawn. He puts his head back, opens his mouth as far as it can go, yawns, and then breathes out, "Ho, ho, ho, ho, ho," like an old Santa toy winding down. Then he takes all his fingers and scratches his wavy grey hair really hard until it's almost bushy, before smoothing it back with his palms. After that he smacks his lips and claps his hands together. "Any coffee going?"

"On the stove, or would you like to be served, your highness?"

"Brilliant." He sits in his chair, rubs his eyes and then his hands down his face. "Two creams, two sugars, two aspirin."

"It's like that, is it?" She gets up and putters around getting a mug.

"Hey, why are you here, anyway? It's Sunday."

"Nothing else to do. Do you want me to make pancakes, Audrey?"

"Sure. Thanks."

I never say no to this, because Aunt Maureen likes making pancakes, even though they're never good. She either burns them or they're gooey inside until she gets the hang of it, so I always ask for the ones on the top of the pile.

"So how was your sailing adventure, Audrey?" Aunt Maureen asks.

"I learned a lot."

"No kidding? Did they let you steer the boat?"

"I found out that I will never step my big toe in a sailboat ever again."

Aunt Maureen nods. "So, you won't be following in your father's footsteps and join the navy."

"I doubt I will ever take a bath again."

"Then the poor kid had an allergic reaction to their dog's fur and couldn't breathe in the middle of the night."

"Dad and Juliette were sleeping together and I had to wake them up."

Aunt Maureen stops pouring Dad's coffee and gives him a stern look.

"Oh, it wasn't like that, Aunt Maureen. They weren't sleeping together because they wanted to. We all had to share beds, because the place didn't have enough bedrooms."

Dad picks up the newspaper and puts it in front of his face. Aunt Maureen goes back to pouring the coffee.

A few days later Dad comes home from work and I know something is wrong instantly. He goes into the living room and sits at the piano and starts to play very sombre music. Tom and I sit with him until he's finished.

"Tchaikovsky's '1812 Overture.'"

"What's the matter, Dad?"

"François was killed today in a car accident."

I burst into tears. "Poor Alain!"

He hugs me.

Dad says I can't go to the funeral because it will be very sad, which I already know, but then I see him in his study with Aunt Maureen, and she is bent over him with her hand on his back, rubbing it. He tells her that François's MG drove straight into the back of a semi-trailer at high speed and he was decapitated.

I run into my room and hide under the covers. Having learned all about Henry VIII and his wives, I know what *decapitated* means. Then I remember something and run back into his study.

"You drive an MG!"

Dad realizes I've been listening at the door. "I'm selling it today and buying the biggest car I can find because I'm driving you around. I've been a selfish old fool. If you ever go back to camp, I'll be able to take you."

The very next day he comes home with a black 1967 Ford LTD 4-door hardtop. It's almost as big as Frank Weiner's Cadillac. I never see the MG again. And then two days later a man and his son show up with a trailer and haul away the old MG from the garage. They are very excited about it and thank Dad over and over again, saying what great shape it's in.

"Will you miss it, Dad?" I ask as they pull away.

"No. It's okay to outgrow dreams. Sometimes you have to move on."

He starts cleaning out the garage and naturally trips while he's holding a bag of glass pop bottles. They go flying and smash onto the cement floor.

"Jesus Christ almighty goddamn bastard son of a bitch!"

"Dad! Do you want poor Mr. Moore to hear you?"

He takes a deep breath and growls low in his throat while I help him clean up.

For a day I'm a bit of a celebrity when I tell my friends what happened to François. Everyone is fascinated by the thought of someone losing their head.

"Did it roll away?" Gloria wonders. "Did it bounce?"

"Like your stupid ball?" Jane snaps. "Of course it didn't bounce. It was probably flattened like a pancake."

"Thanks a bunch. I'll never be able to eat a pancake again."

We're on our bikes at the park, eating Creamsicles because I suggested it. It's not as warm out now as it was earlier in the summer. The green leaves are looking a little peaky and dusty from all the traffic. Sometimes you can feel fall in the air. I'm noticing that the light changes depending on the time of year. Strange how long it takes you to pay attention to things like that.

I squint my eyes. "Is that Pamela over there? Is she kissing that guy?"

Jane takes a bite of her ice cream. "She sure is. I wonder if he has his tongue down her throat."

"That's disgusting!" Gloria says. "Why would you let anyone do that?"

"I wonder what it's like to kiss a boy. Have you ever thought about it?" I ask them.

"I kissed my boyfriend," Jane says.

This is a side of Jane I never knew about. "You had a boyfriend?"

"In Grade One. Burt. He was cute."

I lick my Creamsicle. "There was only one boy in our class I wanted to kiss."

"Let me guess," Gloria mocks me. "Good old Nicholai. You only made goo-goo eyes at him from the minute you walked into the classroom."

"The blond boy in your class?" Jane asks. "Oh yes, I wouldn't mind kissing him myself."

I point my stick at her. "Well, you can't. He's mine. I am proclaiming him as my own. I am sovereign over the country known as Nicholai."

"You are a weirdo, Audrey Parker."

Not only am I a weirdo, I'm going to look like one too. Dad makes me go to the eye doctor with Aunt Maureen because he says I'm squinting all the time. Not that I noticed.

The doctor says I need glasses. Just my luck. Who wants to go to high school wearing glasses?

Aunt Maureen wants me to buy a pair that she likes. Shaped like cat's eyes. "I'm not a hundred years old, Aunt Moo."

Then I spy a pair on the wall that are round. "Look! Just like Mom's opera glasses!"

"What are you talking about? Your mother never owned opera glasses."

"Yes, she did! I have them in my room. I want these."

"You'll look like John Lennon."

"Good."

The eye lady suggests I buy the round tortoiseshell pair instead because a wire pair would bend out of shape easily at my age. And they do look better, but I can't let people know I like them. It's fashionable to say you hate glasses, but golly, I look like a real spy.

It also helps that I can actually see.

Dad thinks they're great. "Very spy-ish." So does my clutch of mothers. Mrs. Weiner shouts, "Fabulous, bubala!" Mrs. Papadopoulos claps her hands. "So flattering, Audrey." And Mrs. Andrews twirls her pearls. "Very nice, dear. Very nice, indeed."

Now Gloria and Jane want glasses. Pamela says I look like a dork, but she smiles when she says it.

I'm picking up fruit at the corner store when I run into Yana and realize that she's wearing round wire glasses. "Hey Yana! We look like twins."

"No. I'm fat."

"Don't say things like that about yourself. You are very pretty. You have the rosiest cheeks."

She blushes, which makes them even rosier.

"How are you getting along with your period? Is it annoying? I haven't got mine yet. Did you ask your mother about it?"

"She doesn't talk."

"I know she doesn't speak English..."

"She doesn't talk about anything, in English or Polish. She gave me a box of pads but that was it. I wish I had another mother. What's yours like?"

"I don't have one."

"You're lucky. See ya."

Poor Yana. I take out my notebook and pencil and write: *Not all kids love their mothers. This is news to me.*

I have trouble sleeping. So does Dad. We're still thinking about François. And I'm thinking about other dead people, like my mother, but I don't catch my dad at a good time. He's only eaten one spoonful of cereal and looks preoccupied.

"Aunt Maureen said my mother didn't own a pair of opera glasses, but I have them in my room."

He shakes his head, wondering what the hell I'm talking about. "What opera glasses?"

I sigh and take them out from underneath my bed. "These. These are my mother's."

"No, I'm sorry. They're not. I found those years ago when I moved into an attic apartment in Old Montreal. They were on the shelf of an old closet. I thought they were interesting, so I kept them."

Suddenly I'm enraged. "Do I have nothing of my mother's? Is there not a scrap of her anywhere? Not a picture, not a drawing, not an article of clothing? Not a bottle of perfume or a pen or a lace handkerchief? Have you thrown away everything of hers? Everything but me? Should I consider myself lucky that you haven't thrown me in the trash too?"

He reaches over and takes me by the wrist, hurting me in the process. "Goddammit, Audrey! What the hell is wrong with you? I can't discuss this right now. I'm late for a meeting, but don't you ever insinuate that I don't love you, or that I'd throw you away! You know me better than that. I don't deserve to be spoken to in that manner."

"Where is my mother, then? Didn't you love her? Don't you have a picture? Explain yourself, please."

"She hated having her picture taken. She said they destroyed pieces of her soul, bit by bit. I wish I had a picture to show you, but I don't. All you have to do is look in the mirror if you want to see your mother. She's right there. Now, we'll discuss this later. I have to go. Aunt Maureen should be here soon. All right?"

I don't look at him. He shakes my wrist. It still hurts. "All right?"

"Fine!"

He lets me go and I slam my bedroom door in his face. After he leaves, I can hear Tom scratching to get in, so I open it. He jumps up and cuddles on the bed with me.

"Why can't people be like cats? Cats don't hide things or pussyfoot around." Despite my fury, I grin at my clever remark. "I'm a spy *and* a writer."

I go into Dad's study and put a new piece of paper in his typewriter and type, SORRY.

Aunt Maureen comes down the hall. "Only me."

We both slump in the kitchen chairs.

"You look grumpy," she says.

"So do you."

"I have reason to be. They're cutting off my tits."

"Bloody hell. Did you tell your sons?"

"They both said I can stay with them, but they live in Toronto. They're busy with their jobs and kids and although their wives aren't my biggest fans, I know they'd help. But I want my own doctor, so it suits me to stay here."

I get up and hug her head. "We'll take care of you."

She nods. "I know."

Dad looks worn out when he comes home and that's before Aunt Maureen serves up corned beef hash for dinner and tells him her news. Now he hangs his head down and looks lost.

"She's going to be fine, Dad. They told her once those suckers are off, she's good to go."

He makes a face and looks at me. "That was their professional diagnosis?"

"Yes," Aunt Maureen says. "Looks like they've caught it early. I'm only having both breasts off because that's my decision. It's not like I need them anymore. It's a two for one sale."

"What do you need us to do, Maureen?"

"I'm not supposed to be alone when I first get home, so I was wondering if I could stay downstairs."

"And sleep on an old sofa? I'm not having that. We'll get you a bed. And I'll put in a new shower."

Aunt Maureen puts her head down on her arms and hides her face. Dad reaches over and rubs her arm. "You're going to be fine. We've got your back."

At bedtime, Dad comes in with some Allsorts. "Got your note. Thank you, I'm sorry too."

I hold out my wrist. "You almost bruised it."

"My humble apology. That was never my intention."

"Oh, I know that."

"Listen, I don't want you worrying about Aunt Maureen. She's a tough old bird. She'll be fine."

"I'm not worried. We've already endured two deaths in as many months. I doubt lightning will strike again."

He reaches into his sweater pocket and takes out a postcard. "Your mother sent it to me. She hated writing letters."

I hold it in my hand. It's a picture of the Empire State Building. When I turn it over, it reads, *On a clear day...you can see forever. R. xo*

"Your handwriting is much better."

"No doubt she wrote that on her lap in a cab."

"Rosemary."

"Rosemary Sullivan. That's right."

"When did she die?"

"When you were three."

"How?"

"Her heart gave out."

"How old was she?"

"Twenty-eight."

"And you were forty-six?

He nods.

"How does your heart give out when you're twenty-eight?"

"Lots of people die young."

"How come she wanted to be with an old man like you?"

"She was crazy."

"Okay. I can't talk about it now. May I keep the card?"

"Yes."

As I brush my teeth, I pull my hair back. Betty said my hair was like my mother's, and Dad says I look like her, but it's hard to figure out what parts. When I get back in bed, Tom comes under the covers with me. I hold onto the card, but I'm not happy with it. She should have written something nicer, like *I miss you* or *Wish you were here*. I'm not sure I like this mother of mine.

—

On the last weekend before the start of high school, Mr. and Mrs. Papadopoulos invite all their children's friends over for an outdoor celebration, with food and drinks and party games. Everything is colourful and fun and I suppose I'm having a good time, but I'm not feeling that great, and then Gloria's brother George squirts me right in the face with a water gun, so that really helps. Gloria says it's because he likes me.

Boys are obviously imbeciles. Blockheads.

I take off my glasses in the hope that he didn't break them and go in search of something to wipe them dry, since the hem of my dress isn't doing anything but producing smudges. Gloria's mother points me over in the direction of the tables, where the men are setting up for the food. Once I grab a cloth napkin, I wipe my glasses and put them back on.

That's when I notice a big barbeque and smouldering fire.

"Oh, Mr. Papadopoulos! Are we having marshmallows?"

He laughs and laughs and tells the men around him that this girl wants marshmallows! "Oh, Audrey, you do make me happy. No, my dear. We're having a Greek favourite. Roast lamb."

"Lamb?" I look at the charred shape turning slowly over the fire and realize it's an actual lamb that's stuck there, with the spit coming out of its mouth and hindquarters.

As in, Mary had a live one, but now she doesn't anymore.

There's a part of me that knows that you have to kill animals in order to eat them. When they are chunks wrapped in paper tied up with string at the supermarket, you don't think about it. But now I see this dear little lamb who was only a baby, suddenly black and dead and stiff, with its mouth open as if still in pain.

It breaks my heart in two. I can feel it crack open.

All the dead things.

Kittens. Young mothers. Nice, smiling, handsome men. Lambs. Aunts? Fathers?

It's too much.

Everything goes black.

Chapter Eight

When I open my eyes, four hundred eyes are staring back at me. This is so embarrassing.

And two hundred mouths are shouting at each other, so I put my hands over my ears. Four hundred arms point in every direction as Mr. and Mrs. Papa gently pull me up off the grass and make me lie down on a lounge chair.

I hear myself say I'm fine, but no one else can hear me because everyone is running around trying to bring me things. Gloria comes over with a glass of water her mother asked her to fetch, George, the jerk who squirted me with water, brings over a cold facecloth, Mr. Papa runs over with a pillow, and Mrs. Papa covers me with a shawl, even though it's really hot out. And then the grandmother hurries towards me with a big bowl and now I know she speaks English.

"EAT! YOU TOO SKINNY! LAMB STEW!"

I throw up all over the shawl.

When I see my father come striding across their lawn, with two hundred people behind him trying to explain that they're sure I'm not dying, I hold out my arms as if I'm an infant. I know he's getting old, but when he reaches down so I can put my arms around his neck and he slips one arm around my back and the other under my knees to lift me out of that chair, it's as if I'm weightless. I'm able to hide my face in his chest, so I don't have to see lambs or pots of lamb stew or grand-mothers or dorky teenage boys or giggling girls I don't know.

"It's okay, sweetheart. I've got you."

Mrs. Papa continues to follow us down the street, chattering nervously behind Dad. "I'm sure she just fainted, Mr. Parker. She didn't have anything to eat or drink, so maybe she got dehydrated."

"You have nothing to blame yourself for, Mrs. Papadopoulos. You have been kindness itself to Audrey and I appreciate everything you've done for her since we moved on this street. Her life is much better because of women like you. Please enjoy the rest of your party. I want to get her home."

She stops then and goes back to her house. I feel terrible about her nice shawl. I must buy her a replacement, but I'll probably never find anything that nice.

Dad puts me to bed and I don't even talk, I feel so rotten. I'm sleeping when I realize that Dr. McTavish is fingering my neck, looking for lumps or bumps or something. Back with the old tongue depressor. He lets me keep it and gives me two lollipops.

Turns out I have a fever and pretty bad strep throat. I have to stay in bed for five days, drink plenty of fluids, gargle with salt and water, and sleep as much a possible with my mooly-moola. That's what I call my humidifier. It looks exactly like a little alien that was on a cartoon once and that's what I've always called it, so I like it when it comes out of the closet and hisses at me at night.

Dad calls Mrs. Papadopoulos to tell her, because strep throat is contagious. She'll be sorry she invited me; there may be two hundred kids missing the first week of high school because of me. Can you believe that? I'll be walking into a class again as a latecomer. And who knows how much work I'm going to miss. Maybe they hand out multiple essays on the first day since this is serious school. It's so depressing.

We really are in a bit of a pickle. I'm sick, Aunt Maureen's surgery was moved up for some reason and she's in the hospital, the plumbers are supposed to arrive and put in a new shower downstairs but they're late, and Dad has to buy a bed, all the while some bigwig is flying in from New York for an important meeting.

Dad's growling gets louder when he roots through the cupboards to find a clean mug for his coffee, and then the coffee, and doesn't find either. He explodes. "Jesus H. Christ! I've got a sick kid with no one to look after her, no clean shirts, no food in the pantry, the house is a goddamn mess with dust and cat fur everywhere. What the hell is going on?"

"You're just noticing this now?" I croak.

"I need a goddamn wife!"

"You're just noticing this now?"

He points at me. "Stop being a smartass and think."

So I think.

"I know, ask Mrs. Weiner. She knows women, apparently."

"Brilliant." And he runs to the back door.

"Dad." I put my hand on my sore throat. "It's seven o'clock!"

"Oh right." He comes back.

"I don't need anyone to look after me, Dad. I'm just lying in bed all day. Mrs. Weiner is here if I need her. I'll answer the door when the plumbers come. After your meeting, call a furniture store and get them to deliver a bed, then pick up your dry cleaning and a few groceries. The only thing we could use is a cleaning lady from time to time."

"What would I do without you?"

"You're just noticing this now?"

I wait for the plumbers to arrive and let them in before I go to Mrs. Weiner's back door. She's horrified once I tell her what's going on.

"Don't worry, bubala. I know a woman. Now get back to bed and I'll be over in ten minutes with some hot chicken soup. I keep a gallon in the fridge at all times."

And that's how Uniska comes into our lives.

If you passed her on the street you wouldn't notice her. A small Ukrainian woman with grey hair always in a bun, a serious face, non-descript really, until she gives you a shy smile and you fall in love with her. But she doesn't smile often, because she's so intent on her work.

She arrives the next morning at seven-thirty with all her equipment, wearing a full body apron. Dad is in a rush to get out the door.

"As you can see, the place is in a bit of a mess. I'm not sure what you should tackle first."

"I'm sure she knows what to do, Dad."

"Yes." She nods. "Don't worry, Mr. Parker."

Dad looks so relieved. "Thank you, Mrs...."

"Call me Uniska."

"Uniska. It's very nice to meet you. Audrey, get back to bed. I'll see you tonight."

We both give him a wave.

"Do you need anything before you start?"

"No, dear. Everyone's house is the same. You go to bed."

It's comforting to hear someone move around your home. Aunt Maureen does, but she's not a great housekeeper and spends most of her time sitting at the kitchen table smoking or watching television and smoking. And knitting. I often wonder if her daughters-in-law ever put her scarves and mitts and socks on their kids. They must stink of smoke.

At one point I ask Uniska if it's okay if I have a bath. The steam helps my throat. She says she's finished in there and she'll do my room while I'm in here. Everything is gleaming. The taps and faucet and mirror shine back at me. The tub and sink look like someone's coming to do a photo shoot. And the toilet water is a blue bubble bath. I never knew a bathroom could be this clean.

By the end of the day, I don't recognize this place. Dad walks in and his mouth drops opens.

"Uniska, you're amazing! Would you be able to come to us twice a week?"

She gives him a shy smile. "Yes, Mr. Parker."

Dad and I and even Tom wonder what the heck we ever did without her.

—

If only Uniska could go to high school for me. This place is too scary for words. We have a homeroom we have to go to first thing every morning, but when the ridiculously loud bell goes off every forty-five minutes, we scramble around and go to other classrooms and I have no idea where they are.

And for some preposterous reason, I can't seem to find Jane or Gloria or Pamela or Yana or Nicholai anywhere. I'd even be happy to see Derek, but there's not one soul who looks familiar here. Where did my friends go? Why are there only ugly pimply guys and girls who seem like they could use someone to talk to, and cool guys and girls who look at you like dirt?

And what is it with me and sitting in front seats? Probably because I missed my first week, I'm stuck in homeroom in the first seat of the first aisle, and I quickly learn this is not where you want to be. The homeroom teacher seems to think I'm an unpaid servant. I'm expected to open the door when someone knocks, close the door if it doesn't close properly, hand out papers, turn on and off lights if we're watching something on a projector, pass notes to the teacher from any other teacher who sticks their nose in the room, gather milk money, or tell the principal where the list is for the field trip. What field trip?

And that's the first hour.

The only thing saving me from utter despair is the boy who sits in the first seat in the last row on the opposite side of the room. His eyes are grey blue. Blue grey. Greyish bluey blue. Bluey greyish grey. They are so startling, and when he looks at you, it's like looking at the tip of an iceberg.

And it seems like he looks at me often, but he doesn't really. He's staring out the window of our classroom door to see what's going on in the hallway.

I don't know one person here in this room, but I am a spy, so when the teacher is called out for a minute, I turn around in my seat and look at the girl behind me. She's a bit vacant, with thick, thick hair but thin, scraggly ends. How is that possible?

"Hi. I'm Audrey. Nice to meet you."

"Okay."

"And you are?"

"Francine."

"Francine, who is that boy sitting in the first desk in the last row?"

"The last desk in the first row?"

"No. The boy in the first desk by the windows."

"Ernie."

"Thank you."

I turn around. She pokes me in the back with her pen. Suddenly I'm pining for Nicholai. I turn around again.

"Want to come to my house?"

"Today?"

"Yeah."

"I'm sorry. I have plans. Maybe another time."

"Tomorrow?"

What the hell have I done?

"I'll let you know."

Maybe it's because I've been sick and in bed all week, but I'm so tired when I walk into my last class of the day, I'm shuffling.

"Perk up, sunshine," says a very cute young teacher. He's a man. I've never had a man teacher before. "There's a seat available here in the front row by me. Lucky you. Know that today is the first day of your career as a writer."

I totally forgot that one of my electives is a typing class. Dad suggested it.

In only ten minutes, my attitude about high school has been flipped on its ear. Maybe it's the clacking of the typewriter keys that brings me such comfort, or the fact that this Mr. Darren is so down to earth. He talks to us like we're real people.

"I was where you are just a few short years ago, and I can tell you, this class is the only one that's going to give you a skill you can use in the real world. This and Home Ec. We should be having classes about changing a tire and managing a household budget, but we're stuck with isosceles triangles. You will never need to know about an isosceles triangle."

Once he shows me how to place my fingers on the keys (which I sort of know already after watching Dad), he writes on the board, *The quick brown fox jumps over the lazy dog.*

"Type this sentence ten times. It uses every letter of the alphabet, so it's good practice."

This is education! I've heard this expression many times, but I never knew why it was so popular. Now I do.

Mr. Darren also doesn't stay behind his desk, he's always moving around, going up and down the aisles, encouraging us with our work.

"Once we get the fundamentals, then we can work on speed! We are going to have races, people!"

All of us smile at each other. When Mr. Darren walks by my desk, I say, "My dad is a writer."

He leans down. "He's a lucky man. I'm trying to finish my novel."

"He doesn't write novels. He writes about the state of civilization and the society we live in."

"So, he's a thinker as well as a writer. You have a lot to live up to— Audrey, isn't it? Sorry you missed the first few days, but you'll catch up. I have a feeling you're a quick learner."

"I'm going to be a writer someday. I have a necklace to prove it." I hold out my gift for him to have a good look.

"It's official then. Well done."

"I'm already a spy, but I'm not supposed to tell people."

"My lips are sealed."

Okay. Now I'm in love with Mr. Darren.

Finally, I spy Gloria as I'm leaving school. "Gloria! Wait up!"

She stops and smiles at me as I approach. "How are you feeling?"

We walk together up the street. "Much better, thanks. I'm sorry about your mother's shawl."

"It's fine. She washed it."

"Did anyone else get sick because of me?'

"No, I don't think so. Is this your first day back? What do you think? I'm having a hard time finding people I know."

"Me too! It's such a relief to see you."

"Jane is in my English class, but she only waved at me. I'm not sure she likes me."

"Gloria, everyone likes you. Jane is a bit of a worrier, so she probably had something on her mind."

"What does she have to worry about? I never worry."

"Everybody's different."

"I'm not supposed to say this, but George was wondering if you're ever coming for supper again. I think we're having lamb souvlaki tomorrow if you'd like to join us."

My stomach heaves. "Thanks, Gloria, but I'm still feeling sort of weak. It's going to take me a while before I feel up to going anywhere." Thank goodness we're now in front of my house. "Maybe I'll see you in the halls tomorrow."

"Okay, see ya."

Tom comes out from under the porch when I put the key in the lock. "Hey you. Waiting for me?"

He rubs his face on my leg to affirm this observation.

The phone is ringing, so I hurry up the hallway and throw my book bag on the kitchen table. "Hello?"

"Hi, Aud. I'm allowed to leave the hospital tomorrow."

"Oh! That's great, Aunt Moo. How are you feeling?"

"Like a piss-hole in the snow."

"Okay. That's a good description. That's how I feel about lamb."

"Lamb?"

"Never mind. Long story. Your bed was delivered and Dad even bought new sheets and two pillows for it. The new shower is installed, so everything is okey-dokey."

"God bless you. I'll take a taxi to your place. I don't want to trouble your dad."

"I think he'd like to pick you up. Call later tonight and discuss it with him."

I just get off the phone with her and have time to go to pee and give Tom his food before the phone rings again. This time it's Jane.

"I couldn't find you today," I say.

"I looked for you everywhere. I only know one person in all my classes and that's Gloria, which is just my luck."

"She thinks you don't like her."

"I don't. She doesn't have a clue about reality."

"That's not her fault."

"And what's up with that stupid ball?"

"She didn't have it today, now that you mention it. I ran into her after school."

"Wanna come over?"

"Not just yet. I'm still feeling not quite myself. Maybe by the week-end I'll feel stronger."

The minute I get off the phone with her and pull my uniform over my head, the phone rings again. "What is going on?!"

I pick it up. "Hello?"

"Hello? Who's this?"

"I should be asking you that question. You called me."

"Is this Jack Parker's number?"

"Yes."

"So you must be...Audrey?"

"That's right. And you are?"

"I'm Joe. Your dad's brother."

"Oh!"

"Is he there?"

"No."

"I'll call back." And he hangs up. Just like that.

Every time I think about my father's family, I get this worried feeling in the back of my mind. Like something isn't quite right. They aren't simple, like Gloria's family or Jane's family. There seems to be this dark undercurrent that wiggles through everything.

It's very unsettling. Troubling.

———

The next day in homeroom, Francine's blasted pen is in my back again. I turn around. "Could you tap me on the shoulder when you want something?" I don't want to tell her that I miss Nicholai whenever she does it.

"Okay." And she taps me on the shoulder. While I'm facing her. Good grief.

"Can you come to my house after school?"

"I can't today, Francine. My aunt is coming home from the hospital and I need to be there. I'll probably have to be with her for at least a few weeks until she gets on her feet."

"Oh." Her face falls, and now I feel bad.

"I promise I'll come over someday."

She brightens up, so I turn around and go back to my work. And then she sticks her pen in my back and taps me on the shoulder. I swivel around and growl, "What now?"

"Ernie is looking at you."

I turn my head to the windows, and sure enough, he gives me a grin. I'm a puddle on the floor. This must mean he likes me. Holy cow! Stuff like this never happens to me. And then the bell rings and everyone gets up and files out the door.

I'm standing by my desk when Ernie walks by. He leans over close to my ear. Is he going to kiss me?

"That weird girl behind you is a real dummy."

Damn it to hell. I glance at Francine and know that she heard him. I can see it in her face as she rushes out.

"And you're just a little bit of a jerk, aren't you, Ernie, with the kaleidoscope eyes."

He scowls and keeps going, along with my love life.

———

When Dad brings Aunt Maureen home, she can't get over how clean our house is. "The woman is a genius."

Dad and I are downstairs with her eating supper. We put a hamburger and fries on a tray so it's easier for her to eat as she sits up in her new bed.

"Are you sore, Maureen?"

"Is the Pope Catholic? It would be like me lopping off your balls, Jack. Sorry, Audrey."

I've missed Aunt Maureen.

"Oh! I forgot to tell you, Dad. Your brother Joe called you yesterday."

Dad and Aunt Maureen give each other a look.

"Did he say what he wanted?"

"No. When he found out you weren't home, he said he'd call back and hung up."

"I wonder what that's about," Dad says.

"Money," Aunt Maureen replies.

"He didn't seem very interested in me."

"He's a harmless old bachelor," Dad says. "Isn't around young people very often. He's okay."

"He was a cute kid," Aunt Maureen says. "Roundish, as I recall."

Dad points his fork at her. "You were all big, but not this fine specimen. Not sure where I came from."

"You're right," Aunt Maureen nods. "Each of us girls was shaped like a Westinghouse fridge."

"Aunt Moo! What an awful thing to say."

"Why? It's true. And strong! My oldest sister was so strong, she tossed one of her husbands right through a plate-glass window."

Dad and Aunt Maureen start to giggle, even though I can tell it makes Aunt Maureen's ribs sore.

"Maybe you were too little, but remember the time Dad held me out the window so I could attach the wire back up to the power grid when they cut off our electricity?"

"DAD! You could've been electrocuted!"

"I wasn't."

"No, I don't remember that, but I do remember when you came home with that tattered five-dollar bill you found buried in the ice and you kicked and scratched at it until you pulled it out. Dad was furious that we couldn't use it, but I thought you were very brave. Your hands were bleeding and raw with the cold."

"I do know that I drank some kind of bleach or lye when I was a year old and Dad crashed his car right through a railway crossing to get me to the hospital."

"I remember that story."

They both smile. It pleases Dad to have this memory of his father doing something heroic for him. Maybe this is the grandfather I'll keep in my mind.

———

Jane and I go shopping with her mother to pick up our gym uniforms. We have to get them at some specialty shop. Mrs. Andrews hands them to us.

"Look at this!" Jane holds up these huge puffy-looking shorts. "They're bloomers!"

"And what's this all about?" I hold up a white blouse with what looks like two fishtails hanging at the bottom, with buttons and buttonholes on either side.

"You button them up between your legs, so your blouse doesn't come out of your shorts while you're running around," Mrs. Andrews informs us.

"That's ludicrous," I tell her. "They're so afraid of us showing our belly buttons that they make us run around with buttons rubbing up against our vaginas for an hour? What if you really have to pee? How are you going to get them undone in time?"

Mrs. Andrews looks aghast. Jane keeps gawking from her mother to me. I finally twig. "I'm sorry, Mrs. Andrews, but I do know what a vagina is and I know where it's located. And it seems to me that these buttons would be a little irritating."

That's when I see the two sales ladies behind the counter, killing themselves trying not to laugh.

Mrs. Andrews is annoyed with me. She doesn't say much on the way home, and when she drops me off, she says, "Just a moment, Jane," and gets out to join me on the sidewalk, the motor still running.

She speaks in a low voice. "I don't know how you're being brought up, and I know you don't have a mother, so that puts you at a disadvantage right off the bat, but in our house, we do not use vulgar words in public."

"Is *vagina* a vulgar word?"

She waves her hand in my face, as if to erase what I just said. "Yessss! And I don't want you to use words like that around Jane. She's still too young for that kind of nonsense."

"I'm sorry, Mrs. Andrews. I really wasn't aware of that. I won't say anything in front of Jane. You have my word."

She pulls down her suit jacket and adjusts it, breathing a sigh of relief. "Thank you, Audrey. Now, we'll say no more about it. Goodbye, dear."

The minute I get inside and hug Tom, I go downstairs to find Aunt Maureen. She's got a crossword puzzle magazine on her chest, and she's dozing, but she opens her eyes when I sit on the old couch beside her bed.

"How was your shopping excursion? As much fun as it was with Mrs. Weiner?"

"The polar opposite." I tell her what happened.

Aunt Maureen stares at me in disbelief. "And she's a twat."

"What's a twat?"

"A cunt."

"What's a cunt?"

"A woman who thinks the word *vagina* is vulgar."

"Are these words I can use in public?"

"Christ, no! Don't tell your father I told you. He'll have my head."

"Dad taught me how to curse, remember?"

"There are words you say and words you don't say. Don't ask me why. But I'll tell you one thing, someone who thinks that the proper word for a body part is vulgar is an uptight old prune."

"No, she's not. I caught her necking with the swimming instructor at camp."

Aunt Maureen laughs so hard she has to hold on to her flat chest.

———

Then comes the day we're let out of class early before lunch—my chance to take a bus to Montreal West High school and ask to look at their yearbooks. I'm determined to see a picture of my mother. If I was three in 1958 and my mother was twenty-eight, that means she was born in 1930, and so she'd be in high school from maybe 1944 to 1947.

The bus takes a lot longer to get to Montreal West than I imagined. I'll probably be late for class, but it can't be helped. I sit right by the bus driver. He says he'll let me know the nearest stop to the school, and he doesn't forget, which I appreciate. I still have a way to walk, but when I finally come upon it, I realize that this building must have had the same architect as my old elementary school. An even bigger rectangle with red bricks and a million windows. Why do schools look like penal institutions?

It's always daunting to walk into a school you don't know—you don't belong, and all the other kids know it—but my mother walked these halls, so I feel a tenuous connection, although it's probably wishful thinking. It's not immediately obvious where the school office is, so I ask an older girl. She blows a bubble and snaps her gum while pointing down the hall. Eventually I find it.

All school secretaries look the same. Harried, exasperated, and flustered. This middle-aged woman looks at me like she can't believe she's being interrupted yet again.

"Yes?"

"Excuse me, please. Would you know where I could find your old yearbooks?"

"Old yearbooks? How old?"

"1944 to 1947."

"Are you joking?"

"No."

"Go to the school library. There might be some yearbooks there, but I doubt we have ones from twenty years ago."

I'm just about to ask her where the library is when she disappears with a pile of papers under her arm. I'm running out of time, so I ask a boy with glasses where I might find the library. He points down the hall. Does no one in this school talk?

Eventually I discover its whereabouts, but there's no one in here. Of course, this is their lunch hour too, so I wander around and try not to panic. I'm so close.

"May I help you?"

Thank heavens. A woman who looks like she knows everything. How do I know that? She has intelligent eyes and a no-nonsense manner. I love women like this and aspire to be one.

"I'm looking for your yearbooks between 1944 and 1947, please. I hope to see a picture of my mother."

She tilts her head and looks at me seriously. No astonishment or reproach, which I appreciate.

"We have some yearbooks here, but I'm not certain we have all of them. Let's look, shall we?"

She takes me over to a section of a bookshelf that is close to her desk. "We have the newest ones here. The older ones might be in storage."

Her finger goes over all the dates on the yearbooks. "Here are the '60s and a 1959, but that's all I can see."

My stomach feels sick. She senses my disappointment. "What's your name, dear?"

"Audrey Parker."

"Well, Audrey, I'm Mrs. Johnson. You tell me your mother's name and I'll do my best to find a yearbook from the forties. It might take me a while. Give me your phone number and I'll call you if I find anything."

"My mother's name was Rosemary Sullivan."

"Was?"

I nod.

"This is very important to you. I'll do my best."

"Thank you, Mrs. Johnson. You know, I'm trying to be a spy, but I'm not very good at it. It's so exhausting because you never find what you want when you want it."

"That's the way it is in life."

"May I ask you something?"

"Surely."

"When you were a kid, did people call you bad names?"

She presses her glasses up to her nose. "You mean because I'm a Black woman?"

"Yes."

"They still do."

"Can you forgive people who do that? Is it possible to know that some people never meant to hurt you?"

"Forgiveness is always possible. It's a choice. But it can get tedious having to do it year after year. And some people very much mean it. I make it my business to stay away from them."

"Thank you for being so nice to me and taking me seriously. I'm collecting a notebook of women I admire and you're going to be in it."

"A very high compliment. Thank you."

I give her my phone number and address and take my leave.

Mrs. Johnson calls me three days later. "You're in luck, Audrey! I found a 1945 yearbook with your mother's picture in it. She was in grade ten. She's not in any of the other years. I'm not allowed to release this book, but I've mimeographed the picture for you and I'll send it to you."

"Thank you, Mrs. Johnson. Thank you so much."

"My pleasure, Audrey. And you look just like her! Take care of yourself, dear."

I hang up, almost unable to believe my luck.

Dad is in the kitchen gathering up the garbage to put in the can outside. "Who's Mrs. Johnson?"

"The school librarian. She found a book I wanted."

"Imagine calling in the evening to tell you that. That was nice of her."

"She's a nice woman." Compassionate.

I'm not sure why I lied. Well, yes I am. This is just for me.

When the envelope arrives in the mail, I take it in my room and sit with it for an hour before I open it. Mind you, a black-and-white copy of a human face is never great, but one thing is quite clear.

I'm the spitting image of my mother.

———

This high school has a pool, which I'm sure they thought was an asset, but I have eyes and a spy's sensibility, and not one girl in my swimming class likes it—except for Lisa Finkel, who has a perfect body, a perfect face, perfect skin, and the most perfect long hair of any human who ever lived. And she likes it because she doesn't care who sees her naked body. Why would she? She looks too damn good. She actually dries her hair with a towel with not a stitch on.

Meanwhile, the rest of us, who have a healthy reluctance to showing the world our business, try to wiggle in and out of our swimming costumes behind small towels. There's nowhere to hide in here. Just walls of small lockers in a straight line with a mile-long bench in front of them.

The school provides the bathing suits, another so-called asset, but after several years of industrial washing machines, these scraps of cotton flannel look just like the socks on our clothesline. They are shapeless enough when they're dry, but the minute they get wet we have to haul up the front of them so our boobs don't pop out, and when we climb out of the pool on the ladder, they're so saggy we look like we're wearing dirty diapers.

I'm standing here in a grump, not wanting to soak myself in chlorine bleach, when I spy Jane! I quickly tiptoe across the slippery tiles and tap her on the shoulder, which momentarily brings Francine to mind. "What are you doing here?"

She turns around and her face lights up. "Oh, hi! I had to switch a class and there was a conflict so they put me in this time slot. What luck!"

Just then a door opens up off the balcony above and a bunch of boys pour in, shouting and catcalling. All the girls, including Jane, scream and jump into the pool. Our teacher blows her whistle frantically, while the male teacher on the floor above corrals his hooligans, pushes them out, and shuts the door. The girls continue to twitter.

Honestly.

As Jane and I hold on to the edge of the pool and flutter-kick, she asks me about the day we went shopping.

"What did my mother say to you when you got out of the car?"

"Nothing. Thanked me for coming."

"Bullshit."

"Jane Andrews! Only I use words like that."

"Tell me."

"She said she didn't want me to say vulgar words like *vagina* in front of you."

Jane screeches, which makes everyone look at her, including our instructor. "Sorry! Just a cramp." Then she spits, "That woman makes me so mad! She treats me like Dixie. She's never going to let me grow up."

"Maybe you should tell her how you feel?"

"She'd have to listen to me, and you know how well she does that."

"Get a rubber ball and bounce it. Gloria says she never worries and I think that's why. It takes her mind off things."

"Keep it up and I'll have to stop talking to you, too."

We smile at each other and then the swimming instructor makes us do laps.

It occurs to me that I should've had Dad write me a note about swimming class. I do one lap and know I can't do any more. I'm still tired from my week at home. Maybe I've got something else wrong with me? While I think about that, I'm hanging on to one of the bars of the ladder. A few girls go up the rungs beside me, but I'm not paying attention. And then a girl I don't know swims up and slides her hand right between my legs, slowly enough that I know it's deliberate.

She continues to climb the ladder as if she didn't do it. She doesn't even look back at me as she heads for the locker room. What just happened? Why don't I say something? Maybe I just imagined it. It's silly that I feel so shaken. Should I tell Jane? If her mother doesn't want me to say the word *vagina*, I'm sure she doesn't want her to know that some girls like to feel them.

When I get home, I check on Aunt Maureen, but she's sleeping and Tom is curled up with her. I sit at Dad's desk and type *The quick brown fox jumps over the lazy dog* about fifty times. Then I start typing, *I don't feel very good. I don't feel very good. I don't feel very good.*

Dad wakes me up at his desk. "You don't feel very good?"

My head shakes no and my eyes leak.

Once more Dr. McTavish is at my bedside.

This time, I have mono.

Chapter Nine

The only thing worse than going to high school is not going to high school.

For the first two weeks I sleep constantly. Don't talk, don't want to eat, don't read, don't even want to watch television because it hurts my eyes. So, I stare out the window from my bed until I sleep and then sleep some more.

In the evenings Dad plays the piano for me and that puts me to sleep. Then I hear his typewriter clicking away and that puts me to sleep. Even listening to Aunt Maureen, Uniska, and Mrs. Weiner at our kitchen table laughing sends me straight to dreamland. That's when I know this is serious. For me to not want to listen in on three women gossiping is major.

"How long am I going to be like this?" I ask my dad.

"The doctor says it can be anywhere from two weeks to two months. Sometimes longer, sometimes shorter. No one knows."

"He's a font of information. I could be a doctor with advice like that."

Dad goes to the school to talk to my teachers, who've only known me for six days, and makes arrangements for them to send me my work, but he tells me to decide when I feel well enough to do it, and right now I don't. Phooey on all of it.

By week three I finally have the energy to take the kitchen phone, lie on my bed, and call my friends.

"You're going to pull this damn phone cord out of the wall," Aunt Maureen gripes. She's grumpy because she's quit smoking and resents every minute of it. She's still here, even though she could go home now, but Dad feels better that I have someone with me, and truthfully so do I. Although sometimes I wish it was just Uniska. She's like a sea of calm next to Aunt Maureen's chaos. She's here every Tuesday and Friday, and sometimes when she comes in to dust my room, she'll sit on the bed and put her hand on my forehead to see how I'm doing. She doesn't say anything, just smiles and then pats my cheek and continues with her work. I added Uniska to my admiration notebook the day after I met her and she keeps earning stars after her name when she does things like that.

It's these moments when I miss having a mother the most.

I call Jane.

"Thank God you're still alive!" she yells in my ear. "I mean, I knew you were, but I wasn't allowed to call you or see you and we didn't get any updates about you from anyone."

"I should've asked Dad to let you know, but I was so sick and he was so worried, we didn't really think about anything else."

"Are you coming back to school?"

"No. I still feel pretty miserable."

"Of course, stupid Gloria says to the girls in English class that she wonders who you were kissing, because you got mono and that's the kissing disease. I told her to keep her mouth shut. She hasn't talked to me since."

"It's called the kissing disease? Fascinating. Tell her it wasn't her brother George, that's for sure. No, don't tell her anything. I don't want you two to quarrel."

"Too late, Audrey. I know you'd like us to be friends, but we're not. I think you might like my new friend Bethany. She's really nice."

A stab of jealousy goes right through my heart. I'm missing everything. "Sorry, I have to go. I'll call again."

"Oh, please do, Audrey. I really, really miss you. You're my best friend."

That makes me feel better. "You're my best friend too, Jane."

"Am I allowed to call you now?"

"Sure. That's something to look forward to."

I'm too tired to call anyone else. And now I don't feel like talking to Gloria anyway.

———

One Saturday afternoon I hear voices in the living room. It doesn't occur to me to look in the mirror to straighten myself up before I go out there. The fact that I want to go out there is enough. Normally I'm in my room twenty-three hours a day.

I show up at the French doors and a short, fat guy with a bald head does a double take. "Jesus! You look like a prisoner of war."

This must be my father's brother, Joe. They say *Jesus* the same way.

Aunt Maureen is insulted on my behalf. "That's a fine greeting. Like you're such a prize."

"Joe, this is Audrey. She's sick with mono at the moment," says Dad.

Joe nods at me. I don't bother nodding back.

"Do you need anything?" Dad asks me.

"No. I'm just being nosy. What are you talking about?"

"Joe's opening a small restaurant," Dad says.

"Which is such a great idea since he can't boil an egg," Aunt Maureen adds.

Okay. Now I get it. Joe is here to borrow money from Dad and Aunt Maureen is annoyed that Dad is giving it to him. Since Dad is the oldest brother and the only one who has some money (despite our modest home), this sibling feels like he can bank here, and Dad has no choice but to hand it over because of his guilt over making something of himself, whereas Joe looks like an unmade bed.

I get a kick out of Aunt Maureen. Dad has helped her many times too, but the difference is, she does her best to help him back. This Joe character I've never met. I'll probably never see him again after today. I have a feeling his restaurant is going to be a dive.

Okay, I have my intel. "Nice to meet you," I say half-heartedly before I wander off.

"Feel better."

I wish I felt better. And then I do, because Mrs. Weiner pops her head in our back door. "Anyone home?"

"Where else would I be?" I smile at her.

She's carrying a big casserole dish and puts it on the stove. "You get some slippers on, young lady, and a bathrobe. I'll make us some tea." Then she hears the voices in the living room. "Oh, am I interrupting?"

"NO! Please stay. It's just my dad's brother asking for money."

She touches the side of her nose. "Say no more."

While she fills the kettle, I bundle up and sit at the table to watch her putter around. She waits with me for the water to boil.

"I made a brisket for your dinner."

"I'm so glad we moved here and that you're our neighbour."

"Bubala!" She pats my hand and laughs. "I'm buttering up so you'll come back and babysit when you're feeling better."

"How are the boys?"

"Monsters! Little terrors! But they're mine."

"They love it when I read to them."

She points at me. "That will be their saving grace. They love to read. Michael will be a doctor and David will be a lawyer."

"They know that already?"

"No. They'll do as they're told. Jewish mothers know you have to go after what you want. Life is not going to hand it to you on a plate. You tell them from the cradle what they will be and they think they thought of it themselves."

"Did Mr. Weiner's mother tell him to sell junk?"

She slaps her hands together and gives a delighted laugh. "Oh, Audrey. You do make me happy. No, of course she didn't. The trouble with kids is, they don't always do what you want, but you have to try anyway. Odds are you'll get one of them."

Aunt Maureen must have heard Mrs. Weiner laugh. She comes up the hallway. "Sharon! So good to see you. I assume you put the kettle on."

"Almost boiled." She takes a package of cigarettes out of her pocket, looks at Aunt Maureen, and puts them back. "Sorry. I forgot. How's it going?"

"Miserable. This is no way to live. I'd rather smoke and die young than go through this."

"That's what I tell my Frank. Eat the sugar! He's beautiful just the way he is. It's his damn doctor who's obsessed with blood pressure. I know what's driving it up: being told he can't have his favourite desserts. The only pleasure that man has in life is sweets. He doesn't drink, smoke, gamble, or womanize. And he loves me to death. Do I want him to be unhappy? I don't think so. Oh, don't get me started!"

She jumps up and puts the tea on, and that's what I love about Mrs. Weiner. She's family now. And I know I'm feeling a bit better because I want to sit here with her.

My tea is mostly hot water and milk with lots of sugar, because she made it. Aunt Maureen takes a package of graham crackers out of the pantry and serves them as cookies. We slather butter on them.

Mrs. Weiner looks around. "How can I tell Uniska was here yesterday? The woman is a living Brillo pad. Everything sparkles. I always get her to come before the holidays, and you have to book her months early. If you're not her client now, there's a ten-year waiting list to get her."

"That's intriguing. So how did we manage to snag her?" I ask.

"Because she loves my Frank. She'll do anything for him. When I called and told her the situation, she didn't hesitate. Whoever she bumped off her list to do this is probably still crying hysterically."

"Why does she like Mr. Weiner so much?"

"He knows her husband. They've worked on construction sites together in the past. One day the elevator door opened and Uniska's husband backed into it with a wheelbarrow full of debris, but there was no elevator. He fell down the shaft and was paralyzed."

Aunt Maureen and I look at her in disbelief.

"How awful! That poor man and dear Uniska, having to deal with that." Aunt Maureen tsks.

"Exactly. He can never work again, and Uniska had to care for him, so she couldn't work at first. The construction company was reluctant to pay damages because technically they said he should have looked to see if the elevator was there. Can you imagine? So, they had no money coming in, and Frank wasn't having that, so he hired a bigwig lawyer and they received a large settlement, so they don't have to worry about money ever again. Uniska went back to work after a couple of years because she just loves to clean, and her husband is free to paint his watercolours. He even sells them. She would move heaven and earth for Frank."

"Wow. What a story." I sigh. "The things people go through."

"So now you see why I want my husband to have a piece of cheesecake!"

Finally.

Finally, I'm being released from my prison. It is now the middle of November, for heaven's sake. The leaves on my maple tree turned red and then fell off, including my cute ones, Snipp, Snapp, and Snurr. They are now covering Sally-Anne's grave.

Dr. McTavish tells me not to kiss anyone, which is his attempt at a joke, and for the sake of my spleen and liver, I'm to cut out gym and swim class for now, just to be on the safe side.

I'm going back gladly, because I am bored out of my mind at this point, but deep down I know I don't have the energy I once did. I'd never say that to Dad, because he worries enough about me. He looks a little older, quite frankly, but then so do I, very pale with circles under my eyes, despite my four thousand hours of sleep.

But the good news is that Mrs. Weiner took me to her hairdressers because she said she'd get a discount.

"Bubala! Your hair is a mop! Something must be done."

My hair is now the best thing about me. I have a pixie cut, though it quickly turns too curly to be fashionable. At least now it's a smaller mop.

Dad delays his trek to work so he can see me off. Aunt Maureen is here too, but I know the minute I'm out the door, she's heading home to smoke her brains out. I hope she does. She's way too crabby.

"Okay! I have my ten pounds of homework with me."

"I made you a chicken sandwich for lunch, and there's cut-up carrot and celery sticks because you have to eat vegetables, and there's maple walnut ice cream in the fridge to fatten you up."

"Thanks, Dad. Jane is coming for lunch to celebrate my return."

"Excellent. I'll bring home a pizza. Good luck, honey! Hope you have a great day."

"I will."

They both hug me a little too tightly, like I'm off to my first day of kindergarten.

"Bye, Tom!"

Tom meows from the piano bench but doesn't bother turning around.

I'm not in homeroom for thirty seconds before I feel a pen in my back and a tapping on my shoulder. Slowly, I turn around.

"Can you come over after school?" Francine says.

"I'm fine, Francine. Thank you for asking. It was a rough go for a while, but I'm back now."

"Well?"

This nightmare will continue until I agree. "Where do you live?"

"Across the street."

Rats. "I'll come for twenty minutes. Then I have to go home and rest. Doctor's orders."

I wait for a response but there is none.

"So is that the plan?"

"I guess."

"I'll be at the front door of the school at three."

She says nothing.

"Have I lost my mind?" I ask my best friend as we walk back to my house for lunch.

"I'll say," says Jane. "Your dad will be furious that you're not going right home after school."

"I'm so desperate to get her to stop nagging me, I just want it over with."

"Who's to say she won't ask you again tomorrow?"

That stops me in my tracks. "Thanks, Jane."

I unlock the door, and Tom rushes out as we go in. Jane brought her own lunch. "Mom put in two sandwiches in case you wanted one."

"That was nice of her." I take my lunch out of the fridge and we sit at the table and grin.

"I love your hair. You look older. I bet Mom wouldn't let me get a pixie cut. Heaven forbid I do something fashionable."

"What have I missed since my Sleeping Beauty routine?"

"Umm, I told you about Bethany. She's in my history class. She's a Girl Guide too, so that's what we talk about mostly. Her troop sounds like they have a lot more fun. Maybe I should go there. It's near Monkland. But Mom will say no to that."

Poor Jane is a prisoner and she's not even sick.

She takes another bite of her ham and cheese sandwich and then remembers something and tries to swallow it quickly. "Oh yeah! I found out about Nicholai!"

Immediately, my eyes get dreamy. "I haven't seen him yet. Not that I've had a chance."

"He's not there."

My sandwich stops halfway to my mouth. "What do you mean?"

"He's gone to another school. His father was transferred or something."

My sandwich is forgotten. "You mean I'll never see him again? Are we always going to be star-crossed lovers?"

"Probably. Unless you can find out what school he's going to."

Of course. I'm a spy. Now I have a mission. I bite my sandwich. "Whoever gave you this information, I'd like to talk to them."

Jane smiles at me. "There are other cute boys in the school. There's one in my French class called Ernie, and you should see his eyes."

"Oh, I know Ernie. He's in my homeroom. He's not that nice— although, now that I think of it, he's not exactly wrong about Francine."

"Call me the minute you get home from her place. If she's as loopy as you say she is, I'm dying to hear all about it."

By the end of the day, I've given my homework to all my teachers and they're surprised and impressed that I typed my work. All except math of course.

Mr. Darren is thrilled with my progress. "You've only been to a few classes and you're my favourite student! How did you get so good?!"

"I typed all my assignments just for something to do while I was home. It was good practice."

"Even if you never show up again, you're getting an A+ on your report card. I love young people who have brains. You're a thinker, like your father."

He remembers our conversation about Dad? Have I mentioned I love Mr. Darren?

———

My Mickey Mouse watch says 3:10. I'm sure it's not cool to wear one in high school, but I don't care, since Dad gave it to me. Francine is late. If she doesn't arrive in two seconds, I'm outta here.

Just my luck, she comes through the door. She points down the street to the left. "We go this way."

No *I'm sorry I'm late*, or *Sorry to have kept you waiting*. The girl has absolutely no social graces whatsoever. If nothing else, this is an experience I can write about. *How some people live.*

Now that I know how some people live, I'm not anxious to explore this subject further, unless it's about foreign lands with ancient cultures.

When we get to her place, it's very dirty and messy. Even Uniska would run the other way. Francine has about five sisters that she doesn't introduce me to, and then her mother walks out of the bathroom stark naked and slams her bedroom door. I don't think she saw me. Everyone is yelling and running around. My ears hurt.

"I have pet fish," Francine says. "Wanna see them?"

"Okay."

She takes me into the bathroom. I'm not sure why she keeps them in here. There's a large bowl with two goldfish in it. To my surprise, it's bright and clean and has fake plants and small pebbles on the bottom and even a little ceramic castle for them to hide in. They look happy enough.

"I have to feed them." She takes a pinch of flaked fish food out of a small container and sprinkles it on top of the water. The two fish immediately come out of their hiding place and rise to the surface with their mouths open, vacuuming up the flakes.

"They were hungry," I say. It's not original, but it's all I can think of at the moment.

"You can't overfeed them."

"Do they have names?"

"Thing One and Thing Two."

There may be hope for Francine yet. "Dr. Seuss! My favourite."

"Who?"

"Never mind."

And then I happen to look down by the toilet and all around it are pads filled with blood. Because I'm a spy, I immediately think Francine's mother has killed someone in here, but then my rational brain kicks in and I recognize that these must be sanitary pads for girls' periods, since there are a lot of girls here. But I always imagined you'd have to fold and wrap up a used pad in toilet paper and put it in a wastepaper basket, because something like that is personal and private. That's what I'll do when the time comes, but who knows when that will be.

I've had enough. "I have to go, Francine. I'm tired."

She looks at me with sad eyes and says nothing.

When I get home, I call Jane.

"So? How did it go?"

"She's fine. She has fish that are pretty neat, but I didn't stay long."

"Well, that's boring. You usually have some horror story or other."

"Not this time."

But I end up telling Uniska when I'm home for lunch on Friday. She sits with me and has hers at the same time. She's so easy to confide in. Now *her* mouth is a steel trap, not like my dear Mrs. Weiner.

"I feel very sorry for her, but I can't tell her that. I can't say, *Well, it's too bad that you live like this and your mother hasn't taught you how to speak to people.* That would be rude. I don't know what to do. I know she wants to be my friend, but I honestly don't have the energy to deal with her."

"You worry too much, Miss Audrey. Some people don't keep their house clean, but if this woman has six children, it's going to be messy. Walking around your own home naked is not a crime, and the pads on the floor, well, there's no excuse for that, but as I say, some people aren't that bothered. This Francine is competing with five other sisters, and so she's probably ignored a lot of the time, but she's still young and she'll find her way. Every twelve-year-old I've ever met is awkward in some way. She'll grow out of it. I'm sure she's as loved as you are."

"Well, she does have some pretty nice fish."

"You see? Her mother lets her keep her pets, and makes her look after them. I'd say that's a good sign."

This makes me feel so much better. I didn't sleep much worrying about Francine. I smirk at Uniska. "How am I awkward?"

She pinches my cheek. "You are an old soul, Miss Audrey. And you think too much. You need to be more carefree. You don't have to be your father's wife or friend. You need to be his little girl. Nothing more. Please remember that."

I understand what she's saying, but it's always been like this with my father. We're a team. How do I stop worrying about him? How can I be more carefree? Is it possible that motherless children are just naturally more anxious? Our mothers aren't around to provide a layer of protection, so we walk around this world without our skin.

And that hurts.

A few weeks later, I decide to bike to a second-hand shop that Uniska told me about. I'm looking for something for Dad for his birthday. He likes old junk, so a second-hand shop may be just the ticket.

It's like Aladdin's cave in here. It's got everything you could ever want—if you want painted picture frames, old china dogs, ugly butter dishes, and cheap dishtowels. Then I find an old tobacco tin in a wooden box. Dad could use that for his pipe tobacco. I like it because it has a sailor on the front of it. *Players*.

Then I come across a tarnished silver rack that looks interesting. I ask the owner what it is.

"That's an old English toast rack. You put your slices of toast in it so they don't get soggy."

"Gosh, I love soggy toast."

"I've seen people use them to hold letters on their desks."

Brilliant. Excellent. I buy both of these items and am very pleased with myself. A woman in an old green coat has been watching me. She's young but looks much older, as if her life has been too hard for her to manage. I give her a brief smile as I head for the door.

"What ya got there?" she says.

"A birthday present for my dad."

"You're lucky. You have money. What's your name?"

"Audrey Parker. Do you need some money?"

"Quit bugging the customers!" the owner shouts at her.

"We better go outside," she says.

I follow her out the door and she holds out her hand. "I could use a little. I want to buy a birthday gift for my father too."

"Okay." I take my Peruvian coin purse back out of my pocket and open it. I'm not sure how much to give the lady, so I put a few dollars in her gloved hand.

She takes it and then looks up at me. "Thank you, Rosemary."

My fingers and toes go numb and my heart swoops down to my belly and then up into my throat and flies away. "What did you say? Did you call me Rosemary? Did you know my mother? Her name was Rosemary Sullivan."

The woman looks confused. "Rosemary Sullivan? But she's dead. You're too young to be her. She was my friend, so you stop pretending you know her! I don't like you!"

She runs up the street to get away from me.

What just happened? My whole body shivers. I'm not telling Dad about this. This woman couldn't possibly know my mother. She has a tooth missing.

Why is the world so scary? Hair-raising? It's best to put the encounter out of my mind. Uniska told me to be carefree. So that's what I'm going to do. It's easier than trying to figure this out. I'm not even going to write anything down about the woman's shabby coat or her grey skin or the way she called me by my dead mother's name.

But I do write one thing. *My mother's friend doesn't like me. And that makes me sad. Maybe my mother wouldn't have liked me either.*

———

Aunt Maureen is totally back to smoking. She doesn't bother to hide it from me or Dad.

"What can I say? I'm a weak woman. I have nothing else in my life. My cigarettes are my best friends."

Dad puts down his fork. "This woe-is-me routine has got to stop. You've just been invited to spend Christmas with your boys and your grandchildren. You've had a good checkup. You're over at Mrs. Weiner's almost every day running your mouth, and you even managed to convince Uniska to stop by for an hour every Saturday morning to straighten up your place. You spend most of your time here eating our food. Your cat lives with us. What the hell else do you want in life?"

"A man."

Dad looks to the heavens. "Well, that I can't help you with."

"Maybe I can, Aunt Maureen. I'm a spy. I can go on a mission. What are you looking for in a man?"

"Someone who looks at me more than once every three months."

"I'm sure that can be arranged. Any other criteria?"

"He's got to have a job. There's no way I want someone sponging off me."

Dad clears his throat and Aunt Maureen hits him with her napkin.

This new assignment will keep me busy, since my mission to find Nicholai is at an end. I found out he moved with his family to the West Island, so unless we happen to bump into each other on the metro someday, the chances of me seeing him again are nil. When people move to the West Island, they never go downtown again, unless it's to the lounge Altitude 737 in Place Ville Marie for a celebration. Dad took me there once. We had lobster. That's when I discovered I didn't like lobster. Dad said he wished he'd found that out at a less expensive venue.

One neat thing has happened. I invited Francine to my house for lunch one day (in desperation to get her to stop tapping me on the shoulder), and Gloria happened to come by to drop off a plate of cookies her mother made for me, and by some strange miracle the two of them hit it off, so now Francine doesn't bother me about going to her place because she's always going over to Gloria's house. I couldn't be happier for her. Mrs. Papa will give her the extra attention she needs.

I read somewhere that elephants may be the most protective moms on the planet. Herds of females and children usually travel together in a circle, with the youngest member on the inside, protected from predators. If one child becomes an orphan, the rest of the herd will adopt her.

It seems to happen in this neighbourhood too.

It hasn't taken me long to catch up with my studies. Dad says that's because I have a big head like him.

"I have a big *brain* like you," I correct him.

"No. Just a big head. I don't know where your smarts come from."

———

It's not until the start of December that I see Pamela for the first time in the hallway at school. Maybe I've seen her before but just didn't recognize her. She's dyed her hair black and it looks terrible. She looks terrible. She has acne on her cheeks that she's trying to hide with makeup and she has an energy about her that I can't shake. It scares me.

"Pamela! It's me, Audrey."

She doesn't seem that interested. "Oh, hey."

"How are you?"

"Okay. You? Haven't seen you around."

"I had mono for two months."

"The kissing disease? You are a dark horse."

"No kissing for me."

"Lucky you."

There is something wrong with this girl. I know it in my bones. But then I remember Uniska saying I have to stop worrying about other people and be carefree. Still. If you know someone's in trouble, shouldn't you do something?

"I like your hair," she says. "It suits you."

"Thanks. Wanna come over after school?"

"No. I'm grounded."

"Oh."

"You wanna come to my place?"

Not really, but I started this. "Okay."

When we walk together back to her house after school, she's smoking. She asks me if I want one but I shake my head. Twelve is too young to be smoking, but Pamela gets away with it because she's so tall and looks sixteen at least. She's always looked and acted older than all of us. Jane told me once she was afraid of Pamela.

When we get to her place, she immediately flops in front of the television and turns it on. All my energy is spent trying to find things to talk about, but she doesn't make it easy. It's like she doesn't care if I'm here or not.

And then I hear someone come down the hallway and she stiffens. This man with a stubby beard walks in. He's carrying a beer. He's weaving like Dad did over at François and Alain's house.

"Hey now," he says. "Is this a friend of yours? You gonna introduce me?"

Pamela gives him a look. "This is Audrey."

"Audrey. Ain't you a pretty little thing? Not as pretty as Pamela here, but then she's my baby girl."

"Shut up!" Pamela gets to her feet and storms out of the room.

"Hey now! Hey now!" he calls after her. "No need for a tantrum."

Pamela told me her father left, so this obviously isn't her father.

"What's your name?" I ask.

He seems surprised that I actually said something. "Well, nosy, you can call me Ace. Yeah, that sounds good. Ace."

"Where is Pamela's mother?"

"Workin'. What's it to you?"

"And why aren't you working? Do you live here?"

"What are you, a detective? Knock it off with the questions. And as a matter of fact, I do work when it suits me, and I do live here. You got a problem with that?"

"Just interested."

He puts down his beer and walks over to the couch where I'm sitting. He stands like a tree trunk in front of me and looks down his nose before breaking out into what I'm sure he thinks is a charming smile. "Just so happens, I'm very interested in you."

He reaches down and puts both his hands on my breasts. He leaves them there. "So how does this feel?"

It's like I'm in the pool again. It's so unexpected that I freeze. I have no words or actions for what this is. And I know I don't have the energy to fight him off, so I just stare at him. This makes him brave and he tightens his grip.

And then he crumples to the floor. Pamela is there with a frying pan in her hand. She has tears running down her face and stares at him on the floor.

I jump up. "It's okay, Pamela. I'm going to call my dad."

Dad comes. The police come. Pamela's mother comes. The neighbours outside are milling around. The man is taken away on a stretcher, but he's as mad as hell about it. Pamela sits in a chair and stares at nothing. I need to be her voice. Even with her mother in the room.

"The man looked like he had too much to drink. When we got here, he said I wasn't as pretty as Pamela and that she was his baby girl and that made her so mad she left the room. He said he was very interested in me and put his hands on my breasts and squeezed them and asked me how it felt. I didn't know what to do, but Pamela saved me. She hit him on the head with the frying pan, and then I called my father."

The policeman thanks me.

"And for what it's worth, I think that man has been touching Pamela. She's not the same as last year. She's been so unhappy ever since her dad left. Just look at her face. When I told her I wasn't kissing boys, she said 'Lucky you,' as if she's always kissing someone against her will."

Her mother takes a drag off her cigarette and makes a mocking noise. "She's been kissing boys since she was eight."

Pamela makes a strangled noise and tries to hit her mother. The policeman intervenes and another one comes over and tells Dad he can take me home.

We say nothing on the drive back. When Dad switches off the engine, he turns to look at me. "That was very brave, Audrey. You did everything right."

"What's going to happen to Pamela? I knew there was something wrong. I could feel it."

"The authorities will have to figure that out, but she's safer tonight than she was last night, and that's thanks to you."

"Why didn't her mother protect her?"

"Grown-ups don't always do the right thing. We're good at ignoring what we don't want to see. But are you all right? That miserable piece of garbage. I could kill him for doing that to you."

"I'm fine. It didn't seem real and then it was over so fast. Fortunately, I don't have big breasts, so it really wasn't worth his while."

Dad grips the steering wheel with his hands and rests his forehead on them. He shakes his head slowly. "Audrey, Audrey, Audrey. What am I ever going to do with you?"

———

A few days later I'm walking home for lunch and I'm happy because Uniska will be there. I'm waiting at the crosswalk and a car stops to let me walk by. Pamela is sitting in the passenger seat. She gives me a big wave, a huge smile on her face. She points at the man driving and mouths, "My dad!"

When I wave at him, he waves back. I blow her a kiss and they drive off.

I never see her again.

Chapter Ten

Mr. and Mrs. Weiner ask the three of us over to their house for the first night of Hanukkah. It's called the Festival of Lights, which sounds amazing.

The library at school had some information and I found out that although you don't exchange gifts, its traditional to give gold gelt coins, or chocolate coins, as a token, so I send Dad on a mission downtown to find some, and luckily he does.

Mrs. Weiner's dining room table looks very festive, and the menorah is on her side table. It's a candlestick with four candle holders on one side and four on the other and a taller one in the middle. The eight candles symbolize the number of days that the temple lantern blazed; the shammash is the helper candle used to light the others. Families light one candle on the first day, two on the second, and so on, after sundown during the eight days of Hanukkah, while reciting prayers and singing songs. You have to light a candle from left to right.

Even though we only have one candle lit tonight, I can see how pretty it makes everything seem, and I make a vow to buy some for us. Dinner is amazing as always. Mrs. Weiner is a wonderful cook. She has matzo ball soup, more brisket, potato latkes, and something called sufganiyot, which is basically a fried jelly donut. Mrs. Weiner puts a big plate of them in front of Mr. Weiner and kisses the top of his head.

"This is a special Weight Watchers recipe, so you can have as many as you like, Frank!"

"Oh boy!" Mr. Weiner looks just like Tom when Aunt Maureen pours cream from the top of the milk bottle into his bowl. Mrs. Weiner winks at me.

I hope I love someone like this one day.

The boys can only stand to be around the table for so long, so I take them into their room and we read more stories from my Junior Classic set, Number 3, *Myths and Legends*. When I hear the adults talk and laugh around the table enjoying themselves, I know this is a gift I can give the Weiners to try and repay them for their friendship to us.

Dad and I are invited to have Christmas dinner with Jane's parents, which is very nice of them, but we decline because we'd have to get dressed up and make polite conversation for hours, and Dad doesn't know them that well. I think Jane's disappointed, but she'll live. Her cousins will be there anyway, so she doesn't need me. The only thing Dad and I want to do is eat our Christmas dinners on trays in front of the TV, wearing our pyjamas.

Naturally, Mrs. Weiner knows a woman who has a catering company, and she prepared two delicious turkey dinners for us, complete with dressing, gravy, and cranberry sauce. We even got plum pudding with it, but I'm not that fussy about it, so Dad eats mine too. Tom is quite content to finish my turkey, even with the gravy on it.

Time to give Dad his birthday presents. We don't tell folks his birthday is December 25 because they grin like fools and say stupid things. Idiotic. Inane.

He loves his tobacco tin. And the toast rack.

"You put it on your desk to sort your correspondence."

"To hell with that. I love crispy toast. That's going on the kitchen table."

It's a wonderful, relaxed evening, and then I realize why.

"It's kind of nice not having Aunt Maureen here, which sounds awful, but you know what I mean."

"I know exactly what you mean." Dad takes a sip of white wine. "She's a great gal, but sometimes her bellyaching gets a bit much. She should be with her boys, anyway. It's their first Christmas without their dad, which is always hard."

"Was it hard for you? Even though your father wasn't that nice to you?"

He stares into the fireplace. We don't light it often, but it sure looks nice and Christmassy.

"It's always a wrench to lose your parent. Especially one who didn't give you what you needed. You want to know why, but they probably don't know themselves. Still, you wish you could've had the conversation."

"I'd like it known for the record that you always give me what I need. Even when you lose your temper, are too impatient with most things, especially driving, and curse too much, I wouldn't want anyone else to be my dad."

He smiles at me. "And you, dear girl, are absolutely irreplaceable. I cannot imagine my life without you." He lifts up his glass of wine. "A toast. To the best father and daughter in the world."

I lift my glass of chocolate milk. "To us! Oh! And Tom! The best cat in the world!"

"Tom," Dad says.

"And Sally-Anne!" I add.

"Sally-Anne."

"And Rollie!"

"Okay, that's enough. And who the hell is Rollie?"

———

Jane, Wanda, and I are up on a chairlift at Jay Peak, a ski hill in Stowe, Vermont. It's only two hours away from Montreal, and the school often organizes ski trips for the day. And it's a very long day. You have to be at the school at 6:45 in the morning, arriving at the hill at 9:00, and we leave the hill at 3:00 in the afternoon to be home at 5:00, but it's often longer with traffic, so it's quite a full day.

Dad doesn't want me to go. He's still nervous about my spleen.

"My spleen told me last night it's never been better. Dad, I've got to get some exercise. I haven't been skiing since last year and I'm dying to do something with my friends. I promise I'll only ski on the bunny hill." (My fingers are crossed when I say it.)

He growls for a while. "If you come home with a broken neck, I'll have your head."

"What would you want with my head if my neck is broken? It'll just flop over."

In the chair behind us are Gloria, Francine, and Patricia, a new member of Gloria's gang. Jane doesn't like her either.

"Jane, what is your obsession with hating Gloria and her friends?"

"Gloria might be nice to you, but she's always got her nose stuck up in the air when I come around."

"Well, I'll forgive Gloria anything because I love her mother. The only downside is that they eat lamb."

"I love lamb," Wanda says.

"Never mind! I'm sorry I brought it up."

The wind is whistling through the evergreens below us. The sky is so blue and cloudless it looks fake. Our cheeks can't possibly get any redder, and I can't feel my fingers. It's so cold up here that our nose hairs are white. And yet breathing in this crystal-clear oxygen is a tonic. After sucking down two months of stale air in my room, I'd gladly freeze to death here on this metal lift and go around and around in circles forever.

"So, Wanda and I have agreed that you have to come back to Guides. We're bored to death with our troop and we need a little fresh blood."

"But I'm so lousy at it," I whine. "I hate crafts and singing songs about ants in rubber pants. And the constant hand-holding and arm-swinging gets to me after a while. I mean, I'd love to earn badges, but I doubt I'd do the work to get them. I'm becoming my father. I'm only interested in what I'm interested in. Having to do other crap is a waste of time."

Wanda sees we're almost at the top of the hill and will have to dismount, so she talks fast. "You can be a Guide and only have one badge. You don't have to be like Miss Perfect here and get every blasted one. You can just spend time with us, and the most you'll have to do is sell some Girl Guide cookies."

"What does that entail?"

"Mostly knocking on people's doors and asking them if they want to buy any Girl Guide Cookies."

This would fit in perfectly with my mission to find Aunt Maureen a man. "Okay. I'll do it."

Wanda and Jane look at each other.

"Well, that was easy," Jane says. "I thought you'd give us a harder time."

"Just don't jump down my throat if I'm lazy, Jane. I know how you get. You're super irritated if someone doesn't do what you say, and I'm telling you right now, I'm not going to do what you say if I don't feel like it."

"You're telling me you're coming but you're going to sabotage me at every turn?"

"Yes."

We run out of time and have to jump off the lift and scurry to the side before it hits us in the back of our heads.

We straighten ourselves out and adjust our ski masks. With the sun blazing on the snow, it's like we're blind. And that's when the other three crash into us when they get off the lift.

"Gloria!" Jane shouts. "Watch where you're going!"

"Why didn't you get out of the way?' she yells back. "You can't stop and powder your nose when you get off a chairlift. Haven't you ever skied before?"

I'm staying out of this. I look at Francine. "How are Thing One and Thing Two?"

"Good! I have a tank now and it's big enough for Thing Three and Thing Four."

"That's great, Francine. And how do you like Gloria's mom?"

Francine smiles. "She's wonderful."

"I know. I love her too. She never gets upset."

We look at Gloria and Jane, still sparring over nothing, and laugh together.

I'm obviously not on the bunny hill, but I'm not completely stupid, so I take my time going down the mountain. All the girls are ahead of me, but I don't care. It's so nice to be out in the wilderness. I hope I get to live near trees someday. Water would be nice too, but only for canoeing. Never sailing.

I've had my limit by two in the afternoon. I rested for an hour at lunch, but my body is telling me to stop. The others are tired too, so we go into the chalet and buy hot chocolate and snacks. The quarrel at the top of the hill is forgotten, at least on the surface. It pleases me to see Francine join the conversation. She's still very quiet, but she doesn't have that vacant look anymore. She's actually listening.

Uniska was right.

The teachers in charge tell us to get our equipment and head for the buses. When we clomp through the ski chalet we sound like elephants, and our legs feel as big and as heavy as elephants, too, with our ski boots on. There are a hundred kids trying to find their skis and poles in the jumble of gear mashed up against the wooden racks outside the chalet.

Everyone finds theirs but me. I wait and wait, letting people clear out so mine will be easier to find, but eventually there's not a soul here and there are no skis or poles left. A teacher comes running from one of the buses.

"What's going on? We have to go."

"I can't find my skis. Or poles."

"Are you sure someone didn't take them with theirs? They're probably on the bus."

"Why would they do that? They've been stolen."

"Stolen? Why would someone steal your skis?"

"They're nice skis. My father only buys the best."

The teacher looks around frantically. "Look, we have to go. We'll call the resort tomorrow to see if they turn up."

"And who is going to drive all the way to Vermont to pick them up if they're found? My father? The school is responsible for this. But in the meantime, I want to speak to the manager of the ski hill."

This teacher, who doesn't know me from Adam, looks like he wants to strangle me. "Look here. I have a hundred kids I have to get back to Montreal before dark or two hundred parents will be down my throat. Now get on that bus and we'll sort it out later."

I could stage a protest like they do for the Vietnam War, but somehow, I doubt my school chums would join me in the freezing cold, so I have no choice. I get back on the bus.

The girls want to know what happened.

"Someone stole my skis. And there will be hell to pay when I tell my dad about it."

Dad is furious, and rightly so. The school can't do anything for us because I signed some piece of paper before I left absolving them of any responsibility for anything. The ski hill said they can't find any missing skis, so that is that.

Dad growls about it for a week.

———

Mrs. Andrews takes me and Jane to the Girl Guides store so I can buy the uniform, sash, belt, scarf, hat, and socks. I make sure I never utter the word *vagina*, although at one point I do say "Shit!" because the Girl Guide pin stabs me.

Dad has a fit when I come home with my loot. "Did you have to buy blue underwear too? What a goddamn money-making racket this is!?"

Very quickly, I remember why I don't like Girl Guides. In that snap decision I made on the ski lift, I forgot one thing. To quote the Grinch: "Oh, the noise, noise, noise, noise. There's one thing I hate, oh the noise, noise, noise, noise."

I'm a girl. But I've never been a girl who likes to scream, unlike some of my counterparts. You can forgive small girls in Brownies for getting carried away, but what is up with girls my age screaming? No wonder this head honcho captain is so sour-looking. Why is she in this game, anyway? She looks like she's having her toenails ripped out. She seemed to like me when I was here the last time, asking her questions, but now she appears to be annoyed that I've come back after such a long absence.

We do the usual nonsense. The only thing I'm happy about is my belt with the small pencil hanging off it and the brown coin purse perfect for keeping my spy notes folded away.

Jane looks at me impatiently. "You were supposed to sew your bluebell badge on your sash."

"I forgot."

"On purpose."

"Don't fuss with me, Jane."

Wanda snickers, so Jane looks at her. "Why did we want her to come back so badly?"

"We love her."

Jane holds out her hand. "Give it to me. I'll sew on your badge—otherwise I'll be asking you this question for the next six months."

"Okay, thanks." I haul the sash off from around my chest and hand it over. The badge is in my change purse, so I give that to her too.

But I do try and find a few minutes to myself to read the pamphlet about badges. There's a badge with a pair of scissors and one with a dog on it, and I like the look of them. I'll try to do whatever it is to get these two first.

Boy, will they be sorry. They don't know I'm a spy and that I will use this to my advantage. My fact-finding is excellent. Just as long as I can get Jane to keep sewing on my badges. But darn it all, maybe that's what the scissors badge is all about. I'll need to conduct more research.

And then the head honcho tells us we need to complete our cooking badges and that we won't pass until we make a meal for her. Not only that, we have to present it to her in her home. In other words, she wants this whole gang of girls, almost twenty-five of us, to make her dinner. Well, she's got this all figured out, hasn't she?

Dad and I grumble all the way home. He has to pick me up because there's too much snow around for me to ride my bike, and he doesn't want me walking home alone in the dark. Jane and Wanda are on the way, so he drops them off too. It's a way of thanking Mrs. Andrews for always hauling me around to stores and camp. But it does mean he has to leave his typewriter and bundle up, wipe the car off if it's not in the garage, and even shovel to get out of the garage if need be, so it's a good half an hour of his evening wasted, which I know he doesn't really mind, but it's a change in his routine and he doesn't like change, because he's an old geezer.

"I think you're right. This Guides thing is a racket. Wanting all of us to cook her dinner at her house. I don't even know where she lives."

"I'm going to talk to Mrs. Andrews about this. I'm sure it's on the up and up, but I don't want you going over there by yourself. You and Jane can present your dishes together."

"What if it's not allowed?"

"Listen, kid. The last time you went over to someone's house I didn't know, the cops got involved. I'm not taking any chances."

So that's how Jane and I end up at the captain's apartment. Mrs. Andrews drives us because she knows where the woman lives. She says she'll be back in an hour. We trudge up the stairs, me holding my tuna noodle casserole and Jane with her apple betty.

The captain is as dour as ever, but the lieutenant is here too and she's always got a smile on her face.

"Hello, girls," she says. "This is a little different, two of you at once, but very nice indeed."

"I only agreed to this because your mother asked me, Jane," the captain says. "I'm not sure what the fuss was about, you two having to do this together."

"My father is a worrywart and the last time I went to someone's house alone, the police showed up."

The captain is holding my casserole to place it on the stove, but she stops and turns around. "The police?"

"There was a happy ending, so all is well."

"You are a strange child."

"I've been told that before."

"Audrey, you can put your coats on the bed in the bedroom."

I do what I'm told. This place isn't very big, and it's sort of messy. I presumed it would be neat as a pin, an army barrack almost, but no. And then my Spidey senses notice that the lieutenant's purse is on the bedside table. Huh.

Apparently, my tuna noodle casserole is a little on the dry side, but they both liked the crumbled potato chips on top. I point at them. "These were supposed to be crushed soda crackers, but I didn't have any so I used the chips."

The lieutenant gives me a big smile. "I like this much better. I'll do this next time."

They both love Jane's dessert. Jane is pleased. "I used cinnamon and a little nutmeg."

"Good choice," the captain says. "Your mother has taught you well."

They tell us we've passed and will be getting our badges at the next meeting. We thank them and go downstairs to wait for Jane's mom. I poke Jane in the ribs. "I think they might be a couple."

"What do you mean?"

"I think they live together. Romantically, I mean."

Jane rolls her eyes. "Two women? Don't be ridiculous. That's impossible."

Mrs. Andrews's face suddenly looms large in my mind. "You're right. That's stupid."

Jane sews on my cooking badge.

And then my scissors badge. I present a Chinese lantern I cut out with scissors and a small throw that I cut strips around and tied together in knots. My demonstration about using scissors with my feet doesn't go well, but the lieutenant says an A for effort. I turn to my research paper on scissors and their actual uses. I'll blow them away with this list.

"Some scissors are self-explanatory, like nail scissors, hair clippers, nose scissors, moustache scissors, thinning shears, hedge trimmers, pruning shears, and grass shears, but then we get into more complicated names like loppers, which are blades for shearing sheep, compound-action snips and tin snips for cutting metal, even hydraulic cutters for old pipes. Then there are the scissors that help us with medical issues, like trauma shears to cut off clothes, bandage scissors, surgical scissors for cutting flesh, tenotomy and Metzenbaum scissors for cutting delicate tissue. And let's not forget embroidery snips, pinking shears, dressmakers' shears, button hole scissors, tailors' scissors, and giant scissors for ribbon-cutting ceremonies."

The captain interrupts. "You were supposed to list three."

"I don't do anything half-assed."

Her face turns purple.

"I apologize for my language. It won't happen again."

Her colouring returns to semi-normal.

I can tell Wanda and Jane are trying not to piss their pants.

My pet badge goes very well at first. I bring in Tom's bed that I made myself. He was annoyed when I lifted him out of it. I also bring in his cat food to show the troop what he eats, and his brushes, telling them a Norwegian Forest cat has to be brushed often or it gets matted. I've even prepared a photo album with pictures I've taken of Tom with my Kodak Instamatic camera. There are pictures of him perched in trees, lapping water from a hose in the summer, hiding in a pile of leaves looking deranged, and curled up on his bed in front of the fire.

The snag comes when I have to go to an animal shelter and report back my findings. Dad and Aunt Maureen take me on a Saturday, but first we stop in to see Joe's restaurant because it's on the same block. There's only one person in it, but Joe seems cheery enough. I like the stools, but that's about it. Dad and Aunt Maureen don't say much when we get back to the car.

When we leave the animal shelter, I'm cuddling a kitten in my hands that looks exactly like Sally-Anne, and Aunt Maureen is holding a very small Maltese dog that had only arrived ten minutes before, after his owner had dropped dead.

Dad rubs his forehead. "Tom's not going to like this."

"He'll have to. No way am I leaving Sally-Anne in that cage. You know I'm right, Dad."

He glances at her as he drives and sticks out his finger to rub under her chin. "The resemblance is uncanny." Then he looks in the rear-view mirror. "And what's your excuse? You only came for the drive."

She holds up the dog. "Look at this face! How could I resist?"

"He's probably just what you need, Maureen. He'll keep you company and then you'll stop coming over to our place all the time."

"I'll just bring him with me. He's small enough to fit in my purse."

"Great."

"What are you going to call him, Aunt Maureen?"

"Elvis."

Elvis, Sally-Anne, and Tom get off to a rocky start, but they eventually settle down. Tom is too confident to be jealous of a kitten, and he soon takes right over, and Sally-Anne loves him more than me. I don't mind. I love seeing the two of them curl up together. It must be lovely for Sally-Anne to feel his fur on her face.

Aunt Maureen is a changed woman with Elvis by her side. She complains about nothing now. Mrs. Weiner is in love with Elvis too and I'm worried she'll want a little dog, but she says straight out, "My two would smother it with love. Not having that."

They'd also smother it with a pillow, so I'm relieved.

———

Winter is hard. We get some real storms, but they never cancel school. We have so many days off anyway between the Christian and Jewish holidays, we can't afford to miss any more. Naturally I always make it to school since I'm two minutes away, but at least I dress appropriately to get there.

There's a girl in my class who trudges to school through snowdrifts with only her knee socks on. She has big legs, so maybe she doesn't feel the cold, but you can see her legs are mottled and red between her socks and her skirt. I always want to go up to her and ask her why she doesn't like snowpants. We have to wear them to avoid hypothermia, but she's the exception. The only other thing about her is that she has a two-headed troll. I'm so envious.

It's around this time that my French teacher suggests I get a tutor. Rats. I ask Mrs. Weiner the name of the woman she knows. Dad talks to her. I'm to go twice a week after school for an hour. She's only about four blocks away. Her name is Mrs. Ivanov.

She fascinating. She lives in a small apartment. When she opens the door, I think I have the wrong place. She's dressed like a fortune-teller, which is intriguing. And then you go in and she's got beads hanging in the doorways. I've only ever seen that in the movies. I'm half expecting a crystal ball somewhere around this joint.

She parts the beads and ushers me into a room that is like a living room, sitting room, and bedroom all in one. And every inch of the walls is covered with old pictures. She's got elaborate quilts and pillows with trim on the bed and on the floor, and even has a rug over top of another one. It's like I walked into a caravan. It's dark and mysterious and there are remnants of burnt candles in holders.

I couldn't care less about French. "Your home is fascinating. Do you know all these people in the pictures?"

She nods. "My family. All dead. The war, you see."

Why did I ask? I feel a heaviness. A great loneliness. She gets up and motions for me to come with her. I ask a few questions at first, but it's like she's forgotten I'm here and rambles on about the past. The poor soul. I know I'm a spy, and I should be writing all this down, but the stories are so terrible and sad, my mind just blanks everything out.

Eventually, she remembers we have work to do, but I can't think. I'm pretending to understand what she's saying about French verbs, but I don't have a clue. At the end of the lesson, I hand over her money and say goodbye. She says she'll see me in a few days.

As I walk down the snow-covered sidewalks and hear the cars go by in the slushy streets, I hold out my tongue to catch snowflakes because I have to do something to make myself feel better.

Dad asks me how the tutoring went and I say fine. Before he can ask me anything else, I try to guess what he had for lunch and that takes his mind off it. After supper I announce I'm having a bath.

"You're going to be a prune with all these baths of yours. My hot water bill is through the roof."

But sitting brooding in a tub is not what I need, so I get out and play with Sally-Anne. She's at the stage where she runs up the hall, hops up in the air several times, runs down the hall as fast as she can, and then tears over to Tom and jumps on him while he sleeps in his bed. He doesn't even move while she bites his ears and bats his tail. I'm sure he can't feel anything because his fur is so thick, but then Sally-Anne only weighs about a pound at this point.

Eventually I wander into Dad's study. He's got his pipe clenched between his teeth. He doesn't even look up from his typing. "Help yourself."

I open his candy drawer and take a handful of Allsorts. "Thank you. Goodnight."

"Night."

The day I have to go back to Mrs. Ivanov, I walk to her apartment and look up at her window. She has a lot of plants. I stamp my feet in the cold, but I'm not moving. I can't go up there. But I have to, so I go inside and tiptoe up the stairs and stand outside her apartment. The minutes pass. Then I take the money and push it under her door and leave. I trudge my way straight to Gloria's house, and Gloria and Mrs. Papa are pleased to see me. We have cookies and milk at the kitchen table. Now Gloria's grandmother doesn't seem so scary. She's eccentric but not haunted.

Mrs. Papa smiles. "Gloria tells me you have a new kitten."

"Yes! She's sweet. Sally-Anne. We have two cats now."

"We used to eat cats," the grandmother says by the sink.

"Mama! You know that's not true."

The grandmother gives me a bit of a grin. Whew. She doesn't hate me now.

Suddenly I'm spilling my guts about Mrs. Ivanov, and how I don't know what to do because I can't go back into that apartment, but I feel so badly about not showing up. "I don't want her to be more unhappy than she already is. What I did today was crummy. I should've told her to her face that I can't come."

"How old are you, Audrey?" Mrs. Papa asks me.

"I'll be thirteen in June."

"Thirteen-year-olds are not equipped to handle adult situations. You tell your father what you've told me and I think you'll find that he will understand. In the meantime, our George is a whiz at French, and I'm sure he'd be happy to help you for an hour after school a couple of times a week." She winks at Gloria.

George? But then, anything is better than poor Mrs. Ivanov.

Dad is annoyed when he gets home. "I had a phone call from Mrs. Ivanov at the office and she says you didn't show up. Then I called here and you didn't answer. Aunt Maureen didn't know where you were. I was a little rattled, to tell you the truth."

"Not so rattled that you came rushing home to see if I was dead on the floor."

"I'm a sensible man. If I was really worried, I would've called Mrs. Andrews or Mrs. Papadopoulos. I knew you were somewhere, just not where you were supposed to be, and that's not like you. I need to trust you, Audrey, if this is going to work. You have a lot of freedom, but that can easily be taken away if you become unreliable."

I tell him what happened and Mrs. Papa was right. He understands and says he'll call Mrs. Ivanov and make some excuse. He actually prefers the idea of me being over at Mrs. Papa's house doing extra work, rather than a stranger's apartment.

He's never going to get over that Pamela episode.

And it turns out that George is not a jerk, and he's really easy to understand. It's too soon to say if I'm developing a crush on him. He'll never be Nicholai, but then I don't think anyone will be.

———

It's April. The long Montreal winter is over, although we still have some days that are quite chilly. But the joy of not wearing winter boots never gets old. It's like your feet are weightless and you can skip down the street and feel like you're flying.

We've been on this street for almost a year, and I can't imagine living anywhere else. This wonderful mood lasts for a few days and then our entire neighbourhood is plunged into sadness with the news that Martin Luther King Jr. has been assassinated in Memphis. Dad and I read about it in the papers and listen to the radio broadcasts all week. I can tell that he is shaken, and that's unsettling. Just when you think the world is great, it quickly lets you know you're mistaken.

But today is the start of my Aunt Maureen mission. I've been waiting impatiently to sell Girl Guide cookies. They are in red boxes like last year to celebrate the centennial.

The captain thinks I'm mad to take so many boxes home. "You've never done this before."

"That means I'll have beginner's luck."

She doesn't know I'm on the hunt for my Aunt Maureen's next husband. Jane and Wanda want me to go with them to sell cookies, but they'd get in my way. I need to be focused. They're a little ticked off at me.

"We know how it's done," Jane points out.

"Does one need a diploma to sell cookies? How hard can it be? 'Knock knock! Wanna buy some delicious cookies you can munch on with your feet up after a long day at the office? I have just the ticket! Melt-in-your-mouth chocolate and vanilla flavours. Best dipped in milk.'"

Jane gives me a great sigh. "You are not going to say that, are you?"

"You'll never know, because you won't be there."

"Fine, you stubborn fool. We'll see how many you sell and how many we sell. I have no doubt who will win."

"Wanda? Is she always this competitive?"

"She's a pain."

"Why do I hang around with you two?!" Jane huffs off.

The first thing I do is go over to Avi's place. He has a big wagon, because sometimes Rollie goes in it if he doesn't feel like walking. He answers the door.

"Avi, it just occurred to me. Do you have parents?"

"Yeah. Wanna speak to them?"

"No. May I borrow your wagon for a couple of days to sell my Girl Guide cookies? That's if Rollie doesn't need it in the meantime. I'll give you two boxes for free as payment."

He spits in his hand and holds it out. "Deal."

Oh God. I have to touch his spit.

I race home with the wagon and pile in as many boxes as will fit. Then I take my order sheet and some pin money for change and the old tin to put money in, and start my journey. I have my pencil hanging from my belt. My plan is to go down one side of my street and up the other, and then move on to the streets to the right first, so I'll hit Aunt Maureen at some point.

"Bubala! How much are they?"

"Fifty cents a box."

Mrs. Weiner passes me a five-dollar bill.

"I'm not sure I have enough change. I only just started to sell them."

"I want ten boxes. Frank loves Girl Guide cookies!"

Trust Mrs. Weiner to help me beat Jane.

When your first customer buys ten boxes, people who buy one or two seem stingy. But Mrs. Papa buys five, so I appreciate that. Then I remember, I don't really care how many boxes I sell. I want to peruse the people who are opening the door, and for the most part it's kids and women, and they're useless in my search for a husband.

One guy does open the door and buys a box, but he looks like someone who would murder you in your sleep. And that's when I remember the one-legged man. I'm almost at his house anyway, but even knowing what Dad said, I'm still nervous as I approach his door. He's probably not going to answer it anyway.

It's a total surprise when he does. And an even bigger surprise that he's not as old as I thought he was and has got a nice face.

"Yes?"

"Oh! Hello. I hope I'm not inconveniencing you. I'm sure you're very busy."

"I'm not, as it happens." He leans against his crutch.

"Well, I'm selling Girl Guide cookies and I wondered if you'd like a box or two. We have vanilla and chocolate flavours and I have it on good authority that they are excellent when dipped in milk. Of course, I would only dip them in chocolate milk because that's all I drink, which my Aunt Maureen thinks is terrible, but now that she has a little dog named Elvis, she's not quite so bossy and doesn't notice stuff like what I'm drinking anymore. You might have seen her walking into our house. Lovely woman. I only live across the street and I've seen you come home in a taxi late at night although that is none of my business and my dad said that maybe you lost your leg in the war and you're a hero and I wondered if you were sad because you never turn on your lights and Dad said maybe you could use some company and if you ever need someone to help you with errands, I'd be glad to because I go to the store a lot on my bike anyway, and obviously it's not as easy for you to get around. The cookies are fifty cents a box, by the way."

What did I just say?

His mouth is twitching. "Um, what's your name?"

"Audrey. Audrey Rosemary Parker. I'm a spy. Oh shit! I'm not supposed to tell you that!"

"Well, Audrey, I'm Mr. McGregor—"

"Are you joking? Like Mr. McGregor's garden? Wouldn't it be funny if you had a rabbit named Peter!?"

"I do, actually."

"You do not!"

"Want to come and see?"

"No! I'm not allowed in strange men's apartments ever again after the last episode. The cops showed up and everything."

"Why am I not surprised? But I do know you live across the street because I have seen you buzzing around the neighbourhood, and I've even seen you peer at me from your living room window at night, so it must be true that you are a spy."

"I apologize for that. I was having a hard time sleeping when we first moved here, but I love it now. I've met so many nice people."

"Well, I'm not one for sweets, but I'll buy two boxes of your cookies and bring them over to my sister's house the next time I visit her in the taxi."

"Thank you so much."

He leaves the door and I wait with the boxes until he comes back. He hands me a dollar bill and a quarter. "That's for you. Buy a Creamsicle or two."

When I look at him with surprise, he smiles. "I'm a spy too."

"Thank you, Mr. McGregor. And would it be all right if I come over someday to see your rabbit? I'll bring my Aunt Maureen as a chaperone so my dad won't worry about me."

"I look forward to it."

Chapter Eleven

When Jane sees how many unsold cookie boxes I have, she tries not to gloat because she's my friend, but the captain looks smug.

"I told you about biting off more than you could chew."

"You were so right. It's a lot harder than it looks. I hope you aren't disappointed in me."

Now she can't say anything. She remembers she's the adult in this situation. "Of course not. You did your best."

No, I didn't. I stopped selling them the minute I left Mr. McGregor's house. Mission accomplished as far as I was concerned. I couldn't care less about selling cookies. These people make enough money off of us. I brought the wagon back and Avi once again answered the door.

"I thought you wanted it for a couple of days?"

"Turns out that isn't necessary."

"I'm keeping the two boxes anyway."

"That's fine. A deal is a deal. Thanks, Avi."

"No problem," he said before shutting the door.

I'm still not convinced he has parents.

And I did keep a few boxes for Dad and Aunt Maureen and paid for them with my babysitting money. Avi's as well.

Jane and Wanda ask me where I went to sell my cookies.

"On my street."

"No! That's the worst place. You have to stand outside banks and liquor stores and drugstores. Anywhere there are people going by at a great rate. It wastes time and energy knocking on one door at a time."

"I'll know next time." There will never be a next time.

The captain and lieutenant have news.

"For our grand finale in June we are going to have a costume contest. Each troop will have to come up with one idea that involves every member of that troop. We will have judges from the community and a prize of twenty dollars will be awarded, to be divided among the winning team. Now, you have almost two months to work on this. It's a fun project that will involve teamwork and lending a hand to others. We are looking forward to the end result."

Jane is beside herself. She gathers her chicks and asks us all if we can think of anything brilliant. Wanda and I have nothing, but then we're not crafty. The minute Jane remembers this she starts to panic. "Oh great. We only have four heads working on this, since you two are useless."

"Sorry," says Wanda.

I hold my hand in the air since Jane got mad at me when I didn't earlier.

"Yes, Audrey?"

"Jane, not everyone gets in a lather about construction paper and glue. Remember, you have to treat us like a team. These three girls can't be useful while Wanda and I are relegated to the useless pile, or you'll have a mutiny on your hands."

She narrows her eyes at me. "So, your sabotage is rearing its ugly head already."

"Already? I've been here for months, more's the pity. And hey, that's an idea. A giant papier mâché Chinese dragon head and everyone in the troop can get under the cloth behind it. You of course will be the one under the giant head, since you're patrol leader."

Jane's face lights up as if Jesus walked in the room. "That's absolutely perfect! And I can't believe it was you who thought of it!"

"You're welcome."

———

Aunt Maureen finally comes over for supper. I've been waiting for two days to tell her my news about Mr. McGregor. It's not something you can say over the phone.

Dad isn't pleased that she keeps Elvis on her lap while she eats the lousy meatloaf she brought with her, but we can hardly complain since we didn't have to cook.

Dad is hearing all about this for the first time too.

"Oh, Aunt Maureen, he's so nice. He gave me money for Creamsicles. And what are the chances that a Mr. McGregor would have a rabbit named Peter!"

"Pretty good, I'd say." Dad nods.

"I told him I wasn't allowed over to see Peter unless I had a chaperone and I said I'd bring you."

Aunt Maureen points at herself. "Me?"

"Did you or did you not ask me to find you a man?"

She's confused. "A man? Why would I want a man? I have Elvis."

I slap my hand on the table in frustration. "A few months ago, you said you had everything but a man and I made it my mission to find you one. And I'm now handing him to you on a plate. He's your age, nice-looking, and he has a rabbit."

"And I believe I said I wanted someone with a job. Does this one-legged man have a job?"

"Fine. I don't care if you don't like him. I still want to go over there and see that rabbit named Peter, and I told Mr. McGregor that you were coming with me, so you have to. It's rude to ask someone if you can come over to their house and then not show up."

"*I* didn't ask him if I could come over."

I shake my head in despair and let out a big sigh. "The things I do for people, and it's never appreciated."

Dad pretends to lift up a violin and play the bow across the strings. He always does this when I'm moaning about something.

"All right! I'll go over with you, but Elvis has to come too."

Peter Rabbit is adorable. He's a lop rabbit, the kind with floppy ears. I drag Dad over to see him too, and once Dad and Mr. McGregor meet it turns out they were both in the navy, so I'm allowed to go over and see Peter without Aunt Maureen, but now she goes over by herself because Mr. McGregor thinks the world of Elvis.

I'm not saying that Aunt Maureen and Mr. McGregor have taken a shine to each other, but the two of them often sit on his front porch and smoke. Mrs. Weiner joins them from time to time while she waits for her little Weiners to kick each other down the street after school.

———

Oh my God.

Jane and Wanda and I are in love with Leonard Whiting's naked bum.

We go to the movies to see Franco Zeffirelli's *Romeo and Juliet* with Leonard Whiting and Olivia Hussey, and all of us want to kiss Romeo and be Juliet.

None of us have seen a boy's bottom before, but we all agree it's amazing.

"Well, technically, I saw my brother's rear end once when his towel slipped, but it definitely wasn't as gorgeous as that!"

"Can you imagine looking like Olivia Hussey?" Wanda sighs. "Wow."

"I *love* the name Olivia. I'm going to call my daughter Olivia," Jane announces.

"I think you're getting ahead of yourself, my friend. You've never dated and already you know your child's name?"

"Don't tell me you never think of things like that, Audrey."

"Never."

"Weirdo."

"Hey! I thought of the dragon head, so you better be nice to me." She smiles. "That's true."

Today we're watching the movie *Yours, Mine & Ours*, with Henry Fonda and Lucille Ball. It's really good. I sit down first; Jane is beside me and Wanda is in the aisle seat. There's only one other person in our row, and he's sitting at the other end.

While I munch on my popcorn a quick movement makes my eyes dart to my left. The man I thought was sitting at the very end seems to be closer, but he's still far away. Maybe I'm dreaming. Quickly, I'm immersed in the fun of the blended family trying to eat breakfast around the table before school. I'd never survive the noise.

While I'm laughing, it appears that the man is closer to me, and I'm aware of it but my attention keeps wandering. He's allowed to sit where he likes. This is a movie theatre, after all. My spying is making me paranoid. Not everyone is out to get me.

Something is crawling on my skin. I have a skirt on. I glance down, hoping it's not a spider, and there's a finger. I leap out of my seat and the man runs down the row and disappears up the other aisle. The girls look at me.

"What's wrong?" they ask.

I don't want to ruin their fun. "Nothing. A bug, I think."

But I have no idea how the movie ends. The girls have enjoyed it and I pretend it's great. Wanda and Jane ride off on their bikes towards their houses and I go the other way to mine. I wave to Aunt Maureen, Elvis, and Mr. McGregor on his porch. I notice Peter in a small cage getting some air by his owner's foot.

I turn down the driveway and Dad and Mr. Moore are sitting on a sawhorse by Mr. Moore's garage. I wave at them too and ride my bike right into our open garage. On my way to my room, I see Tom and Sally-Anne asleep in Dad's basket in the study. I shut my door, lie on my bed, and scream into my pillow.

What is wrong with me? What am I doing that is inviting these men to either stare at me through binoculars, grab my breasts, or try and put their fingers in my underpants? And not just men. What about that girl in the pool? Am I looking at people the wrong way? Am I dressing the wrong way? I feel this big knot in my stomach. Uniska says I worry too much, or maybe she said I think too much, I can't remember. But this odd feeling is settling into my bones and I'm not sure if it will ever leave.

———

The dragon head has become a major headache for everyone but Jane and her mother. Mrs. Andrews has taken over their garage, and the dragon head is being constructed on the cement floor, which is now covered with a half-acre of old sheets, newspapers, and rolls of plastic.

Not only am I expected to show up for Guides on Monday night, I have to be in the garage on Wednesday after school and Saturday mornings. And let's not forget Tuesday and Thursday afternoons, when I'm over with George. He asked me to call him G. He says it's cooler. Poor old George doesn't realize he'll never be cool.

And now, thanks to some universal stroke of luck, my Wednesday and Friday nights are taken up with rehearsals for the school play. I auditioned after a dare from stupid Ernie. He keeps flicking eraser bits at me from across the room as if he was in grade two, so according to Gloria, he likes me. She seems to be the authority on boy behaviour, and I guess she is since she has three brothers.

We're doing the Broadway musical hit *You're a Good Man, Charlie Brown*. I don't audition for any specific role, so when the play director yells from the stage, "And the role of Charlie Brown will be played by Audrey Parker," I look around. I didn't know there was another Audrey Parker in the school. Then Gloria, Jane, Wanda, and Francine start jumping and screeching in my ear. Even Jane's friend Bethany joins in.

Oh, the noise.

Suddenly, I'm famous. Dad and Aunt Maureen don't shut up about it.

"It's not like I'm going to Hollywood!"

"Aud, will you just let us enjoy this?" Dad pleads. "You've been chosen out of all the kids in high school to play the lead and you're only in Grade Eight. Be proud of yourself! I've told everyone in the office and the AAA Club."

"And Ian is coming as my date on the big night," Aunt Maureen informs me.

"Who's Ian?"

"Mr. McGregor. And he goes *nowhere*, so it's a big deal."

"Ian. That's a nice name."

"Although I wonder why they didn't ask a boy to play Charlie Brown," she muses. "Wouldn't that make more sense?"

"You know theatre types. The director said he was looking for heart, not sex."

Dad grins. "Then he picked the right kid."

Mrs. Weiner is predictable when I bump into her the day after the news breaks. "Mazel tov!!" She kisses my cheeks all over. "I'm so proud! So proud!"

Mrs. Papa makes me a cake, which doesn't surprise me. She presents it to me while George and I are trying to conjugate these damn French verbs I hate so much.

"We are very pleased for you, Audrey. And I'm not surprised you got the part. You're a little sparkplug."

"I am?"

"You light up every room you walk in. Doesn't she, George?"

George turns bright red.

I could get used to this. But the adulation stops with Mrs. Andrews. She says she's very happy for me while we soak strips of newspaper in water and glue around the dragon's nose, but I can tell she doesn't mean it. Jane looks pissed off, but is it with me or her mother? When she gets up to get another bucket of water, I follow her into their laundry room.

"Are you okay?"

"Ugh! She makes me so mad! Did you see her in there? 'Oh, I'm very happy for you, Audrey.' No, she's not! She's furious that I didn't get the part of Charlie Brown. Or Snoopy. Or Lucy. Or Linus. I only auditioned because she wanted me to. I hate being on stage. And now she's sulking because I failed."

"I've never known you to fail at anything, Jane. You are the most gifted girl I know, and you put your heart and soul into everything you do. I wish I had your tenacity and drive, but I know I'll always be a lazy slob. I make you sew on my badges for me, so what does that tell you? Your mother would be pulling her hair out if I was her daughter."

"You're very sweet. I just wish it was my mother telling me this."

As I bike home, I stop and take out my notebook to scribble, *A mother's opinion is the one most sought after by her children. Take Jane. She has a nice father, and two sets of really nice grandparents, even super aunts and uncles, and they love her dearly, not to mention great friends, and yet she still frets about what her mother thinks of her. Why is this so important? I wish I knew that for myself.*

Why do I get myself in these situations?

The play director, Mr. Keillor, loves to hear himself talk, and not just talk but emote, and not just emote but yell his head off, and by the time we finish rehearsals, my ears are always ringing. But that's not the only annoying thing about him. Sometimes we have to rehearse at lunch time, so while we bring in a small sandwich for ourselves, he sits at the side of the stage and pontificates with his mouth full as he eats three-course meals out of Tupperware containers.

I had to ask him. "Who makes these meals for you?"

"My mother."

When I get a chance, I write down this observation. *The need for mothers to feed their offspring seems to last a lifetime. This must be a genetic trait to save mankind.*

But today our director's yammering is incessant and Snoopy and I are fed up.

Simon (Snoopy) is in grade ten and he towers over me, which Mr. Keillor thinks is hilarious. "Snoopy looming over his owner, since he is clearly the more dominant personality in this relationship."

Simon whispers, "What a load of garbage. He's a dog."

"But he's a good dog, Simon."

He smirks at me. "You're a cute kid. I can see why this nutcase picked you. Now pardon me while I lie on this very uncomfortable doghouse with my feet hanging off the end of it."

"Did you learn the words for your solo, 'Suppertime'?"

"You mean, 'Sup-per, super duper supper, sup-per, super duper supper'? That one? Yeah, I think I have it down pat."

We giggle.

"CHARLIE BROWN AND SNOOPY, STOP GOOFING AROUND AND PAY ATTENTION!"

Something has to give. I'm getting worn out and Dad notices at the supper table. Sally-Anne is clinging to my sock and kicking my heel with her back paws as fast as she can. It's so cute.

"You have bags under your eyes. I'm not having it. You have to give up something. Your health is more important than anything. Let's talk about it."

The relief I feel now that's he's brought it up makes that knot in my stomach lessen.

"I need to get out of Guides. It gives me heartburn. And that dragon head is going to be the death of me. I know Mrs. Andrews will kill me—"

"Mrs. Andrews? You mean Jane."

"No! This dragon has become her personal mascot. Jane and Wanda will forgive me because they know how much it takes out of me to sing in circles, but Mrs. Andrews has assigned all of us a colour, and since red is pretty essential to the Chinese dragon, I'll be screwing up her system if I don't come back."

"Tough titty on Mrs. Andrews. Why is she involved, anyway? This is supposed to be a project for you girls."

"She wants it to be perfect."

"The woman needs a tranquilizer. Okay, so that frees up Monday night, Wednesday afternoon, and Saturday morning. Good choice. Now what about French?"

"I don't think I have to go two days a week anymore. I'm getting better."

"So now Tuesday after school is free. Obviously, there are a lot of people counting on you for this play, so this is more difficult, but say the word and I'll call this Mr. Keillor myself."

"No, the play is fun, even though Mr. Keillor is louder than a fog-horn. Simon and I keep each other's spirits up. The girl who plays Lucy really thinks she's a psychiatrist. 'Snap out of it! Five cents, please.' She says that to everyone and it's getting ridiculous. I could be running around saying 'good grief' every three minutes, but I don't."

"All right. Problem solved."

Not really. I have to tell Jane first because it's Monday night—Guides night—and she'll be expecting me to bike over to her house.

Sally-Anne is still hanging onto my sock with her little sharp claws as we get up from the table. Dad starts to wash the dishes. Tom is perched on the top cupboard watching the action. He goes up there when he needs a break from this little scrap of fur.

I pick up the phone and call Jane. Mrs. Andrews answers.

"Hi, Mrs. Andrews. Is Jane there?"

"No, she just left. She was waiting for you. You're late. Why are you still home? You were supposed to meet early tonight to go over the final plans for the project."

"Oh, gosh. I forgot all about that."

"You forget a lot of things, don't you, Audrey? You're not exactly reliable, which is why it surprises me that they've asked you to be the lead in a play. That's a great responsibility, and you are much too cavalier to my way of thinking."

"I'm sorry..."

"Jane was very disappointed that she didn't get the lead, but she's too nice to tell you that. She would have made a wonderful Charlie Brown. And what in heaven's name is wrong with you, making her sew on your Girl Guide badges? She's not your personal servant, you know."

"I'm sorry..."

Dad turns around from the sink with a puzzled look on his face. I'm trying not to get upset, but he clearly sees that I am. He crosses the kitchen. "Give me that phone."

I don't really get the chance because he grabs it out of my hand. "Mrs. Andrews? What the hell are you saying to my daughter?"

She's obviously giving him an earful too. He stands with his hand on his hip, a dishtowel over his shoulder, looking incredulous. I can tell he's had enough.

"And you, madam, are pathetic. Running around making this damn dragon's head. The girls are supposed to be doing that, not you. And telling me Audrey shouldn't be Charlie Brown? Did you want that role for yourself too? And if Jane is willing to sew on a badge for her friend, why is that any of your business? It shows me that she's a kind person, unlike her mother. But let me assure you that you won't have to worry about any of this anymore, because my daughter is never going to attend another Girl Guide meeting again or put one more dab of paint on your precious dragon's head. So, stick that up your very uptight ass, Mrs. Andrews."

He bangs the phone down. "That woman is a disgrace!"

I immediately start blubbering, which not only horrifies him, it horrifies me too.

He bends down and holds me by my shoulders. "What's the matter, princess?"

"Jane's going to hate me! She'll never talk to me again. You were rude to her mother, and a mother's opinion is very important to a child."

"She was discourteous to you. And I'm not having that. You don't deserve that kind of treatment, and don't ever think someone can speak to you in that manner. I highly doubt that Jane will hate you. She'll be upset, because no doubt her mother will cast us in a bad light, but so be it. I believe that Jane knows what you're capable of and what her mother is capable of, and she'll know the truth in her heart, even if it takes her a while to admit it."

I wipe my eyes on my sleeve. "That all sounds great, Dad, but when you're my age, friends matter the most. If I lose Jane, I know other girls, but they aren't her. She's my best friend. She knows my secrets. And now Wanda or Bethany will be her best friend."

Now he looks upset. "You're right. I'm sorry. I got carried away. Just because Mrs. Andrews was impolite to you, I had no business insulting her. Let me sort this out."

"What are you going to do?"

"Be an adult." And he puts on his jacket, goes out the door, and drives away. To Mrs. Andrews's house, I'm guessing.

I call Aunt Maureen and tell her what's happening.

"Poor Jack. He's trying to protect you, Audrey."

"You mean I shouldn't have said that to him?"

"No. You're absolutely right. I remember being your age and friends are your whole world. Just don't blame him for this. Mrs. Andrews started it. This is her doing, not his. And Jane will forgive you. Maybe."

"Maybe?"

"She's just a little bit like her mother, don't you find?"

And that's why I'm worried.

Dad comes home and looks like he's been dragged through a knot-hole. We go into his study and eat candy.

"Obviously Jane wasn't there because she was at Guides, but her little sister was, and what a handful she is. Reminds me of you."

"Get on with it, Dad."

"We talked. Mr. Andrews came in and I apologized for my language. To tell you the truth, he seemed annoyed, but not at me. I'm sure he knows what his wife is like. I asked Mrs. Andrews not to say anything to Jane about Guides, to give you a chance to tell her yourself. I told them why we decided you can't attend anymore, because of your health, and naturally Mrs. Andrews asked why you're not quitting the play too. That's when her husband told her to knock it off. I thought I better leave. So, unless she breaks her word and says something to Jane tonight, you'll be able to tell her tomorrow at school that your good old dad is making you quit because he's a worrywart. Blame me. A parent is handy for that kind of thing."

The minute I see Jane in the hallway at school in the morning, I know her mother has told her everything. Her version of everything, anyway. She looks sad too.

"I'm sorry I'm not coming back to Guides. But I know you're going to win the contest."

"Like you care." She slams her locker door and walks away.

It takes me until lunchtime to track down Wanda. I find her in the girl's bathroom. "She hates me, Wanda. What can I do?"

"Tell your dad not to curse at her mother."

Now my hackles are up. "Mrs. Andrews was abusive to me on the phone and Dad was trying to protect me. He even went over and apologized. Obviously, she never told Jane that, did she?"

Wanda hesitates. "No, she didn't. Jane just said your father cursed over the phone and told her mother that you weren't coming back because you hate Guides, and we all know that's true, so what was she supposed to think?"

"Girl Guides is not my thing, but that doesn't mean I didn't love spending time with you two. I want you to win that contest. Dad says

I'm getting worn out with all this running around and he's right. I am tired."

"So, like Jane said, why don't you quit the play and stay with Guides and your supposed best friends if you love us so much?"

I can't do this anymore, so I walk away.

———

After school I head straight to George's house to tell him I can't come in.

"Why not?"

"I'm only going to come once a week. Dad says I'm looking very tired with all my extra activities. I've never really felt the same since that mono episode."

"Come on in and forget about Thursday."

"That makes sense. I'm here now."

But I'm not here, and he knows it after five minutes. Mrs. Papa delivers her fabulous cookies with a big smile and hums on the way out. I eat them half-heartedly, so my doldrums are obvious.

"Look, Audrey. You can get away with not coming at all. Your French is good enough to pass this year. I'll miss you, but you need to get better."

His kindness brings a lump to my throat. I can't swallow my cookie. He passes me a glass of milk, which I drink readily, even if it isn't chocolate.

"Thank you. I really needed to hear that today. But I'd miss coming here. I love your mother."

"She loves you. You can still come; we'll just eat cookies."

"You're such a nice friend, George."

When I go home, wonderful Uniska is packing up to leave. That's right; she's here on Tuesdays. My cookie day will have to be changed.

"This house smells so clean it's almost minty fresh."

"Thank you." She opens the fridge. "I had some leftover cabbage rolls. I brought them for your dinner."

"You didn't have to do that, Uniska. You're too kind to us."

"It's easy to be kind."

I look at the floor. "For some people, maybe."

"Kindness is a decision."

Dad is wolfing down Uniska's delicious cabbage rolls. When he asks me how it went at school with Jane, I downright lie.

"She understands completely. She told me not to worry about a thing. That my health is more important than a dragon's head or a Girl Guide meeting."

Dad seems surprised. "Well, I have to give Mrs. Andrews credit for keeping her word. I told you that things would be all right."

"Thanks, Dad, for making it better. You saved the day."

He kisses me on the top of my messy head. "That's quite all right, Charlie Brown."

—

The next night Aunt Maureen, and Elvis come over with a pan of lasagna because she knows I need to be at play rehearsal at six thirty. Elvis, Tom, and Sally-Anne run up and down the basement stairs in some kind of frantic relay race only they understand. After twenty minutes, the three of them are pooped. So is Aunt Maureen from all the laughing.

"Don't you find that funny?" she wheezes. "Oh my God, I love this dog. Why did I never have a dog before?"

"Uncle Jerry didn't like dogs."

"Your uncle Jerry was an idiot."

"Maybe you were the idiot for not getting one anyway."

"Oh, Christ. You're right."

Dad comes home and after changing out of his suit, he washes up and comes out of the bathroom, rubbing his hands together with glee. "Do I smell lasagna?"

I don't eat much. Aunt Maureen remarks on it. "No good?"

"It's great. It's just hard to sing on a full stomach. I better go."

I see my father and his sister look at each other, so I bend down, grab their faces, and give them five kisses each. "Farewell, loved ones! I'm off to Good Grief my heart out!"

They're laughing as I go out the front door. The minute I shut it, my shoulders droop as I slowly make my way down the sidewalk. It's a lovely May evening, with new leaves on the trees. New little Snipp, Snapp, and Snurrs. I must remember to pick out which leaves are the cutest on my maple tree out back. I notice Ian McGregor has his upper window open. Peter Rabbit is in his cage on the window ledge, sniffing the night air. Now that his father is feeling brighter, Peter's life has changed for the better too.

———

Snoopy gives me a sideways glance on stage. "Wanna lie down on top of my doghouse?"

"Is my lack of enthusiasm noticeable?"

"Just a tad. A turnip is more animated."

"Sorry."

"You can always tell me. I'm your best friend, remember."

"And you're a good dog."

"You are such a cute kid. What's wrong?"

"My other best friend has decided she hates me."

"Listen, Charlie Brown, take it from someone who is older and wiser—"

"You're fifteen. How wise can you be?"

"Shut up. You will have many, many best friends before they cart you out of here. I've gone through at least thirty."

"How do you stop being friends with someone?"

"You punch them in the nose."

"SNOOPY AND CHARLIE BROWN! STOP GOOFING AROUND AND PAY ATTENTION."

———

As I walk up the stairs after school the next day, Mrs. Weiner pokes her head out of her front door. "Audrey, are you going to your French lessons today?"

"No, as it happens. I'm only going once a week to eat cookies."

"How odd. My mother just called. She's in a bit of a jam. Her tooth fell out of her head and her dentist can see her right away, but my father has gone somewhere in the car and she can't track him down. She wants me to take her. Do you mind?"

"Not at all. I'll go grab a book and be right over."

"My angel in heaven!"

Today I read Junior Classics Number 2, *Stories of Wonder and Magic*. It keeps the boys' attention for an hour, which is pretty darn good, but now that the days are nicer, they want to play outside, so we go out back. While they tear around on their bikes between the driveways, I go over to my maple tree and pick out some cute leaves to keep my eye on throughout their life journey. There's quite a few in this new fresh bunch.

Whenever I'm under the tree, I always pat the ground over Sally-Anne's grave. "I still miss you, little one. Your sister is very sweet, but I wish you were here too. Although it would get confusing. I'd have to call one of you Sally and one of you Anne."

Just then Tom wanders out of Mr. Moore's garage, with Mr. Moore behind him.

"Is he bothering you again?"

"Nay, child. He's great company. Your father was telling me that you have the lead role in the high school play. I'd like to come and see it. He's very proud of you."

"I'll make sure you get a ticket, Mr. Moore. Dad and Aunt Maureen will be happy to take you along."

"That's grand. Something to look forward to. I haven't been to a theatre production since my Edie died. We used to take our children to *The Nutcracker* every Christmastime, even when they were grown up."

I can't help but wonder: "Was your Edie a good mother, Mr. Moore?"

He smiles. "Oh, aye. But she was the strict one. I was too quiet to do much good, so she was the one who gave the kids their marching orders."

"So you were a real team. Kind of like Mr. and Mrs. Weiner."

He gives me a sly smirk. "Edie wasn't quite as loud as Mrs. Weiner. She's in a league of her own, bless her."

"Gosh, I better go check on the boys. I'm supposed to be babysitting."

"Oh, aye. The scallywags. Nice little chaps when they're not trying to kill each other."

The boys are nowhere to be found. Damn it. I should've been paying more attention. I circle our two driveways a few times but can't see them. I'm willing myself not to panic, but I am.

"Mr. Moore!"

He comes out of his garage.

"I can't find the boys!"

"You start up the street. I'm right behind you!"

My feet are going fast, but if I run, I can't look down all the driveways properly. Please don't let Mrs. Weiner drive down the street in her big-ass Caddy at this moment. They have to be somewhere. I was only talking to Mr. Moore for a minute. And then I see Michael's bike laying on its side down an overgrown pathway near the top of the street, so I rush over and luckily see David, straddling his bike, looking in the bushes. Thank God.

"David! I couldn't find you. Never go anywhere without telling me. Where's Michael?"

He points in the bushes while he sucks on a lollipop.

"Where did you get that?" I crouch down and push the branches out of the way. There's Michael with a lollipop in his mouth as Jacques takes down his pants.

"Let go of him!"

Jacques whips around, and when he sees me, he tries to scurry away, but I jump on top of him. I can't hold him for long, and before I know it, he's got me pinned to the ground, the two of us wrestling, getting whipped by the sharp branches.

And then Mr. Moore is there. He grabs Jacques by the back of the neck and pulls him off of me. Jacques is still struggling to get away, but Mr. Moore takes one of his arms and twists it behind his back and Jacques is quickly on his knees, whimpering like a baby.

"Audrey, take the boys home. I'll deal with this."

"Are you sure, Mr. Moore? You don't need any help?"

Even in this drastic situation he gives me a little smile. "Oh, aye. I survived the trenches, remember?"

I gather up my little charges, who are now shaken, and take them home, the two of them walking their bikes down the sidewalk. I make them give me their lollipops and throw them into a sewer grate where they belong. I'm so furious that I let this happen and then I'm furious that this unwanted mauling could happen to little ones. They're six! Is no one safe in this world?

By the time Mrs. Weiner comes home, the boys are watching television with hot fudge sundaes I made for them. They beam at her.

"Hello, my darlings! Did you have a nice time?"

They both nod and raise their treats. "Look what Audrey made for us!" says Michael.

"Marvellous!"

"Mrs. Weiner, could we speak outside for a moment?"

She can tell right away that something's wrong. "All right."

We go out on the porch and I see Mr. Moore by his garage. "We need Mr. Moore."

So, we go down the stairs and over to him. Between the two of us we explain what happened, and I'm so surprised that Mrs. Weiner is not running around in circles at the news, but she's very calm.

"I can't thank you enough for what you did for my children today. Frank and I will deal with this. We need to get the police involved."

Mr. Moore raises his hand. "Nay, missus. I wonder if you wouldn't mind me dealing with Jacques."

Now she gets upset. "He's a little bastard!"

Mr. Moore remains calm. "Oh, aye. Being raised by an even bigger bastard. I talked to the lad and he poured his heart out. It's not a pretty picture, Mrs. Weiner. But instead of punishing him, I think he could use a little compassion. This is behaviour he's learned. I told him I want him to spend his days after school and on weekends helping me in the garage. Get him interested in something. His own father does nothing for him. I should have acted sooner and I regret that now. But Audrey saved the day today. I think your boys will be fine."

She nods her head, considering what he's said. "All right. Let's give the boy a chance. But if he ever goes near them again, I'm going to rip his face off."

Mr. Moore grins. "Spoken like a true mother."

When Mr. Weiner comes home from work, he knocks on our back door. He's such a gentle soul. He just cries and hugs me.

"It's okay, Mr. Weiner."

He sops up his tears with his linen hanky that Mrs. Weiner irons for him. He starts to say something but can't, so he blows his nose. Then he spies Mr. Moore and hugs me again and runs down the stairs to embrace his heroic neighbour. Poor Mr. Moore looks like a salmon caught in the paws of a giant grizzly bear.

That night, as I soak in my hot bath, which is quickly becoming my go-to spot for mulling things over, I think about what Mr. Moore said. That instead of punishing Jacques, he could use a little compassion. That this is behaviour he's learned.

I think about Jane. Instead of being upset with her, I think she needs compassion too. Her mother only told her one side of the story. This quick rush to judgment is a learned behaviour. Her mother is so intolerant when things don't go her way, she lashes out at people, and that's what Jane is doing. Jane doesn't hate me. She's upset that I'm not coming to Guides, which means she's going to miss me. Which tells me she loves me.

Then I remember what Uniska said. My decision is to be kind and leave Jane be. Let her figure this out for herself.

But if Mrs. Andrews ever comes after my father like that again, I'll rip her face off.

Spoken like a true daughter.

Chapter Twelve

It's now June. My birthday. Only three weeks left of school.

To tell you the truth, I'd envisioned my thirteenth birthday with Dad taking me and my friends to one of our favourite restaurants, Piazza Tomasso, but I tell him I don't want a fuss.

"You're a teenager now! Who doesn't want a fuss?"

"Dad. It's my birthday. I get to decide what I want to do."

He looks puzzled, and then the deep wrinkles in his forehead become even deeper. "Now that I think of it, I haven't seen Jane around here. Please tell me you girls are still friends."

"Sure we are. But I've been so busy with the play and she's distracted with her dragon. It's not easy to get together."

"Bullshit. I know when you're lying."

"No, you don't. I lie to you all the time and you don't have a clue."

He bursts out laughing. "Oh, Aud. What would I do without you?"

"You can do one thing for me. When I tell you I don't want a fuss, believe me. Pizza with Aunt Maureen and Elvis is as crazy as I want to get. I'm saving my energy for opening night tomorrow.

"All right. Pizza it is. And I'm assuming we can have a cake, or is that off limits?"

"A cake is fine."

I get five cakes. Dad flouted my rules and told our neighbours it was my birthday, so every one of them comes bearing a cake: Aunt Maureen (she said hers was from Mr. McGregor too), the Papadopouloses, the Weiners, Mr. Moore, and Uniska, even though she doesn't technically live on this street.

It ends up being a pretty jolly party. I'm glad Dad ignored my Gloomy Gus directive. Everyone wishes me good luck for tomorrow night, and all of them say they will be there.

Now I'm anxious about tomorrow. I haven't been nervous this whole time, my mind being wrapped up in my feud with Jane. Too bad it isn't as easy for girls as it is for boys to break up with a friend. Snoopy's advice about punching noses is a bit drastic. Is it really that simple for them? A girl's heart seems to be a lot gooier. Pieces of us stick to each other and we can't extricate ourselves easily.

I'm sitting up in bed, talking to Tom and Sally-Anne, trying to get their take on the situation. They both have their heads sideways, as if deep in thought. My blind is down, but I put it up during the day now. Lately my spying on neighbours is not quite as ardent as it was, and not just because the opera glasses aren't as special anymore. What I've learned over time is that people have the same routines every day, which is behaviour of vital importance to keep society from tumbling into chaos. The trouble is, it makes for dull spying assignments, but it's not enough to stop me altogether. My problem is I'm addicted to *noticing* things.

But what I love about the world is that we are very similar, despite our differences. Take the friends at my party. Jews, Greeks, Scots, Brits, Ukrainians, Canadians. We all like each other.

Dad knocks on my door.

"Enter."

He holds out some Liquorice Allsorts. "Dad! I'm stuffed."

He pops them in his mouth. "More for me then."

"Thank you for my party."

"Oh, phew," he says, munching away. "You forgive your old man? I couldn't let the day pass without some kind of celebration. The happiest day of my life was the day you were born."

"Was my mother happy?"

"Very, very happy. You were, and always will be, a gift from whatever gods are roaming about."

"You don't believe in that stuff."

"As you get older, and your time on this planet gets shorter, you start to wonder about what's out there."

"DAD! I don't want to think about that. Why aren't you young like other dads? Then I wouldn't have to worry about you dropping dead."

"I'm going to live to a ripe old age. You wait. You'll be pushing me around in a wheelchair and get so tired of it, you'll want to push me right off a cliff."

"Keep talking like that and I'll push you right out the window, like your sister did with one of her many husbands."

His face lights up at the memory. "Oh God. That was so good. By the way, I forgot to give you this." He holds out a long, thin box.

I take off the cover. It's a green fountain pen, just like his.

"Every teenager needs a serious writing implement."

"It's perfect. I love it."

"I knew you would. Okay, you have to get some sleep for your big debut. Night-night." He kisses my head.

"Thanks for tonight, Dad."

"You're welcome, sweetheart." He goes out the door and then pokes his head back in. "And Audrey?"

"Yeah?"

"Don't despair. Jane will come around. You'll see."

———

The gymnasium is packed to the rafters. Everyone in NDG seems to be here. Me, Snoopy, Lucy, Linus, Patty, and Schroeder huddle together behind the big curtains to peek out at the sea of people.

"Who knew this was such a big deal?" I whisper.

"I think I'm going to be sick!" Lucy says.

"Oh God...where did I put my blanket?" Linus runs off in a panic.

Schroeder spins around to make sure his toy piano is where it's supposed to be.

Mr. Keillor roars over and pushes us all away from the curtains. "Take your places! Snoopy, up on your doghouse. Charlie Brown, remember, you set the tone for everyone else. Most people will be looking at you."

"They will?"

"You're Charlie Brown! You're a good man! Don't let me down! Choosing you was a decision I had to fight for, but I know I made the right choice. Remember that." He gives my shoulder a squeeze and runs off.

He had to fight for me? I didn't realize I was so important. So, this isn't just a silly high school production. This man is counting on me. And by the look of the audience out there, it seems like a big deal for a lot of people. Stop thinking that you're just Audrey Parker. You are Charlie Brown, and your best friend is lying over there on his dog-house looking nervous, and Lucy is behind her psychiatrist's stand in imminent danger of throwing up, while Linus is twisting his blanket into knots.

I'm out front on stage. I turn to all of them and hiss, "We've got this!" I give them a thumbs-up and they give me one back.

Don't even ask me how it went. I can't remember anything but the lights in my face, the colours swirling around, the school orchestra bowing, huffing, drumming, and strumming below me, and the sound of laughter as we sing, dance, and run around the stage. It's a giant dream and then the six of us line up, hold hands, and take a bow, and the entire audience gets to their feet and applauds wildly. I look to the left of the stage and Mr. Keillor is crying happy tears.

I try to find my dad and Aunt Maureen in the crowd, but there are too many people, and now that the curtains close on our little Peanuts gang, we hug each other and jump around with excitement. Mr. Keillor runs over and grabs us.

"You were all amazing! Thank you for your hard work. I don't think people will forget this production for a long time. It's the high-light of my career! I'm delighted I was right about you, Audrey. Your facial expressions were priceless! The more you mugged for the audience, the louder the laugher. And we get to do it two more times, so keep it up!"

I forgot about that. I hope I have the stamina. But I'm so pumped with adrenaline that I feel like I could fly. Simon lifts me off my feet and swirls me around. "You are such an adorable kid, Audrey. Only you could've pulled this off. Your energy is infectious. You have no idea how much it helped me. You really should consider going into the theatre. You were born to be an actress."

"And you were born to be a really good dog!"

He laughs with delight and kisses my cheek.

My first kiss. I'll never forget it.

The school hallways are jammed with people, everyone wanting to congratulate us. The six of us are trying to find our families, but it isn't easy. At one point I think I see Mrs. Weiner waving one of Mr. Weiner's hankies in my direction, bawling her head off, but she's so far down the corridor I can't get to her. She's carrying a bouquet of long-stemmed roses. Are those for me?

I'm surrounded by people touching me, smiling at me, congratulating me. It's a very strange experience. All these faces I don't know, and I just want to see my dad.

And then I spy the woman in the green coat from the second-hand store. There's a buzzing in my head. People are jostling us. I call after her, "Hello! Hello!"

She's disappearing into the crowd, but I'm not going to let her get away this time. I push and elbow my way through the departing audience and keep my eye on the dirty green coat. I manage to snag a piece of her cuff. "Stop! Please!"

She whips around and gives me an alarmed look.

"Please! Do you remember me? I gave you money. You knew my mother, Rosemary Sullivan. How did you know her? Please tell me. I don't know anything about her." I pull out her folded-up picture from my pocket. I carry it with me every day. "This is her when she was young."

She looks at it but doesn't touch it. She appears more alert today.

"We were waitresses together at a bar in Côte-des-Neiges. She died the day the bar closed down. I lost a friend and my job. But God, you look just like her close up. It's as if she's right here. It's too much."

She quickly slips away. I call after her. "Wait! What's your name?" She doesn't stop.

It's like I've been doused with cold water. But my father and friends are waiting for me. Back down the hall I go, trying to catch my breath. I'm frantic to find Dad. I need a hug.

Finally, I see my street gang. They're standing close together with delighted smiles on their faces and they clap and hoot and holler when they see me. I run into Dad's arms as if I'm a toddler, and he picks me up and twirls me around just like Simon did. He makes me happy again in this moment. When Dad puts me down, everyone kisses me in turn, so not only do I get my first kiss from a boy tonight, I get another three, because George, Nicolas, and Philip all take a turn. Gloria and her parents squeeze me, even her grandmother, and Mr. and Mrs. Weiner are both crying as they pass me the bouquet of flowers. Michael and David were allowed to stay up late and accompany their parents and they look at me with their eyes shining, as if I'm something special. It's strange to see Aunt Maureen without Elvis and Mr. McGregor without Peter, but they are obviously delighted. Mr. Moore keeps touching his cap to salute me. Uniska is here with her husband in a wheelchair, and I get to meet him for the first time. He's lovely, and he's painted a picture of Charlie Brown and Snoopy for me. I'm speechless.

Then Wanda, Francine, and Bethany come screaming up to me. Oh, the noise.

I miss Jane.

We walk out of the school en masse. Ernie is in the doorway and he smirks before throwing an eraser bit on my messy head. I stick my tongue out at him.

I decide not to tell Dad about my encounter with the woman in the green coat because I don't want to deal with it right now. Which was exactly my reaction the last time I met her, but now there are two more shows to get through, and I'll never be able to concentrate if I start digging up old bones.

Besides, he hasn't stopped talking about how marvellous the production was, and how wonderful I was, and how he thinks maybe I should take drama lessons.

"Girl Guides smothered your creativity, but being in a dramatic society would allow you to blossom. I can't believe how talented you are. I mean, I knew it, but I didn't know it. And where did that voice come from? You certainly didn't get it from me."

He pours himself a Scotch. "Want one?" he says absentmindedly.

"What?!"

"Oh. Sorry." He lifts his glass. "To my little girl. Someday the toast of Broadway!"

"Dad, for God's sake, calm down."

My cats and I are under the covers. They love it under here, and it's cozy. We hide from the world together. They want to know how it went.

"I became someone else tonight. I felt powerful for the first time in my life. It's an extraordinary feeling. But something happened. I met that woman again, the one who knew my mother, but she doesn't look like someone my mother would know. She has a tooth missing. She's obviously fallen on hard times, but I always imagined my mother knowing ballerinas and going to the opera. I'm just a bit unnerved, to tell you the truth."

Dad and Aunt Maureen insist on coming to the next two shows as well. It's nuts. But they are just as happy each time, and seeing as how we get the same reception for the next two shows as we did the first, the fame is going to our heads.

Mr. Keillor rushes over at the end of the last show with a copy of the *NDG Monitor*. "Look! We've made the front page! *Westmorland High's stage production of the Broadway hit* You're a Good Man, Charlie Brown *is as good as it gets for amateur theatre. The entire cast is marvellous, but a special shoutout goes to Miss Audrey Parker as Charlie Brown. This girl is going places. A fantastic evening's entertainment, thanks to director Mr. Ken Keillor.*"

We look at each other in disbelief.

"I'm taking you all out to celebrate!" Mr. Keillor shouts.

As we sit around the table at our local St-Hubert barbeque restaurant, I realize that friends come in many different varieties. At this moment, although the six of us cast members, all from different grades, would never have talked to each other in the hallways at school, right now we're bosom buddies.

Mr. Keillor takes a big bite out of his drumstick and waves the bone at us, thankfully swallowing most of his mouthful before he makes his point. "I don't want any of you to forget this experience. It just goes to show what you can achieve when you get the right people on the right project. Magic happens. You think you're nothing special, but clearly you are, and I want you to believe in yourselves like I believed in you. You need to take this spark of creativity and nurture it in your hearts your entire lives, because things like this don't happen very often. I'm so proud of you."

We are terribly embarrassed, because Mr. Keillor is practically shouting by the end of his spiel, and other diners are giving us odd looks. When he gets up to pay the bill, we snicker together about his dramatic pronouncement, but when I'm alone under the covers in my room with my cats, I'm grateful for his belief in me. In all of us.

There's only a couple of weeks of school left, but it's amazing how much has changed. People hang off me. One day Snoopy walks down the hall surrounded by adoring fans and he gives me a smirk.

"Enjoy it, Charlie Brown. They'll forget all about us come September."

He's right. This is not going to last. But even with these new so-called friends, I still long for only one. I've seen Jane from time to time. She always scurries the other way if she catches sight of me. Obviously, she and her mother would have to be living under a rock not to know about the success of the show, and while it gives me a petty thrill to know Mrs. Andrews is probably spitting nails about it, I have the feeling Jane would love to come and congratulate me, but she doesn't know how. I wonder if she saw the play? How I'd love to get her take on it. It's one thing to be in the middle of it, but I also wish I'd been able to watch it like everyone else.

———

It's early in the morning. I'm just about to put two slices of toast in the silver toast rack when Dad comes out of the bathroom holding his razor, his cheeks and chin still covered in shaving cream. He looks traumatized.

"What's wrong?"

"They shot Bobby."

"Bobby?"

"Robert Kennedy is dead. First Martin Luther King and now Bobby. This is madness. What is wrong with the world? It's petrifying."

You never want to hear your dad say that. It's really scary.

———

Dad is annoyed that I'm late for supper.

"Where were you?"

"At the NDG library, studying for exams."

"Well, please leave a note next time. Aunt Maureen didn't know where you were when I called."

"God! I can't go anywhere!" I slam my bedroom door behind me, which isn't a bright thing to do when he's in a foul temper. And right on cue, he slams my bedroom door back open.

"What is your problem, young lady? It's reasonable for a parent to want to know where their child is when that child is very late. And for the last week, you've been like a bear with a sore paw, anyway. One minute you're my little star and the next you're a black hole. What's going on?"

"Nothing."

"Bullshit."

I flounce on my bed and cross my arms. "Find a better word!"

"Horseshit."

"I've been trying to do research and I'm not getting anywhere. I'm the world's lousiest spy."

"Explain."

I can't keep this to myself any longer. "Look, on opening night I saw a woman who once called me Rosemary at a second-hand shop. She told me she worked with my mother at a bar in Côte-des-Neiges and my mother died the night the bar closed. She couldn't get over how much I looked like her. And I couldn't get over how odd she was. She had a missing tooth and seemed rough somehow. I can't explain it, but it bothered me. For some ridiculous reason I thought if I could find the name of the bar, I could track her down again. I didn't get her name. So, I've been going to the library and searching through their microfiche of community newspapers in 1958 for a bar closing, and I can't find anything. That doesn't mean it didn't happen. I did find the announcement of a bar closing in 1962, but that's four years after my mother died, so it can't be the right one. She's the only person I know besides you and Aunt Maureen and that Betty woman who knew my mother, and I'd like to see if she can add anything. But I'm almost afraid to ask her, because I don't know why my mother would know a woman like that."

When I stop to take a breath, I realize my father has turned white.

"Dad? What's wrong?"

"Nothing. Nothing, honey."

"Dad. Who was that woman? Did my mother really know her?"

"I don't know, Audrey. I didn't see her."

"Why was my mother working in a bar when I was three? Wasn't she home looking after me?"

He doesn't answer me. It's like he's not even in the room.

"Dad! You're worrying me."

"I'm sorry, Audrey. I don't feel very well. Would you excuse me?"

He goes into his study and quietly closes the door. If he'd slammed it, I'd feel better. Immediately, I call Aunt Maureen.

"You better get over here. I think Dad might be sick."

She and Elvis come bursting into the house. She's still got her slippers on, and from the state of them, she must have run from her place. It didn't occur to her to use the car.

"Where is he?"

"In his study. When I knock, he asks me to leave him alone."

"Oh, shit."

She goes up to the door and knocks. "Jack? It's me. I'm coming in."

When he doesn't say anything, she hands me Elvis and goes in the study and shuts the door. Now I'm left in the hallway wondering what on earth is happening.

Tom and Sally-Anne come out from my room because they smell Elvis, and the three of them totter off to go sniff shoes or whatever else they get up to. It doesn't look like Dad and Aunt Maureen are coming out of the study anytime soon, so my heart stops racing. He's obviously not having a heart attack or Aunt Maureen would be on the blower calling for an ambulance.

Somehow the news of this mystery woman caught him off guard and he's trying to sort things out before he speaks to me about it. The only thing I can do is wait. I wander into the living room and sit at the piano. It's time for me to learn how to play this thing, since it's in my blood.

Whatever Dad is going to say to me, I know it's the truth. He never lies to me.

I play "Chopsticks" on the keyboard to pass the time.

And then the front doorbell rings. This isn't a good time. I stay where I am. Whoever it is will have to go away. Now someone is banging on the door as if they're in trouble. Maybe it's Mr. Moore. I race to the door and open it.

It's my father's brother Joe. He's drunk. I recognize the stance now.

"Is your father here?"

"He's busy at the moment. Perhaps you could come back at a later time."

He screws up his face. "What are you? A little secretary? Jack! Jack! I need to speak to you."

He pushes past me and looks in the living room. "Where is he?"

Aunt Maureen comes out of the study and walks down the hallway. "Joe, this isn't a good time. I suggest you go home and sober up. Audrey doesn't need to see this performance."

"Fuck Audrey."

I hear Dad push back the chair from his desk and march down the hallway. He grabs Joe by the front of his shirt. "Have some respect."

Joe points a finger in Dad's face. "You gave me money, and now that I need a little more, suddenly the well's gone dry? I'll lose my restaurant because of you and your stingy attitude. Meanwhile you sit high on the hog."

Dad looks around. "Yeah, this is a bloody castle, isn't it? I got where I am by working my ass off. Something you know nothing about. You won't lose that restaurant because of me. You've done that all by yourself. And I'm tired of bailing you out of every scheme you've ever had.

Maureen was right when she said I don't owe you anything. You're not going to get another dime out of me, so go find a legitimate back-breaking job and save your money for once in your miserable life, like everyone else in the world."

Joe staggers around, Dad still holding his brother's shirt front. "You fucking big shot. You always did think you were better than all of us."

Dad looks straight at me and points. "Go to your room. Now!"

I immediately run down the hall and shut my door. I've never seen two men arguing like this. It's worse than on television. Your whole body gets shaky just listening to it. What if he hurts my dad? What about Aunt Maureen? I should do something to protect them.

The voices are getting louder and it sounds like there's a scuffle going on. I'm so afraid of what's happening. Then I think I'll call the police, so I open my door and run over to the phone, but my fingers are shaking. One peek down the hallway shows the two of them still hanging onto each other as if they're dancing.

"For God's sake!" Aunt Maureen yells. "Audrey is here. Stop it!"

"Oh please," Joe slurs. "Jack knocks up a drug addict and gives her money to get rid of the kid, but now suddenly she's important?"

I drop the phone receiver and it crashes to the floor.

The ringing in my head becomes deafening. I see Dad turn to look at me but I can't hear it when his fist lands on his brother's face, splattering blood everywhere, and while I know Aunt Maureen is screaming, there's no sound, and that makes it more frightening. Dad and Joe are on the floor, and Dad is still pounding on Joe's face. Aunt Maureen pulls at his arm to get him to stop. I'm above my own head as I run out of the kitchen and thump on Mr. Weiner's back door. He opens it, sees me pointing at our house, and runs past me. Mrs. Weiner grabs me and her mouth is moving, but I can't hear her either. She just holds me next to her and I hide my face in her chest.

———

It might be ten minutes or five hours later when I whisper to Mrs. Weiner that I'd like her to take me home so I can go in my room with my cats. I hide my face in her dress as she escorts me into the back porch, through the kitchen to my bedroom. She pulls the covers off my bed, and when I crawl in, she tucks the blankets around me.

"I'll be right back with a drink and the cats."

She opens and closes my door.

First Tom is delivered, then Sally-Anne. She comes back with a big glass of chocolate milk and sits on my bed while I drink it. The cats look nervous and spooked.

No wonder.

Mrs. Weiner reaches out and brushes my hair from my forehead. "I don't know why this happened, Audrey, but right now, your dad is downstairs with your aunt Maureen and he's bloody and bruised but he's going to be okay. Frank took your uncle home. I know it must have been very scary, but sometimes brothers get into fights. You and I know that very well. It doesn't change just because they're grown up, unfortunately. It was a stupid thing to do in front of you, but in the heat of the moment, sometimes these things happen. I'm sure your father feels very badly about it."

"My father feels badly because I found out that he wanted to get rid of me when my drug-addict mother became pregnant."

Poor Mrs. Weiner. I feel sorry for her. She's trying not to cry in front of me.

"Audrey, if you'd like to sleep at our house tonight, you can bring the cats with you."

"If I go back to your house now, Mrs. Weiner, I'll have to live there forever. I'm better off here, despite the fact that I'm terrified. The only reason I'm brave enough to stay is that you and Mr. Weiner are next door. If I need you, I'll come for you."

She grabs my hand. "Promise me you will, bubala."

"I promise. I'm going to sleep now."

She kisses my forehead and closes the door behind her.

I fall asleep. But it's more like I just lose consciousness.

—

When I open my eyes, the sun is peeking out of the edges of the blind. My poor little pussycats need to pee. They're at the door looking desperate, so I get up and let them out. Aunt Maureen is sitting at the kitchen table looking awful. She's not even smoking.

She starts to say something, but I hold up my hand. "Don't. I'm not talking to anyone about this. I have five exams in the next four days, and that's what I'm worried about. Ask Dad to please stay at your house, and you can come here if you must, although I'll be fine if you don't. I'm not ready to see him and I certainly don't want to hear what he has to say. Tell him I'll decide when that happens and not before. Can you do that for me?"

She nods.

"Where is he now? I don't want to see him."

"He's not here."

"Good."

My observation about having a routine to keep civilization from tumbling into chaos is pretty much on the money. I go to school, write my exams, come home and play with my cats, eat the occasional frozen dinner, and go to bed. Aunt Maureen is here, but she spends her time in front of the television with Elvis. She knows that's all I want from her.

Even Mrs. Weiner doesn't come near me, but she blows me a kiss from her clothesline one day as I head out on my bike.

Finally the tests are over, and we're doing nothing in school on these last few days. I spend my last typing class clicking furiously. Mr. Darren comes over and puts his hand in the way.

"Stop wasting ink. You made your A+."

"It's therapy."

He looks at my paper and then back at me. "Are you okay?"

"Peachy."

"Which is why you're typing every curse word I've ever had the pleasure of saying."

I nod.

"A kid with a brain. I love it."

And he walks away and leaves me alone.

I'm cleaning out my locker when Wanda comes over and rests her head on the locker beside me. She looks downcast.

"Spill it," I say.

"We didn't win."

I'm so shocked, my mouth drops open. "What the heck happened?"

"Oh my God. It was a nightmare. But you should have seen that dragon. It was absolutely beautiful. The judges were gasping when we walked in with it. Everyone knew we were going to win. Mrs. Andrews was there because we could only get it to the church in her station wagon. Jane was so proud. I was really happy for her. And then the captain announced the winner and it wasn't us. It was the Sunflowers."

"What did they do?"

"The leader's costume was a big red apple and the troop were dressed as apple seeds. They did a funny skit together and even handed out apple recipes and had a big bowl of apple crisp and apple cider for everyone It was pretty cool, actually."

"So, we lost because everyone didn't have a part. You guys were under the fabric of the dragon's body but didn't do anything else. That kind of makes sense."

"I suppose that's true, but actually we were disqualified. Someone squealed about all the work Mrs. Andrews put into it. The captain said if she'd wanted the parents to enter the contest, she would've put it in the rules. And Mrs. Andrews gets up and shouts that she's a miserable bitch and insinuates that it's not normal for the captain and lieutenant to always be together and they should be disqualified from being Girl Guide leaders in case they pervert young minds. Jane starts crying and runs out of the room and all hell breaks loose with the judges and the girls and the poor lieutenant is crying. You know how nice she is. I felt terrible for everyone. But especially Jane. She was so embarrassed by her mother."

"Oh dear. Poor Jane."

"I'm telling you, don't go over there. She didn't come to school today. Things need to calm down. I went home and told my mother I've had it with Guides and I don't care if she's in the Trefoil Guild. She says I'll feel differently in September. Mothers! I can't figure out adults, can you?"

"Not lately."

As I walk home, I remember last year when I was so excited about the summer coming up and how Jane and I travelled the streets on our bikes, laughing and following the ice cream truck. Right now, I feel a hundred years older than that girl.

When I get home, Dad is sitting in the living room. He still has the remnants of a black eye and he looks a hundred years older himself. "Please sit down, Audrey."

"I'm not interested in talking to you." I start up the hallway.

He stands up. "Sit the hell down. You're in my house and you'll do what I say."

My school bag hits the floor and I'm fuming as I park myself on the piano bench.

"Maureen!" he yells. "Get in here."

Aunt Maureen shows up looking very unhappy, holding Elvis in a tight grip. She slinks over to the farthest chair and tries to disappear.

"I don't want you to talk, Audrey."

"Good! I'm never talking to you again."

"Fine. But in the meantime, you need to know the facts, and not that garbled bullshit you weren't meant to hear."

"It's not like I was snooping. I was calling the police. So, now you're going to tell me he was lying? How convenient. I'm starting to think that *you're* the liar. The fibber. The deceiver."

"Audrey..."

I take out my notebook and open it. "Let's go over my observations, shall we? You looked like a ghost when I told you about that woman at the play. So that makes me think that you know her, but you left the room when I asked you who she was. You and Aunt Maureen never talk about my mother, even to mention something funny she might have done. You talk more about Elvis and Tom than my actual mother. I ask to see her pictures, but you don't have any. You tell me she didn't like to have her picture taken. I don't believe that. I ask to see something of hers and you eventually come up with a lousy postcard. Then we meet that Betty at Orange Julep, and she's very pleasant, but suddenly you're sad about mom being dead just when I want to ask her a few questions about their friendship. What an opportunity for me, but what did you do? You drove away as fast as you could and I ended up feeling sorry for you. Did you know I found a picture of my mother in her yearbook from Montreal High School? I didn't feel I could tell you about it because of your reluctance to share anything with me. Where are the pictures of her and I together? Or the three of us? There aren't any. Is that because neither of you wanted me in the first place?"

"Have you finished?"

I put my notebook back in my pocket, fold my arms across my chest, and stare into the fireplace because I don't want to look at him. Sally-Anne wanders in and jumps into my arms, so I hug her instead.

"You're right, Audrey. I am the deceiver, the false witness. And I don't intend to lie to you ever again. You don't deserve it. And as you say, you're too good a spy. You know when you're being hoodwinked, and that's what I've been doing to you for years." He takes a deep, shaking breath. "I'm ashamed of myself. I thought I was protecting you, but no one can hide from the truth forever. And what I'm about to tell you is the truth. But it's going to hurt."

My heartbeat is in my ears and my cheeks are on fire. This is the moment I've been waiting for. Maybe I don't want to know after all.

"Aunt Maureen, would you get me a glass of water, please?"

She jumps up like a jack-in-the-box, obviously thrilled to get out of this room, if only for a moment. But she returns all too quickly and slumps in her chair once again. I drain the glass and put it on the piano, but Dad points at a coaster on the coffee table and I put it there. He's so protective of this damn piano.

Dad takes a deep breath.

"I met your mother in the spring of 1954. Rosemary Sullivan. I was at a fancy literary party and she was one of the caterers serving drinks off a tray. I noticed her right away because she had this light that shone out of her eyes and a sideways grin that you knew meant mischief. She didn't take anything seriously. I knew she was a free spirit and much too young for me, but when I left the party, she was outside trying to light a cigarette and not having much luck, so I held out my lighter and she cupped her hands around mine. I knew I was smitten and had no business being so. I should've walked away then, but she asked me if I wanted to get a drink after dealing with all the stuffed shirts at the party and I laughed and said yes.

"She was funny and clever and completely without guile. I asked her why she was a waitress when it was clear to me that she could do anything she wanted. She told me she was a poet, and didn't I know that poets never made money? She was a waitress to put food on the table. When I mentioned I was in the publishing industry, her eyes lit up and she started rooting through her pockets to gather up folded scraps of paper with her poetry on them. Just like you with your bits of paper, Audrey. You get that from your mother."

My chest relaxes a bit. This piece of information is just the kind of thing I've been waiting to hear all my life.

"We started dating, and she wanted me to do something for her with her poetry, but it's a difficult genre to place. Rosemary thought it was just a matter of me publishing it myself, but I didn't do that sort of work, and she became quite frustrated with my dithering. 'I thought you were somebody important,' she said to me once. 'You're just as useless as the rest of them.'" He looks over my head and out the living room window for a moment, then clears his throat.

"But we had some fun times. The only thing I didn't like was that she was always smoking pot. She said it relaxed her and that she needed to get out of her own head from time to time because there were too many words stuck inside.

"And then came the day she told me she was pregnant. She was initially very upset because she said she had no business being a mother. That she'd make a hash of it like her own mother did. And if I'm honest, I was flustered as well, because I'd never had any desire to be married or have children. I thought that at the ripe old age of forty-two all that was over for me. She blamed me and I blamed her, which sounds terrible when I say it to you, but we didn't know *you* would be the one coming into our lives. When you can't see a baby and you don't even see a bump, it's easy to speak in abstract terms. You're not discussing a child. It's just a problem that needs sorting. She told me she didn't want the baby and I had to give her the money to get rid of it."

Now Dad looks stricken.

"It feels wrong to tell you this, but you deserve the truth." He nods, more for himself than for me. "She insisted and I gave her the money. I'm ashamed I didn't try harder to talk her out of it, but she informed me in no uncertain terms that it was her body, not mine, and to mind my own business. The day I thought she had the abortion I felt sick all day. And then there was a knock at the door and Rosemary was standing there. She laughed and said, 'Well, that was a stupid idea.'"

I give a big sigh. My mother sounds lovely.

"We got married at City Hall and you arrived that June. Your mother loved you so much. She said, 'I want to call her Audrey because there was a woman on our street who always brought me in and gave me a cookie when I had to sit outside because my mother was so-called *entertaining*.'"

Oh no. I can't swallow.

"Please know, Audrey, that your mother loved you with all her heart. She said you were the best poem she ever wrote. She tried so hard. But she was a troubled soul. She'd gone through things that I only learned about after we had you, and she started to drink and take drugs to stop the nightmares and delusions. I tried to help her but didn't know how. She absolutely refused to see doctors, had a pathological fear of them, and she resented me for interfering, saying I'd never understand." He looks down and hesitates, wringing his hands.

"Finally, one day I came home and she was on the floor. You were three and must have been crying for a long time. There was smoke coming from a pot that had been left on the stove. The whole place could've gone up in flames if I hadn't arrived when I did."

"She died in front of me? That makes me so sad. I don't remember that."

Dad collapses on the chesterfield. "This is the devastating part, Audrey."

"What?"

"She didn't die that day. I told you she did. She died in 1962. When you were seven."

I jump off the piano bench and stand in front of him, trembling. "Say that again!"

"She might as well have died that day. I was so incensed that you might have been hurt because she was stoned out of her mind. We got into a huge argument and she said she wanted nothing to do with either of us ever again. And she walked out of our lives. Of course, I felt awful and tried to persuade her to come back to us, but by then she was taking cocaine and heroin and I didn't recognize her anymore. At one point she was living in the streets and would spit at me if I tried to come near her. I knew it wasn't Rosemary. It was the drugs addling her brain, and now I'm sure she had a mental condition, maybe schizophrenia. She was adamant that she didn't have a husband or child and that I was the devil. It's so exhausting to try and help someone who refuses that help. And I couldn't have you around that. I needed to protect you."

I'm clenching my teeth so hard my jaws ache. And he needs to stop talking. "So, when you kept asking for your mother, I told you she died. Because the mother who knew and loved you did die, Audrey. Aunt Maureen stepped in to try and help me raise you as best we could, but it wasn't easy. She had her own family to worry about.

"Most of the time I felt terrible, because I knew your mother was out there. I thought I was keeping you safe, but clearly, it was the biggest mistake of my life. Maybe if she'd met you again when you were older, she'd have had something to live for. But she died of an overdose. I knew the woman you met at the school. She'd be there when I'd drop money off for Rosemary at the bar. Which was apparently another thing I shouldn't have done, because she didn't use it for food, just needles in her arm.

"I will never forgive myself for messing this up so badly. I love you with all my heart, Audrey, and I've failed you in every way. I know you hate me at this moment, and I don't blame you. Not one bit. But please know I didn't do it out of malice. Any time you brought up the subject of your mother, I wanted to pass out. I was so frightened that you'd hate me forever."

"I *do* hate you forever, Dad! I will always hate you forever! I could have passed my mother on the street and I didn't know it. And was she cremated and blown to the four winds, or was that a lie too, so you wouldn't have to show me the date on her gravestone?"

He begins to sob then.

Aunt Maureen whispers, "I know where she's buried."

"How could you do this to me? How could you take even that away from me? A place I could go and talk to her and bring her flowers, like I do with Sally-Anne. I've always wanted just a little piece of my mother and you erased her like she was nothing."

I can't stay here. I run out of the room and out the front door and jump on my bike, pedalling as fast as I can. Streets whiz by. A few times cars honk at me because I'm not watching where I'm going. I'm trying to breathe, to get enough air in my lungs so I can keep living, but do I want to? The pain is too intense. There's no way to survive it.

It's dark now, and I'm exhausted and not sure where I am. I can't bike anymore, so I use my bike as a crutch to keep walking. There are no thoughts. Just an all-consuming ache. And then I see the United Church, which means I've been going around in circles.

Now I know what to do. I keep walking until I stop.

At Jane's front door.

Chapter Thirteen

Mrs. Andrews opens it. Even in my state I can see she looks dreadful. "Audrey. What do you want? Come to gloat?"

"I need to see Jane, Mrs. Andrews."

"She doesn't want company. Least of all yours."

"Shouldn't she decide that for herself?"

Her face hardens and she opens her mouth to say something, but Dixie shows up. "Oh, hi, Audrey! Where have you been? I've missed you."

Here I am smiling, and I never thought I'd smile again. "I've missed you too, Dixie. What's new?"

"I gots tap shoes!"

"Lucky girl."

Then Mr. Andrews comes from somewhere and gives me a welcoming smile. "Hi, Audrey, it's so nice to see you, dear. We've missed you."

"Thank you. I'd like to talk to Jane, but Mrs. Andrews says she doesn't want company."

He gives his wife a quick glance. "I believe she's mistaken. Jane would love to see you. Feel free to go up to her room."

"Thank you." I don't even look behind me, just rush up the stairs and quickly knock on Jane's bedroom door.

"GO AWAY!!"

I open the door and close it again and a pillow hits me in the face. When Jane sees it's me standing there, her face crumples and so does mine. She jumps off the bed and I run over to embrace her.

"I knew you'd come," she whispers into my shoulder.

I can't speak. It's enough to just be here with her. She takes my hand and we crawl back on the bed. There's a big box of Kleenex by her and about thirty scrunched-up pieces of tissue strewn everywhere. Her eyes are bloodshot and her nose is red and raw.

"You heard about the great debacle then?"

"Wanda told me."

"I knew in my heart that my mother had no business helping us like she did, but I got so carried away at the end I refused to think about it. I'm furious with her for acting like a spoiled brat when we lost, but I'm just as mad at myself for not telling her to keep out of it."

"Jane, you did your best. That's all you can do. You made a beautiful dragon, and who cares if you didn't win the lousy twenty dollars? Your take would've been about three bucks anyway. It kept you happy for weeks, so it wasn't all a waste."

"I wasn't happy. I was heartbroken because we weren't talking to each other."

"Me too. And I'm so glad we're talking now, because I don't know what to do."

The story pours out of me. She hands me tissue after tissue until the Kleenex box is empty. By the end of it, I'm limp, with not enough energy to lift my head.

"What am I going to do?"

She lies beside me and we both stare at the ruffled canopy she hates so much.

"Suddenly the dragon episode seems ridiculous. Mom is a pain the ass, but she's always been here for us."

"My mother's light went out more easily, I guess."

"Your mother loved you very much. Who wouldn't love you? But I know your dad loves you too. Wanda told me he came and apologized to my mother. She never mentioned it, naturally. At least he wanted to fix things for you."

"But he's lied to me my entire life. I must have given him a hundred opportunities to say something when I'd ask about her, but it was a subject he always deflected. Don't you think that's willful on his part?"

"You should believe him when he says he was frightened. My dad cried like a baby when Dixie ran out on the street in front of a car once. I didn't know fathers did that."

"Right now, I hate him."

"That's okay."

"I've got such a headache."

"You can stay here tonight if you like."

"That's very tempting, but I think I want to go home and get in my tub. I need to be with Tom and Sally-Anne under the covers."

"Dad and I will take you home."

As we drive back to my place, Jane turns around in the front seat. "Dad and I went to see *Charlie Brown*. You were insanely good! I was so proud of you. I'm sorry I didn't have the courage to tell you that at the time."

"Thanks, Jane. I was wondering if you were there."

"I wouldn't have missed it."

We pull up to the house and say goodnight. Mr. Andrews takes my bike out of the back of the station wagon. "Here you go, honey."

"Thanks, Mr. Andrews."

He puts his hand on my shoulder. "Thank you for coming to see Jane. She's missed you terribly."

"I've been lost without her."

I wheel my bike down the driveway and lean it up against the garage door because I don't have the strength to open it. I trudge up the back steps and walk into the kitchen. Mrs. Weiner is sitting at the table with her back to me, talking on our telephone.

"What are you doing?"

She turns around and jumps to her feet. "Oh, thank God! Never mind, she's here! We're coming!" She hangs up and grabs her keys. "Audrey, I'm sorry to tell you this, but we have to go to the hospital. Your father had a heart attack and your Aunt Maureen is with him. I said I'd stay here until you got home, but we need to hurry."

———

This is my fault.

It doesn't matter what Aunt Maureen or Mrs. Weiner say. I'm not listening to them. We're sitting in a waiting room. Then a doctor comes in and Aunt Maureen gets up to talk to him but I can't hear what they're saying. The doctor leaves without looking at me so I run after him down the corridor and grab the back of his gown. He turns around, dismayed.

"Tell my father I don't hate him."

He looks like he doesn't know what to say to me.

"Promise me? I don't hate him."

He nods and then turns around and keeps walking.

Aunt Maureen catches up to me and takes me by the shoulders to bring me back to the waiting room. Mrs. Weiner is wringing her hands.

"What's the latest?"

"He's had the bypass surgery, but he's still poorly. The doctor says we can't see your father tonight, so we might as well go home and they'll call if there's any change."

I need to get this straight. "We have to go home without seeing him?"

"I'm afraid so."

"He won't know I was here?"

"I'm sure he knows you're here." Aunt Maureen starts crying and Mrs. Weiner gives her a hug. "Let me take the both of you home. We'll come back in the morning."

Another dark car ride through the city, and nothing has been accomplished. I watch the windshield wipers go back and forth, wiping away the tears falling from the sky. My father is probably dying tonight, and he thinks I hate him because I told him I did, and that's why his heart exploded.

No one will ever convince me that I didn't make this happen.

———

Nobody will let me see my dad for three days. Now I'm thinking he's dead and they're just not telling me. I've been lied to before. There is not one person I trust. Except my best friend.

"Of course he's not dead," Jane tells me over the phone. "My father says they don't like little kids running around hospitals, so they're probably just keeping you out of the way for now."

"I'm a teenager."

"Or maybe he looks terrible, and they're just giving him a chance to look more normal before you see him."

"I don't care if he looks like Quasimodo! They have no right to keep me away."

"I'm just trying to think of something to say to make you feel better."

"I know that. And thank you. I never would've survived this if I couldn't call you every hour of the day. I'm not allowed to have anyone over in case we have to go to the hospital in a hurry, but it's sure nice to know you're at the end of this line."

"Just a sec, Audrey. Someone wants to speak to you."

Probably Dixie.

"Audrey?" It's Mrs. Andrews.

"Yes?"

"I'm very sorry about your father, dear, and I'm mortified that I was so prickly with you both. There was no need for it and I'm ashamed. You are welcome to our home, and if we can help in any way, we're here for you. I'm very glad that you are Jane's best friend. Do you accept my apology?"

"Thank you, Mrs. Andrews. I do. You've made me feel so much better about everything."

"I'm glad. Here's Jane, dear."

Jane gets back on the phone. "Thanks, Mom. You can shut the door. Can you believe that? I've never heard her apologize to anyone in my life! I might have to faint."

"I'm going to faint if any more strange people walk in here. It's like a game show: *Have a Heart Attack & Meet Your Family!*"

I do know Aunt Maureen's sons. They come down for a few days to support their mother. I meet three of Dad's sisters and they are all indeed shaped like fridges, but the one who threw her husband out a window lives out west. She calls, and so does one of Dad's brothers. He's in the States. The other brother doesn't show up, which is just as well, because if he did I'd have to borrow Mr. McGregor's crutch and beat him to death.

We have more food than I've seen in a lifetime. Between the Weiners and the Papadopouloses, we will never have to buy groceries again.

I'm under the covers with my pussycats when Aunt Maureen knocks on my bedroom door the next morning.

"Your dad is allowed one visitor. He wants you."

He's so small and old and grey on the hospital bed. There are wires everywhere.

"Hi, princess," he whispers.

I'm afraid to touch him, but he holds his hand a few inches off the mattress and I put my cheek against it. "I don't hate you."

"I know. I got your message."

We don't talk after that. There's nothing more to say.

———

It turns out Dad is the world's worst patient. At least that's what Aunt Maureen says.

"For the love of Christ!" she yells. "Stop ringing that Jesus bell!"

Aunt Maureen's neighbours must wonder if she actually lives on their street or ours. She's moved in here again, though I tell her it's not necessary. School's out for the summer and my days are my own, so I can be here whenever Dad rings his dumb bell, which he does constantly.

But eventually he finds a rhythm that suits him. As long as he can be at his desk for an hour or so, sit and play the piano a while, lounge outside under the maple tree with Mr. Moore while rubbing Tom's head, and accompany me for a walk down the street since he's supposed to get some exercise, his complaining is not as dire as it was at first.

When he comes home from a doctor's appointment, I know something's wrong, and in the spirit of keeping me in every loop from now on, he sits me down immediately. We're both on his bed, Sally-Anne between us, biting her own tail.

"Despite the operation, I've had some damage to my heart. The doctor thinks I should retire, which comes as a dreadful shock, I have to admit. I love my job, and the thought of just sitting around doing nothing petrifies me."

"You can finally finish writing your own book, 'The Ultimate Society.'"

He smiles. "Thank you for thinking of that. I'll always write, it's who I am, but that particular project isn't singing to me anymore."

"What do you mean?"

"I had something to say at one point in my life, but that time is long gone. Just like my MG, it feels right to let it go."

"What will you do?"

"I'm going to think about that for a while."

Since Aunt Maureen insists on being here, and now that Mr. McGregor comes over to sit on our porch with her, in case Dad needs something, I have a few afternoons to hang around with Jane at the tennis club pool, or bike with the girls to get Creamsicles.

One day Jane, Wanda, Bethany, and I meet Gloria, Francine, and Patricia and we have a game of baseball in our old elementary school playground with a few other kids who happen to be hanging around. It's a lot of fun, but we're dying of thirst after a while since it's so hot out. Gloria tells us to come over and get a drink from her father's hose since she lives so close, but naturally her mother makes us go into the backyard and comes out with a big pitcher of lemonade with lemon slices in it, along with a huge batch of brownies. We lie on the grass in the shade and laugh at nothing.

But as delightful as this is, and as grateful as I am to be back with my girlfriends, I feel as if I'm a lot older than they are. There's a space between us that was never there before. I'm not the carefree girl I was last summer. I often cry at night under my covers, which is something I've always hated, but now I don't. It feels right to cry for my mother, so I have no wish to interrupt my tears on their journey down my face.

Because my father and I have made a pact to always tell each other the truth, no matter how difficult, I go to him one evening as he's playing the piano, and sit beside him on the bench.

"That's nice. I've never heard you play it before."

"It's your mother's favourite. 'Love is a Many-Splendored Thing.' It came out the year you were born. That's why she always loved it."

I rest my head on his arm. "I need to see her, Dad."

"All right, princess."

It's just an ordinary little grave in an ordinary little graveyard about ten minutes away by car. I can bike here if I want to.

Of course, I research what kind of roses a daughter gives her mother and every source says pink, so I place the pink roses I bought at the foot of the marker.

Rosemary G. Sullivan Parker

Beloved wife and mother

1930–1962

"I'm glad you put beloved wife and mother. What does the G. stand for?"

"Gertrude. She always hated it, so I knew she wouldn't appreciate it carved in granite."

"It's not stupid to miss someone you don't remember, is it?"

"It's probably the best reason to miss someone."

I feel so much better now. I know where she is and I can come back whenever I want. I'll be back tomorrow so she and I can have a real chat. Dad is still recovering and I don't want his heart to be any more upset than it already is.

Before I go to bed, Dad comes in my room. It's so odd to see him in a housecoat now. I miss him in a suit. He's holding a very worn-out, thick journal with bits of paper hanging out of it. It's held together with an elastic.

He gives it to me. "This is your mother's notebook. Her observations about life, her poetry, some very disturbing imagery and drawings. I never wanted you to have it because so much of it is dark, but it's your mother's and you want to know her, and I'm not going to protect you from this. Like your favourite teacher, Mr. Darren, says, you're a girl with a brain."

"Thanks, Dad."

Something tells me I shouldn't read it just now, so I hug it to my chest. It's enough to know I am my mother's daughter; she loved notebooks too. She's right here with me.

———

Jane goes to camp with Wanda in mid-August. I'm not interested, since I'm staying close to Dad. As I hang out the wash on the line, Mrs. Weiner joins me with a load of laundry herself.

"Glorious day for hanging out clothes." She sniffs the air. "There is nothing nicer than hanging sheets in the sun and smelling the outdoors when you're in bed. Frank loves it."

"Remember when you taught me how to do this?"

She gives a great shout, "Oh, bubala! Will you ever forget that terrible wash? I felt dreadful. Who knew you'd take everything to heart?! Whenever I hear the word *scrub*, I smile and think of you scrubbing the life out of your socks. I tell people that story all the time."

"We've had some nice times, haven't we, Mrs. Weiner?"

"The very best. Funny how it happens when you live in these duplexes. I say hello to the people who live upstairs, but we don't even know their names."

"We don't know the woman who lives upstairs from us either. Maybe because they don't have a back deck. I'm sure they're allowed to sit out here in the yard, but they never do."

"Would you, with these hooligans running around?" She laughs.

Michael and David and four other little boys are dressed up like cowboys and Indians, running around the yard shooting arrows and guns at each other. Mr. Moore is outside his garage, and when Michael points a gun at him, he grabs his chest and staggers around like he's been shot.

"DON'T KILL THE NEIGHBOURS, MICHAEL! AT LEAST NOT THE NICE ONES!" his mother yells.

I notice Jacques painting some boards at the front of Mr. Moore's garage. His little sister is also there with a paintbrush. He's been no trouble since Mr. Moore took an interest in him. I must write that down. A little attention from someone goes a long way in making you feel good about yourself.

"Do you think your dad is up to coming to dinner with us tomorrow? We'd like to have you both and your Aunt Maureen. Around six?"

"He'll be fine. He's feeling better every day. It's over six weeks now. He's putting a little weight on too."

"Good. He'll love my roast chicken with dried fruit."

We have a wonderful time with our friends and the food is superb as always. "Once again, I wish I was Jewish." I wipe my mouth with an ironed napkin that still smells like the outdoors.

"That can be arranged." Mr. Weiner chuckles.

"I'll read with the boys so you can enjoy your tea."

"Stay, Audrey," Mrs. Weiner says. Suddenly she looks not quite so jolly. Her eyes fill with tears and she waves at Mr. Weiner because she can't talk. This must be a first.

"Is everything all right?" Dad sounds concerned. "Anything we can help you with?"

Mr. Weiner smiles and looks at his boys, who are serious for once. "Everything is fine. But we hate to tell you, we're moving."

"Oh, thank God!" Aunt Maureen cries. We all look at her. "Sorry! I thought someone was dying!"

"It feels like a death." Mrs. Weiner sniffs into her napkin. "I mean, we're happy about it. This house is getting too small, and the boys need a big backyard to play in now that they're getting older, and Frank is doing so well with his business, we can afford to move into much nicer house. It's actually huge, probably too big, but why not. I have relatives to impress. But we do love this neighbourhood and the friends we've made."

"Are you going far?" I ask.

"Only to Hampstead. About seven minutes by car. I needed to be sure we'd be able to get to you for babysitting purposes! You're not getting off that easy."

"When do you leave?" Dad asks.

"Not until November," Mr. Weiner says. "We're having work done on the house, but Sharon couldn't keep this locked up any longer. She feels like she's lying to you by not mentioning it, so I suggested we tell you now."

"Well, we're going to miss you terribly," Dad says.

"I can't talk about it!" Mrs. Weiner wails before she runs into her bedroom and slams the door. The boys chase after her.

Mr. Weiner gives Dad their new address. Obviously, we have lots of time with them still, but right now we're pretty sad, so we thank Mr. Weiner for dinner and go back to our place to sit and brood.

"I can't imagine living here without them," I say.

Sleep doesn't come to me that night. It's shocking how lonely I am at the thought of Mrs. Weiner not being near me. Maybe it's the recent upset with Dad, but if another adult I love leaves me, my world won't feel safe. I want to stop being a kid and grow up fast.

It's like the shine has worn off the rest of my summer. Dad is busy in his study talking on the phone a lot. Since Jane's at camp, I wander over to Gloria's, but she's not here. She and Francine are over at Patricia's house. So I sit with Mrs. Papa and her mother. They're blanching great batches of a very green vegetable I've never heard of. Kale.

"I bet Peter Rabbit would like this stuff."

You can't say anything to Mrs. Papa. She immediately takes a bag and puts some kale in it. "Take this to Peter."

"Thank you. The Weiners are moving to Hampstead in November."

Mrs. Papa looks up, surprised. "Oh dear. You'll miss her terribly. She's such a nice lady."

The grandmother makes a face, like she doesn't agree. But now I know she does that with everything, so I don't pay attention.

"She still wants me to babysit."

"Hampstead is not far."

"I know. But I don't seem to like change."

"Audrey, the only thing you can count on in this world is change, so you better make peace with it. If you had never moved from your apartment in Westmount, you'd never have known the Weiners. Think how dull your life would've been."

"You're right. And I wouldn't have known you, oh gosh."

"So, you see? Change is good."

I deliver the bag of kale to Peter. He's on the front step of his house in his cage, nose twitching, smelling the summery smells, while his father and Mr. Moore chat.

"Compliments of Mrs. Papadopoulos." I hold a piece through the wire and Peter immediately starts nibbling. "He loves it."

"Thank you, Audrey." Mr. McGregor smiles.

"Did you hear the Weiners are moving?"

Both men nod. "Maureen told us. But that's life, especially in this neighbourhood. People come and go all the time."

"I'm not happy about it."

They exchange grins.

Then I see Avi and Rollie coming up the street, so I say goodbye to the gentlemen and join the boy and his dog on their daily parade. "What's new, Avi?"

"My mom had another stupid baby."

"How many stupid babies does she have?"

"Just me. And now this ugly looking fellow named Noah. I said, 'Where's his ark?' She didn't think that was funny."

"You'll be great pals one day."

"I doubt it. I've got Rollie, and he doesn't like anyone but me."

"I don't know about that. He's always been very friendly whenever I see him."

Rollie gives me his huge grin. He's fifty pounds of love.

"Well, this Noah kid better think twice about wanting to take Rollie for a walk. We have our routine."

"Noah won't be walking for another year, and then I doubt your mom will let him walk Rollie by himself for at least three or four years after that, so I think you're good."

"I suppose that's true. Thanks."

And off they go. I guess I'm dismissed.

———

Dad calls me into his study a week after that. He's wearing a casual shirt and corduroy pants, so he looks more like Dad. This is my old life and it puts me at ease. Seeing him in pyjamas for days on end bothered me.

"What's up?" I sit in the chair opposite his and he pushes his Liquorice Allsorts across the desk. I grab a handful and pop one in.

"As you've probably noticed, I've been spending a lot of time in here on the phone."

"Uh-huh."

"That's because I've officially retired and have now sold my business."

I chew really fast. "Do you mean to tell me that I'll never see that glorious desk in the Linton building again?"

He laughs. "We can go and see it today if you like. The man who bought the firm is an old friend. I'm sure he'd let you sit under it as often as you like."

"You're really going to leave that desk behind? Maybe we should bring it here."

"Well, the fact that it weighs about six thousand pounds and would never fit through the front door suggests we better not. I can let it go. It's not singing to me anymore."

I nod, and put more candy in my mouth. "So, what are you going to do now that you've retired? You said the thought of it spooked you."

"I'm going to travel the world."

My body goes limp as all my blood seems to have drained into my feet. He quickly realizes I might faint again, so he holds out his hands. "Wait! That didn't come out right. I'm not going alone. You're coming with me."

"WHAT?!"

"That's if you want to. We have to talk about it. If you'd rather not, then I'll think of something else."

Now I have to shake my head to get it to stop buzzing. "Dad, you are the world's worst person to talk to. You just blurt out this stuff instead of easing into it. I'm going to be the next family member who has a heart attack because of this foolish practice of springing things on people out of the blue."

"How else should I have said it?"

"'We have to discuss it, but I was thinking maybe you and I should travel the world together.'"

"You're right. That's much better. Sorry."

"Are you out of your ever-loving mind?"

He shrugs. "Maybe."

"Explain."

He leans forward and clasps his hands together on the desk. "I've sold the business and if we decide to travel the world for say, two years, we can afford it. We'll sell the house."

"Sell the house?"

"We can always move back to the neighbourhood when our journey is over. I've invested my money over the years. My retirement portfolio will keep the wolf from the door. You can look that phrase up. Now, I've researched this, and young people are allowed to be homeschooled, meaning we would get the curriculum for grade nine and ten, and you would do at it your own pace as we travel from country to country, much like you did when you missed school for two months. My only reluctance is the thought of you missing your friends and perhaps the chance to be in more school theatrical productions. I honestly think it's your calling. So being in school is important and we need to consider it, but I also think that seeing the world and different cultures is advantageous to a young mind. I travelled in the navy and I always longed to see more, but life gets in the way and you never seem to have the time."

I watch his face. It's getting more serious.

"This is not meant as a tactic to blackmail you. I've been given a second chance here. Our reality is that I won't be around when you're old and grey, so it might be to our advantage to make a lifetime of memories now, while we still can."

I shake out more candy. My blood sugar must be low. His words are sinking in.

"What does your doctor say about all this? I assume you talked to him about it."

"He thinks I'll be fine now that you don't hate me anymore."

"DAD!"

"He said we should wait another month before going just to make sure I'm in fine fettle when we leave. And we'll need that time to get things organized anyway. But I reassured him we had no interest in running around like fools. We'll just mosey our way across whatever landscape we want, and if we feel like staying in Paris for a couple of months, we will."

"Paris?"

"London, New York, Moscow."

"Golly! We always said the world lived on this street. Now we get to see it. We can ask our friends where we should go."

"Does this mean you like the idea?"

"In theory. It's slightly less painful now that I know Mr. and Mrs. Weiner are moving. The thought of them not being here really bothers me. But what about our other neighbours? The Papas? And Jane, for goodness' sake! Oh, my God, what about Tom and Sally-Anne? And Aunt Maureen and Elvis?!"

"Yes, we have to consider all that. Now, for the record, we're not going forever. Aunt Maureen, Elvis, Tom, and Sally-Anne will be here when we get back. I know she'll look after them for us."

"She doesn't like cats, remember?"

He waves his wrist at me. "She does so! Those cats are all over her and Elvis. She just didn't like her husband."

"So, you really think this is a good idea?"

"It's doable, and you and I need to take some time together to recover from this terrible trauma we've been through."

"The heart attack."

He smiles sadly. "No. Finding out about your mother. That lie made me heartsick, quite literally. You were very ill with mono and I know your energy hasn't recovered yet. And you haven't had a chance to process your mother's story, because my heart attack pushed everything to the sidelines, but you need to grieve. We need to grieve together. I want us to have the time to talk about her, to tell you all my memories, because there are sweet memories of the three of us. We need to get away from here, princess. We need to go and find your mother."

Dad holds out his hand. I reach over and take it.

"Let's do it."

—

What the hell are we thinking?

Aunt Maureen is smoking three packs a day over this and snivelling between puffs.

"Jesus Christ! You must really hate me! It's bad enough you don't want to see my face for two years, you expect me to take your stupid cats!"

"You have to take the cats. Elvis would be heartbroken without them," Dad reminds her.

"Oh sure. Lay that guilt on me. And on top of it, Sharon's moving away!"

"It takes seven minutes to drive from this street to her new street."

"Who knows if I'll ever get over there? My car is a piece of shit."

"I'm leaving you my car, Maureen."

This never occurred to her. "You are?"

"We're not packing it in our suitcase. It's yours. To thank you for all you've done for us this year."

She brightens a little. "Oh. Well, that's nice of you."

"We'll be selling the house."

"WHAT?! What about all your stuff?"

"Will you take the piano for me?"

"The piano? Where am I going to put it? My kitchen? I have no room. But I'll take your new La-Z-Boy and your new television, since mine's toast. And the new bed you bought me. Too bad I couldn't take that shower."

"I can hardly rip that out of the wall. Okay. I'll put my desk, chair, typewriter, bookshelves, books, stereo, records, and piano in storage. Also my World's Greatest Dad mug. What about you, Audrey? Anything you want to keep safe in storage?"

"Of course. I've already made a list in my notebook."

I pull it out of my pocket and open it, checking things off with my pencil. "I want the old tin with your bits of writing in it, the covers on my bed, all my books and Encyclopaedias, the opera glasses, my Russian dolls, my sombrero, my Indian jewelry box, my Girl Guide belt, and my picture of Charlie Brown and Snoopy. I'll be taking my mother's notebook and postcard, my Peruvian change purse and the Expo 67 bag. And of course, my typewriter necklace that I never take off. Also, my Mickey Mouse watch. And Aunt Moo says you have a picture of your grandfather around here so we need to take that too. Oh, and my camera and flash cubes. I plan on taking pictures of Aunt Maureen, my pets, my room, my friends, neighbours, the houses, the schools, the corner store, the clothesline, Sally-Anne's grave, my maple tree, my bike...that reminds me. What should we do with my bike?"

"Why don't you give it to Jacques's little sister? Hers looks pretty dreadful."

"It'll be too big for her, but I supposed she'll grow into it."

"We'll donate everything else to Goodwill."

Aunt Maureen is in a halo of smoke. "By the time Audrey finishes her list, there won't be anything left. But promise me you're not going for more than two years!"

"That's the plan."

I'm starting to understand my father a little better. He didn't promise her anything. He didn't say yes or no. Fascinating.

———

I'm feeling like Mrs. Weiner. I've got this secret and I'm not sure if I should blurt it out now or wait until the last minute.

There's a part of me that doesn't believe this is real.

Wanda happens to call me. "We just got back from camp last night and Jane and her mother aren't speaking to each other, as usual. Those two exhaust me. And oh my God! I saw Mrs. Andrews kissing the swimming instructor! Can you believe it?"

"Gee whiz. Don't ever tell Jane."

"Why not? Maybe if she knew her mother wasn't so flawless, she might feel better."

"Would you want to know if your mother was kissing someone other than your dad?"

"True."

Instinctively I know I have to make my pilgrimage to Jane's house. This is probably going to be a shit show.

That's something I should work on. My bad language.

Thank Christ, Jane answers the door. "Hey! I was going to call you tonight. I'm unpacking. Come on up."

We hurry up the stairs to her room and sit on her bed.

"Guess what happened?" she says.

"I hate this game, as you well know."

"Jeffery Weinberg kissed me!"

"On the mouth?"

"Well, sort of. He's got braces and one of his elastics came loose so he fumbled around."

"Sounds delightful."

"You're just jealous!"

I give her a weak smile. She immediately frowns. "What's wrong? I can always tell."

"I'm leaving."

"Leaving where? The planet? This room? Be more specific."

"I'm travelling the world with my father for the next two years. We're selling our house."

She jumps off the bed and starts to pace back and forth, her hand on her forehead. "Okay, this is a joke. Are you and Wanda up to something? This isn't funny. Your father just had a heart attack. There's no way he's going to roar around Europe."

"We are not going to roar. We are going to purr and growl around Europe."

It's hitting her that I'm telling the truth. She sits back on the bed. "For real?"

"Yep."

"And you want to do this? Leave your house and your street and your friends?"

I pick away at a hangnail so I don't have to look at her. "I'm going to miss everything. All of you. Especially you. But my dad nearly died and he's not a young man. He's the only parent I have. He says he wants

250

us to spend time together while we still can. How can I say no? When you think of it, it makes perfect sense."

She flops on her back and stares at the ceiling, or she would stare at the ceiling, but the ugly canopy is in the way. "I don't know what to say. Suddenly grade nine feels like it's going to be lonely."

I lie back on the mattress with her. "I'll write to you. How about I send you postcards from all the places we go and you can make a collage of them for your Girl Guide troop?"

"I don't want to go back to Girl Guides. Too many bad memories."

"Jane! You love Girl Guides. Go to the troop in Monkland with Bethany. You just need a change. Don't let what happened with that damn dragon spoil the fun. You're a natural-born Girl Guide, and Dixie will want to follow in your footsteps."

She appears to be mulling it over. "Maybe. But you know what I'm going to do first?"

"What?"

"Rip this miserable canopy off the bed and set it on fire."

"I'll help!"

We stand on the mattress and can't get our balance—it's not easy to stand on a mattress—so we jump up to rip the material off in strips. We hoot and holler and throw the pieces on the floor. Jane looks for something else to destroy. "Let's rip up the ruffled bedspread!"

We take the ends and pull at it until it starts to fray and then tear it up as fast as we can. We don't even see that Mrs. Andrews standing in the doorway with a look of utter astonishment on her face.

"What are you girls doing?"

"Mother, for the last time: I hate ruffles. I hate canopies, I hate, hate, hate this room. I'm going to paint it and decorate it the way I want to from now on!"

"Oh, no you're not. This is my home and I like it to look a certain way. I'll not have a thirteen-year-old dictate to me how things are going to be decorated."

"Then I guess I'll just have to tell Dad that you and the swimming instructor are still going at it."

Mrs. Andrews looks like she's been stabbed. She grabs the edge of the doorway and steadies herself. Then she backs away and walks into her bedroom, shutting the door quietly behind her.

Jane looks triumphant. "Boy, that felt good. Sorry I had to involve you in a family quarrel, but I know you won't say a word."

"Your secret is safe with me."

She smiles at me. "I know you know about my mother. I saw you that night, and that's when I knew you were a true friend. Which is why I'm going to miss you more than anything."

———

School has started and even though I'm only going to be here for two more weeks, I go to classes and have meetings with the guidance counsellor to make sure the package with my curriculum for the next two years is in order. It also gives me a chance to say goodbye to the small circle of friends I've accumulated over the past year or so.

The Peanuts gang and Mr. Keillor take me to lunch one day, which is a lovely surprise, and I get quite emotional when they present me with a picture of the six of us on stage. They've even signed it for me. I will make sure to add this to my pile of treasures.

Mr. Darren sees me in the hallway on my last day and gives me a smirk. "What am I supposed to do with all the brainless kids I have in my class?"

He sticks out his hand and I don't mind shaking it. "You are going to go far, kid. It's been a pleasure."

Our house is put on the market and the first couple who come to see it don't even get as far as the kitchen and they say they want to buy it. That's because Uniska makes it extra sparkly, which hardly seems possible.

Both Dad and I have a hard time saying goodbye to this quiet, gentle soul. But she says she's very happy for us and tells us to make sure to visit the city of Kyiv in Ukraine. "It's where we were married."

Mr. Moore and Mr. McGregor and Peter Rabbit wish us all the luck in the world. I make sure I go over to Avi's house to say goodbye to him and Rollie.

When Avi answers the door, Rollie is beside him and the baby is sound asleep in his arms. He's got a burp cloth over his shoulder.

"Just wanted to say goodbye, Avi. I'm moving away."

"Oh yeah? Well, have fun."

"I'm glad you like Noah."

"He's okay."

I look past him. "Are your parents home?"

"Yeah. Wanna talk to them?"

"No." I reach out to pat Rollie's giant head. "You're a good dog, Rollie. I'll never forget you." He licks my hand.

"Sorry, gotta go. Noah might get a chill. See ya." And he shuts the door.

I've been dismissed.

It's tough saying goodbye to the Papas. Gloria's mother holds me for a long time. "Remember, Audrey," she says, "change is good."

"I'll never forget what you did for me," I whisper.

"You are very welcome," she whispers back. "You will do the same for someone else one day."

Of course, when we tell the Weiners, they all start crying. The boys cling to my legs. "Don't go, Audrey!"

Which gives me a great idea. "Just a sec!" I run out of their house and back into my room to grab all ten of my Junior Classic books.

"Here! Now, I want you to read all these stories and by the time you do, I'll be back."

That placates them for now.

Dad is telling them our plans, and how we're getting rid of everything except the piano and things to go in storage.

"Don't put them in storage," says Mr. Weiner. "Our house is huge. Embarrassingly so. Please feel free to store anything you want with us. That way you'll know it will be safe."

"And you'll have to come back and get it!" Mrs. Weiner adds.

"That's so kind of you. If that's the case, please feel free to use the piano in the meantime."

Mrs. Weiner is still wiping her tears with a hanky. "Are you crazy? I'm not letting these two monsters near it! They will *never* learn to play the piano! Do you hear me? *Never.*"

Suddenly the boys think piano lessons are a fabulous idea, which I believe was her ultimate goal. Oh, this woman is clever.

I hang onto Mrs. Weiner for quite a while. "Come back to me, bubala."

The worst is saying goodbye to Aunt Maureen, Elvis, Tom, and Sally-Anne. They are now living over at Aunt Maureen's and seem quite content, which makes me happy but annoyed at the same time.

I bawl my head off. I make Aunt Maureen promise to send me pictures of them every week.

"Every week?! Once a month, maybe."

"They have to sleep under the covers on your bed or they won't be happy."

"You've told me that already."

"And Tom likes his milk heated a bit."

"Tough luck, Tom."

"Aunt Moo!"

"Okay, okay."

"We'll call you often, Maureen," says Dad. "We'll always let you know where we are. If we settle some place for a while, maybe you'd like to come over for visit."

"Get on a plane and leave Elvis? Are you nuts? No, thank you! Just make sure you're here two years from now."

"That's the plan."

The three of us hug in silence, because we know we can't say anything else without crying. I hold my cats and tell them I love them.

Then we get in the taxi waiting outside with our luggage and drive away, but only down our street. We have to look at the house again, and I run out back to kiss the ground under the maple tree and say goodbye to my first Sally-Anne and thank her for being in my life.

It's mid-September now and the green leaves on the tree look a bit weary. I take three of them, Snipp, Snapp, and Snurr, and stuff them in my pocket. I'll press them in my notebook.

I'm hurrying back to the taxi when Jacques steps out of Mr. Moore's garage and gives me a small wave, so I give him one in return.

We have one more stop, and that's to my mother's grave.

Dad has brought an impressive bouquet of pink and red roses and we place them on the ground.

"Rosemary, I'm off to show our girl the world. You'll be with us every step of the way."

"Goodbye, Mama."

We straighten up, and he holds out his hand. "Let's go, princess."

 Epilogue

All my life, I've remembered that year in NDG. It will always be one of my favourites, and I've lived for sixty-six years now.

The street, the houses, the neighbours, the feel of the air on my face as I raced my bike along the city sidewalks in the sun and the rain. The classrooms and the kids who shared them with me. The close friends, the not-so-close friends, the teachers, the Guide leaders.

But mostly the mothers.

These women nurtured me, each in their own unique way. I once made a list of things that, if I were ever a mother, would be the most important to me.

A clean house.

Always being there, even if your kids don't want you to be.

Welcoming your children's friends and making them feel special.

Yelling at them when they need it.

Delicious meals.

Letting them have as many pets as they want.

Giving them books to read, and a thesaurus, and expecting them to use their brain. (That's a Dad trick.)

Poor Aunt Maureen. We were gone for five years. I finished high school and CEGEP on the other side of the world. Every time we thought maybe we should head home, some new adventure would pop up. And then it was obvious to me that Dad was so happy, the thought of him sitting around in retirement doing nothing would break his spirit.

After the first few months of really missing my cats and Elvis, Aunt Maureen's pictures and cards assured me that they were quite content, even when she gathered them up and moved to Ontario to be with her family, which Dad was very relieved about. I was surprised she left Ian McGregor behind. I thought he was her boyfriend, but when I asked her, she wrote back and said Elvis was her one true love. Apparently, she and Ian were only friends and now they were pen pals, which suited her just fine. "Who needs a man buggering up your life?" were her actual words.

We kept in touch with the Weiners, of course. They were my touchstone to that world, even if they weren't technically on that street anymore. They helped remind me that it all wasn't just a dream. Being so far away, it sometimes felt like it.

I sent Jane postcards at first, and got a couple of letters back, but since we were always travelling, she didn't know where to send them, so we lost touch. I wonder if she and her mother are still arguing.

I still think of Mrs. Papa. I'm sure she had twenty grandchildren who adored her and her endless trays of goodies. And I often wondered if Mr. Moore was able to hang around long enough to make a real difference to Jacques and his little sister. That's the trouble when you move away. It's like you close a book and suddenly the characters who walked through your life are not there anymore. You miss them.

Dad and I decided early on that both of us would write about our adventures in journals. Even after all these years, I'll take them out and read a few pages at my desk on rainy afternoons.

Monday, May 5, 1969. Dad and I were in a tiny bookstore in Oxford this afternoon and while he nosed around the bins, I took up my position near the back. I could peek out from behind the books on the shelf in front of me. There was a couple having an argument in the corner but they didn't want anyone to hear them so there were a lot of facial gestures and finger pointing. She accused him of being unfaithful, or maybe she said hateful. He called her a witch or a bitch and she said he was a wanker. Have no idea what that means, so I'll look it up. Then she hit him over the head with a book and he did the same thing to her. She went crying to the owner about how the man was abusing her, so I stepped out of my spot and told the bookseller that she started it. All of the adults looked at me and Dad grabbed me by the shoulders and steered me outside. "Mind your own damn business. I'm too old for this aggravation."

Sunday, June 10, 1969. Dad bought me a pair of real binoculars for my fourteenth birthday. He said they were for birdwatching, or peering up at castle towers or counting the ships at sea. Nice try, Dad. So far, I've watched a drug deal go down in a local pub, saw a couple roll around under an oak tree in a cemetery, and spied a policeman drag a guy out of his house wearing only underpants. He kept shouting and hitting the cop but never lost the cigarette hanging out of his mouth. That has to be some kind of talent. I almost lost my binoculars in Venice when I leaned too far over in a gondola and landed in the canal. The gondolier plucked me out of the dirty water looking like a drowned rat. Luckily my binoculars were still around my neck.

Saturday, Oct. 3, 1970. Dad and I stood in the middle of the Swiss Alps today and sang "Ain't No Mountain High Enough" by Diana Ross at an ear-splitting level. Two old ladies gave us dirty looks, which made us sing it again!

When we accumulated too many journals, we'd ship them to the Weiners, who added them to "our room." We tried very hard not to buy too many souvenirs, but some things we couldn't pass up, like the beautiful silk fabric we found in India that I planned on putting on my wall someday just like Mrs. Papa. And Dad had to have a vintage bronze Viking dragon ship he found in Copenhagen.

My father told me about my mother as we sipped lattes in cafes in Lyon, ate fish and chips at the seaside in Cornwall, went sightseeing in Kyiv, walked along the Great Wall of China, and oh my, slowly trekked our way along a fiord in Norway.

Together, our hearts healed completely as if they were brand new. I remember we laughed every day and made a pact to stop swearing so much, but neither one of us were very good on that score. Who cares? It was our thing.

We were leaning over the railing of a sightseeing boat on Loch Ness in Scotland, watching an eagle glide just above the choppy waves, when he turned to me. "This is it, Audrey. Right here, this minute with you. My ultimate society. All my life I've been searching for it, trying to describe it in words, when all I ever needed to do was live it. And share it with you."

"This is pretty spectacular, Daddio."

"Amazing."

"Breathtaking."

"Stupendous."

"Incredible."

"Flabbergasting."

"Phenomenal."

"Mind-blowing."

"Fucking awesome."

"Okay, missy. That's enough."

We were on the Greek island of Santorini, on lounge chairs by the beach, gazing out at the aquamarine water, when I told Dad that I wished Mr. Papadopoulos could see me now. He didn't answer me.

He never did again.

I scattered his ashes on that beautiful water. It was the last thing he saw in this world, and I felt it was appropriate for a navy man to be buried at sea. But I needed him, too, so I kept a small vial of his ashes and eventually put them in the Viking dragon ship.

When I went home, I enrolled in the National Theatre School of Canada on Saint Denis Street in Montreal. Mr. Weiner and a few of his workers helped me bring over the piano and all of our belongings to my older walk-up in the Latin Quarter. He even had Dad's La-Z-Boy chair that Aunt Maureen left behind before she moved to Ontario. She felt guilty about taking the chair, he said. We laughed that she didn't feel guilty about the bed, the television, or the car.

One of the first things I did was go to the pound. There was a fat bulldog in a cage who looked like he could use a good walk. Rollie and I walked at least three times a day for the next eight years. I also took piano lessons so I could play my father's music. It took me a long time to get any good at it, but just sitting on the bench gave me great solace.

A highlight of my week was having dinner with the Weiners. I never had to buy groceries. Sharon (she insisted I call them both by their first name) would load me up. "You're a starving student, bubala! We've got to get some meat on your bones!"

It was at one of these dinners that I met Frank's nephew Caleb. He looked exactly like his uncle, a big teddy bear with a mop of curls and round glasses, so I knew we were kindred spirits. He was shy and sweet and I fell so hard, it's a wonder I didn't crack the tiles on Sharon's kitchen floor.

I knew nothing about boys, obviously. I'd only been kissed a few times, which seems ridiculous to say now. I was eighteen, and so naïve. It's not like I had necked with strangers with my dad hanging around. Well, there was that time in Norway when I bought an ice cream cone and the boy who served it to me was going off duty so he got one too and we went down to the shore, ate our cones, and then kissed for the rest of the afternoon. That was a good day.

But my best day was marrying my Jewish sweetheart, despite the fact that Michael told everyone at the wedding reception about the night I tried to smother him with a pillow.

"GOOD!" Sharon yelled, with a glass of champagne in her hand. "I ALWAYS KNEW I LOVED THIS GIRL!" Aunt Maureen laughed so hard she spilled her drink all over Frank.

I kept my maiden name, much to my father-in-law's annoyance, but Nosy Weiner just doesn't have the same panache.

Michael took over his father's junk business and is now a millionaire several times over and his brother David became a high-powered lawyer, so Sharon was correct. One out of two ain't bad. David also grew about six inches taller than Michael, which he never lets his brother forget. But they're the loveliest boys you'll ever meet. They adore each other. And both their wives are exactly like Sharon.

Snoopy was right: I became quite successful with my career in the theatre, but it eventually became evident to me that I loved watching and writing plays much more than acting in them. My spying on people helped me to understand the human condition and I've become a well-known Canadian playwright. Which is an oxymoron, I know. But I'm doing as well as I could have hoped.

The most important thing to me is Caleb and our children. Caleb is a pediatrician (a bit like Dr. McTavish), but he's mostly doing research now on obscure childhood diseases. We've lived all our married lives in a rambling brick house on Lansdowne Avenue in Westmount. We bought it so I could be close to the Westmount Library. It's usually messy and despite an army of cleaning ladies over the years, it has never come anywhere near to being Uniska- clean.

We have six children: John, Rosemary, Rachel, Avi, Caroline, and a little boy who came into our lives when his mother left him in the emergency department every weekend, saying he was sick, just so she could party. Caleb would stay late to read to him as the baby lay in the crib crying until finally my sweet husband couldn't stand it, so Angus became ours after much paperwork and his mother's signature.

We now have four grandchildren, and my love for them knows no bounds. If you can believe it, one of them is named Tom, and the newest baby is Sally-Anne. That's what you get for telling your kids the same stories over and over again. (No one has taken up the cause for Elvis yet, but you never know.)

I've always been on the lookout for waifs and ragamuffins, and have nurtured quite a few that our gang have dragged home over the years.

Aunt Maureen died when she was ninety, only ten years ago. She visited us often and would sometimes stay for months. Always with an Elvis in her arms. She finally stopped smoking the day she accidently burned her third Elvis on the nose with her cigarette. That was the end of the smokes. I believe she had eight Elvises over the years, but we shouldn't talk. We're on our fifth Rollie and have had about eighty-four stray Sally-Annes.

It was on the plane coming home from Toronto after Aunt Maureen's funeral when a man sat next to me and gave me a quick smile before he put on his seat belt.

"Nicholai?"

He looked me. "Yes?"

"Oh my God! I'd know you anywhere! It's Audrey! Audrey Parker!"

He looked at me with no recognition, of course. Why would he remember me? Meanwhile, he's still God's gift to the universe.

"We were in grade seven together. You sat behind me in Mrs. Fuller's class. Remember, the teacher who used to throw chalk at us?"

He breaks out into a big grin. "Of course! Audrey. The brave girl."

"Brave?"

"I thought you were. You stood up for yourself, and I never did."

"I remember I was heartbroken that you moved away and didn't go to our high school."

"That was my parents' decision. The boys in school were giving me a very hard time."

"Really? Why?"

He gives me a delighted look. "Audrey. Think about it. I carried tissues and hand lotion in grade seven."

I'm gobsmacked. "Oh! No way!"

"Would you like to see a picture of my husband and children?"

"Only if I can bore you with mine!"

"And for your information, Snipp, Snapp, and Snurr were Swedish, not Norwegian."

"I can't believe you remember that."

It was only two months later when my darling Sharon Weiner died. Her last word to me was "Bubala."

Frank didn't last three weeks without her.

It was many years before I had the courage to read my mother's notebook. Knowing what we know now, she was clearly mentally ill. But oh, so talented. I've used her poetry in a lot of my work. Much of it is disturbing, but very profound and wise.

But my absolute favourite piece is on a little scrap of paper I found tucked into the fold at the back of the notebook. I mounted and framed it so I can see it when I'm at my desk, next to a picture of my father at his typewriter.

It's dated the day I was born.

Hey my little blueberry,
with the blueberry eyes.
If you were in a field of blueberries
I would wander by
And pick you.
Every time.

And really, that's all I ever needed to know about my mother.

Complete your collection with the new Lesley Crewe Classics series, available at fine bookstores everywhere.

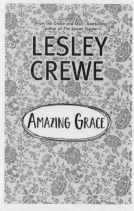

978-1-77471-085-2

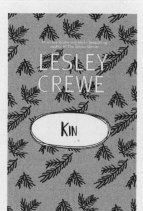

978-1-77108-964-7

978-1-77471-032-6

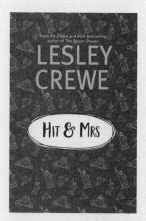

978-1-77471-121-7

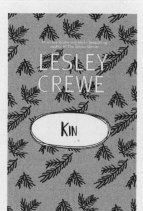

978-1-77471-030-2

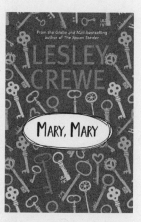

978-1-77471-122-4

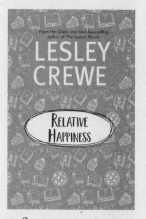

978-1-77471-123-1

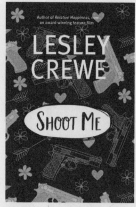

978-1-77108-963-0